W9-CEF-666

# The Marsh King's Daughter

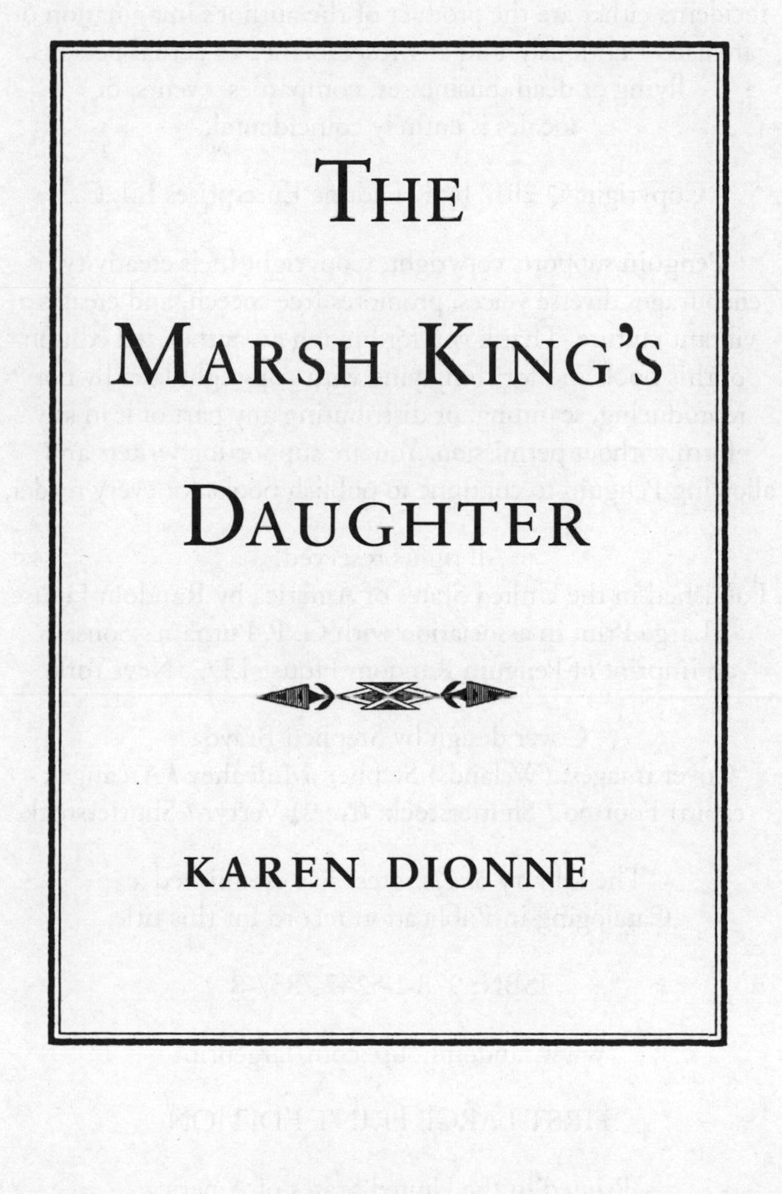

# THE MARSH KING'S DAUGHTER

KAREN DIONNE

RANDOM HOUSE LARGE PRINT

This is a work of fiction. Names, characters, places, and incidents either are the product of the author's imagination or are used fictitiously, and any resemblance to actual persons, living or dead, businesses, companies, events, or locales is entirely coincidental.

Copyright © 2017 by K Dionne Enterprises L.L.C.

Penguin supports copyright. Copyright fuels creativity, encourages diverse voices, promotes free speech, and creates a vibrant culture. Thank you for buying an authorized edition of this book and for complying with copyright laws by not reproducing, scanning, or distributing any part of it in any form without permission. You are supporting writers and allowing Penguin to continue to publish books for every reader.

All rights reserved.
Published in the United States of America by Random House Large Print in association with G. P. Putnam's Sons, an imprint of Penguin Random House LLC, New York.

Cover design by Stephen Brayda
Cover images: (Welands) Stephen Mulcahey / Arcangel; (cabin) Foottoo / Shutterstock; (trees) Vertyr / Shutterstock

The Library of Congress has established a Cataloging-in-Publication record for this title.

ISBN: 978-1-5247-7837-8

www.randomhouse.com/largeprint

FIRST LARGE PRINT EDITION

Printed in the United States of America

10 9 8 7 6 5 4 3 2 1

This Large Print edition published in accord with the standards of the N.A.V.H.

**For Roger, for everything**

To be fruitful provokes one's downfall; at the rise of the next generation, the previous one has exceeded its peak. Our descendants become our most dangerous enemies for whom we are unprepared. They will survive and take power from our enfeebled hands.

—Carl Gustav Jung

# The Marsh King's Daughter

From its nest high on the roof of the Viking's castle, the stork could see a small lake, and by the reeds and the green banks lay the trunk of an alder tree. Upon this three swans stood flapping their wings and looking about them.

One of them threw off her plumage, and the stork recognized her as a princess of Egypt. There she sat without any covering but her long, black hair. The stork heard her tell the two others to take great care of the swan's plumage while she dipped down into the water to pluck the flowers she imagined she saw there.

The others nodded and picked up the feather dress and flew away with her swan's plumage. "Dive down now!" they cried; "thou shalt never more fly in the swan's plumage, thou shalt never again see Egypt; here, on the moor, thou wilt remain." So saying, they tore the swan's plumage into a thousand pieces. The feathers drifted about like a snow shower, and then the two deceitful princesses flew away.

The princess wept and lamented aloud; her tears moistened the alder stump, which was really not an alder stump but the Marsh King himself, he who in marshy ground lives and rules. The stump of the tree turned round, and was a tree no more, while long, clammy branches like arms extended from it.

**The poor child was terribly frightened, and started up to run away. She hastened to cross the green, slimy ground, but quickly sank, and the alder stump after her. Great black bubbles rose up out of the slime, and with these, every trace of the princess vanished.**

—Hans Christian Andersen,
**The Marsh King's Daughter,**
1872 translation by Mrs. H. B. Paull

# Helena

If I told you my mother's name, you'd recognize it right away. My mother was famous, though she never wanted to be. Hers wasn't the kind of fame anyone would wish for. Jaycee Dugard, Amanda Berry, Elizabeth Smart—that kind of thing, though my mother was none of them.

You'd recognize my mother's name if I told it to you, and then you'd wonder—briefly, because the years when people cared about my mother are long gone, as she is—where is she now? And didn't she have a daughter while she was missing? And whatever happened to the little girl?

I could tell you that I was twelve and my mother twenty-eight when we were recovered from her captor, that I spent those years living in what the papers describe as a run-down farmhouse surrounded by swamp in the middle of Michigan's Upper Peninsula. That while I did learn to read thanks to a stack of **National Geographic** magazines from the 1950s and a yellowed edition of the collected poems of Robert Frost, I never went to school, never rode a bicycle, never knew electricity or running water. That the only people I spoke to during those twelve years were my mother and father. That I didn't know we were captives until we were not.

I could tell you that my mother passed away two years ago, and while the news media covered her death, you probably missed it because she died during a news cycle heavy with more important stories. I can tell you what the papers did not: she never got over the years of captivity; she wasn't a pretty, articulate, outspoken champion of the cause; there were no book deals for my timid, self-effacing wreck of a mother, no cover of **Time.** My mother shrank from attention the way arrowroot leaves wither after a frost.

But I won't tell you my mother's name. Because this isn't her story. It's mine.

# 1

"Wait here," I tell my three-year-old. I lean through the truck's open window to fish between her booster seat and the passenger door for the plastic sippy cup of lukewarm orange juice she threw in a fit of frustration. "Mommy will be right back."

Mari reaches for the cup like Pavlov's puppy. Her bottom lip pokes out and tears overflow. I get it. She's tired. So am I.

"Uh-uh-uh," Mari grunts as I start to walk away. She arches her back and pushes against the seat belt as if it's a straitjacket.

"Stay put, I'll be right back." I narrow my eyes and shake my finger so she knows I mean business and go around to the back of the truck. I wave at the kid stacking boxes on the loading dock by the delivery entrance to Markham's—Jason, I think is his name—then lower the tailgate to grab the first two boxes of my own.

"Hi, Mrs. Pelletier!" Jason returns my wave with twice the enthusiasm I gave him. I lift my hand again so we're even. I've given up telling him to call me Helena.

**Bang-bang-bang** from inside the truck. Mari is whacking her juice cup against the window ledge. I'm guessing it's empty. I bang the flat of my hand against the truck bed in response—**bang-bang-bang**—and Mari startles and twists around, her baby-fine hair whipping across her face like corn silk. I give her my best "cut it out if you know what's good for you" scowl, then heft the cartons to my shoulder. Stephen and I both have brown hair and eyes, as does our five-year-old, Iris, so he marveled over this rare golden child we created until I told him my mother was a blonde. That's all he knows.

Markham's is the next-to-last delivery of four, and the primary sales outlet for my jams and jellies, aside from the orders I pick up online. Tourists who shop at Markham's Grocery like the idea that my products are locally made. I'm told a lot of customers purchase several jars to take home as gifts and souvenirs. I tie gingham fabric circles over the lids with butcher's string and color-code them according to contents:

red for raspberry jam, purple for elderberry, blue for blueberry, green for cattail-blueberry jelly, yellow for dandelion, pink for wild apple-- chokecherry—you get the idea. I think the covers look silly, but people seem to like them. And if I'm going to get by in an area as economically depressed as the Upper Peninsula, I have to give people what they want. It's not rocket science.

There are a lot of wild foods I could use and a lot of different ways to fix them, but for now I'm sticking with jams and jellies. Every business needs a focus. My trademark is the cattail line drawing I put on every label. I'm pretty sure I'm the only person who mixes ground cattail root with blueberries to make jelly. I don't add much, just enough to justify including **cattail** in the name. When I was growing up, young cattail spikes were my favorite vegetable. They still are. Every spring I toss my waders and a wicker basket in the back of my pickup and head for the marshes south of our place. Stephen and the girls won't touch them, but Stephen doesn't care if I cook them as long as I fix just enough for me. Boil the heads for a few minutes in salted water and you have one of the finest vegetables around. The texture is a little dry and mealy, so I eat mine with butter now, but of course, butter was nothing I'd tasted when I was a child.

Blueberries I pick in the logged-over areas

south of our place. Some years the blueberry crop is better than others. Blueberries like a lot of sun. Indians used to set fire to the underbrush to improve the yield. I'll admit, I've been tempted. I'm not the only person out on the plains during blueberry season, so the areas closest to the old logging roads get picked over fairly quickly. But I don't mind going off the beaten path, and I never get lost. Once I was so far out in the middle of nowhere, a Department of Natural Resources helicopter spotted me and hailed me. After I convinced the officers I knew where I was and what I was doing, they left me alone.

"Hot enough for you?" Jason asks as he reaches down and takes the first box from my shoulder.

I grunt in response. There was a time when I would have had no idea how to answer such a question. My opinion of the weather isn't going to change it, so why should anyone care what I think? Now I know I don't have to, that this is an example of what Stephen calls "small talk," conversation for the sake of conversation, a space-filler not meant to communicate anything of importance or value. Which is how people who don't know each other well talk to each other. I'm still not sure how this is better than silence.

Jason laughs like I told the best joke he's heard all day, which Stephen also insists is an appropriate response, never mind that I didn't say anything funny. After I left the marsh, I really struggled with social conventions. Shake hands when you meet someone. Don't pick your nose. Go to the back of the line. Wait your turn. Raise your hand when you have a question in the classroom and then wait for the teacher to call on you before you ask it. Don't burp or pass gas in the presence of others. When you're a guest in someone's home, ask permission before you use the bathroom. Remember to wash your hands and flush the toilet after you do. I can't tell you how often I felt as though everyone knew the right way to do things but me. Who makes these rules, anyway? And why do I have to follow them? And what will be the consequences if I don't?

I leave the second box on the loading dock and go back to the truck for the third. Three cases, twenty-four jars each, seventy-two jars total, delivered every two weeks during June, July, and August. My profit on each case is $59.88, which means that over the course of the summer, I make more than a thousand dollars from Markham's alone. Not shabby at all.

And about my leaving Mari alone in the truck while I make my deliveries, I know what people would think if they knew. Especially about leaving her alone with the windows down. But I'm not about to leave the windows up. I'm parked under a pine and there's a breeze blowing off the bay, but the temperature has been pushing upper eighties all day, and I know how quickly a closed car can turn into an oven.

I also realize that someone could easily reach through the open window and grab Mari if they wanted to. But I made a decision years ago that I'm not going to raise my daughters to fear that what happened to my mother might also happen to them.

One last word on this subject, and then I'm done. I guarantee if anyone has a problem with how I'm raising my daughters, then they've never lived in Michigan's Upper Peninsula. That's all.

BACK AT THE TRUCK, Mari the Escape Artist is nowhere to be seen. I go up to the passenger window and look inside. Mari is sitting on the floor chewing a cellophane candy wrapper she found under the seat as if it's a piece of gum. I open the door, fish the wrapper out of her mouth and shove it in my pocket, then dry my fingers on my jeans and buckle her in. A butterfly flutters through the window and lands on a spot of sticky something on the dash. Mari claps her hands and laughs. I grin. It's impossible not to. Mari's laugh is delicious, a full-throated, unself-conscious chortle I never get tired of hearing. Like those YouTube videos people post of babies laughing uncontrollably over inconsequential things like a jumping dog or a person tearing strips of paper—Mari's laugh is like that. Mari is sparkling water, golden sunshine, the chatter of wood ducks overhead.

I shoo the butterfly out and put the truck in gear. Iris's bus drops her off at our house at four forty-five. Stephen usually watches the girls while I make my deliveries, but he won't be back until late tonight because he's showing a new set of lighthouse prints to the gallery owner who sells his photographs in the Soo. Sault Ste. Marie, which is pronounced "Soo" and not "Salt," as people who don't know better often say, is the second-largest city in the Upper Peninsula. But that isn't saying much. The sister city on the Canadian side is a lot bigger. Locals on both sides of the St. Mary's River call their city "The Soo." People come from all over the world to visit the Soo Locks to watch the giant iron-ore carriers pass through. They're a big tourist draw.

I deliver the last case of assorted jams to the Gitche Gumee Agate and History Museum gift shop, then drive to the lake and park. As soon as Mari sees the water, she starts flapping her arms. "Wa-wa, wa-wa." I know that at her age she should be speaking in complete sentences. We've been taking her to a developmental specialist in Marquette once a month for the past year, but so far this is the best she's got.

We spend the next hour on the beach. Mari sits beside me on the warm beach gravel, working off the discomfort of an erupting molar by chewing on a piece of driftwood I rinsed off for her in the water. The air is hot and still, the lake calm, the waves sloshing gently like water in a bathtub. After a while, we take off our sandals and wade into the water and splash each other to cool off. Lake Superior is the largest and deepest of the Great Lakes, so the water never gets warm. But on a day like today, who'd want it to?

I lean back on my elbows. The rocks are warm. As hot as it is today, it's hard to believe that when Stephen and I brought Iris and Mari to this same spot a couple of weeks ago to watch the Perseid meteor shower we needed sleeping bags and jackets. Stephen thought it was overkill when I packed them into the back of the Cherokee, but of course he had no idea how cold the beach gets after the sun goes down. The four of us squeezed inside a double sleeping bag and lay on our backs on the sand looking up. Iris counted twenty-three shooting stars and made a wish on every one, though Mari snoozed through most of the show. We're going to come out again in a couple of weeks to check out the northern lights.

I sit up and check my watch. It's still difficult for me to be somewhere at an exact time. When a person is raised on the land as I was, the land dictates what you do and when. We never kept a clock. There was no reason to. We were as attuned to our environment as the birds, insects, and animals, driven by the same circadian rhythms. My memories are tied to the seasons. I can't always remember how old I was when a particular event took place, but I know what time of year it happened.

I know now that for most people, the calendar year begins on January 1. But in the marsh there was nothing about January to distinguish it from December or February or March. Our year began in the spring, on the first day the marsh marigolds bloomed. Marsh marigolds are huge bushy plants two feet or more in diameter, each covered with hundreds of inch-wide bright yellow blossoms. Other flowers bloom in the spring, like the blue flag iris and the flowering heads of the grasses, but marsh marigolds are so prolific that nothing compares to that astonishing yellow carpet. Every year my father would pull on his waders and go out into the marsh and dig one up. He'd put it in an old galvanized tub half-filled with water and set it on our back porch, where it glowed like he'd brought us the sun.

I used to wish my name was Marigold. But I'm stuck with Helena, which I often have to explain is pronounced "Hel-LAY-nuh." Like a lot of things, it was my father's choice.

THE SKY TAKES ON a late afternoon quality that warns it's time to go. I check the time and see to my horror that my internal clock has not kept pace with my watch. I scoop up Mari and grab our sandals and run back to the truck. Mari squalls as I buckle her in. I'm not unsympathetic. I would have liked to stay longer, too. I hurry around to the driver's side and turn the key. The dashboard clock reads 4:37. I might make it. Just.

I peel out of the parking lot and drive south on M-77 as fast as I dare. There aren't a lot of police cars in the area, but for the officers who patrol this route, aside from ticketing speeders, there isn't much to do. I can appreciate the irony of my situation. I'm speeding because I'm late. Getting stopped for speeding will make me later still.

Mari works herself into a full-on tantrum as I drive. She kicks her feet, sand flies all over the truck, the sippy cup bounces off the windshield, and snot runs out her nose. Miss Marigold Pelletier is most definitely not a happy camper. At the moment, neither am I.

I tune the radio to the public broadcasting station out of Northern Michigan University in Marquette, hoping for music to distract her—or drown her out. I'm not a fan of classical, but this is the only station that comes in clearly.

Instead, I pick up a news alert: **"—escaped prisoner . . . child abductor . . . Marquette . . ."**

"Be quiet," I yell, and turn the volume up.

**"Seney National Wildlife Refuge . . . armed and dangerous . . . do not approach."** At first, that's all I manage to catch.

I need to hear this. The refuge is less than thirty miles from our house. "Mari, stop!"

Mari blinks into silence. The report repeats:

**"Once again, state police report that a prisoner serving life without parole for child abduction, rape, and murder has escaped from the maximum security prison in Marquette, Michigan. The prisoner is believed to have killed two guards during a prison transfer and escaped into the Seney National Wildlife Refuge south of M-28. Listeners should consider the prisoner armed and dangerous.**

**Do NOT, repeat, DO NOT approach. If you see anything suspicious, call law enforcement immediately. The prisoner, Jacob Holbrook, was convicted of kidnapping a young girl and keeping her captive for more than fourteen years in a notorious case that received nationwide attention . . ."**

My heart stops. I can't see. Can't breathe. Can't hear anything over the blood rushing in my ears. I slow the truck and pull carefully onto the shoulder. My hand shakes as I reach to turn the radio off.

Jacob Holbrook has escaped from prison. The Marsh King. My father.

And I'm the one who put him in prison in the first place.

# 2

I pull back onto the pavement in a spray of gravel. I doubt anyone is patrolling this section of highway in view of everything that's happening thirty miles to the south, and even if someone is, getting stopped for speeding is now the least of my concerns. I have to get home, have to have eyes on both of my daughters, have to know that they're with me and they're safe. According to the news alert, my father is heading away from my house and into the wildlife refuge. Only I know he's not. The Jacob Holbrook I know would never be that obvious. I'll bet any amount of money that after a couple of miles, the searchers are going to lose his trail, if they haven't already. My father can pass through the marsh like a spirit walker. He wouldn't lay down a trail for searchers to follow unless he wanted them to follow it. If my father wants the people who are looking for him to think he's in the wildlife refuge, then they're not going to find him in the marsh.

I clench the wheel. I picture my father lurking in the trees as Iris gets off the bus and starts up our driveway, and I press down harder on the pedal. I see him jumping out and grabbing her the moment the driver pulls away, the way he used to leap out of the bushes when I came out of the outhouse, to frighten me. My fear for Iris's safety isn't logical. According to the news alert, my father escaped between four and four fifteen, and it's now four forty-five; there's no way he could travel thirty miles on foot in half an hour. But that doesn't make my fear any less real.

My father and I haven't spoken in fifteen years. Odds are he doesn't know I changed my last name when I turned eighteen because I'd had all I could stand of being known only for the circumstances in which I grew up. Or that when his parents passed away eight years ago, they willed this property to me. Or that I used the bulk of the inheritance to have the house where he grew up razed and brought in the double-wide. Or that I'm living here now with my husband and two young daughters. My father's granddaughters.

But he might. After today, anything is possible. Because today my father escaped from prison.

I'M ONE MINUTE LATE. Definitely not more than two. I'm trapped behind Iris's school bus with the still-shrieking Mari. Mari has worked herself into such a state, I doubt she remembers what set her off. I can't pull around the bus and into our driveway because the stop sign is extended and the red lights are flashing. Never mind that mine is the only other vehicle on the highway and that's my daughter the driver is delivering. As if I might accidentally run over my own child.

Iris climbs off the bus. I can see by the dejected way she trudges up our empty driveway that she thinks I've forgotten to get home in time for her again. "Look, Mari." I point. "There's our house. There's Sissy. Shh. We're almost there."

Mari follows my finger, and when she sees her sister, just like that, she shuts up. She hiccups. Smiles. "Iris!" Not "I-I" or "I-sis" or "Sissy" or even "I-wis," but "Iris," plain as day. Go figure.

At last the driver decides that Iris is far enough from the highway to turn off the caution lights and the door hisses shut. The second the bus starts moving, I swing around and pull into our driveway. Iris's shoulders straighten. She waves, beams. Mommy is home and her world is back on its axis. I wish I could say the same for mine.

I shut off the engine and go around to the passenger side to strap Mari into her sandals. As soon as her feet touch down, she takes off across the front yard.

"Mommy!" Iris runs up and wraps her arms around my legs. "I thought you were gone." She says this not as an accusation but as a statement of fact. This is not the first time I've let my daughter down. I wish I could promise it will be the last.

"It's okay." I squeeze her shoulder and pat the top of her head. Stephen is always telling me I should hug our daughters more, but physical contact is difficult for me. The psychiatrist the court assigned to me after my mother and I were recovered said I had trust issues and made me do trust exercises, like closing my eyes and crossing my arms over my chest and falling backward with nothing to catch me but her promise. When I resisted, she said I was being belligerent. But I didn't have trust issues. I just thought her exercises were stupid.

Iris releases me and runs after her sister into the house. The house isn't locked. It never is. The downstaters who own the big summer homes on the bluff overlooking the bay keep their places locked and shuttered, but the rest of us never bother. If a thief had a choice between an empty, isolated mansion filled with expensive electronics and a double-wide that sits within sight of the highway, we all know which one he'd pick.

But now I lock the door to the house and head for the side yard to make sure Rambo has food and water. Rambo runs along the line we strung for him between two jack pines and wags his tail when he sees me. He doesn't bark because I taught him not to. Rambo is a Plott hound, a brindled black and tan with floppy ears and a tail like a whip. I used to bring Rambo bear hunting with me and a couple other hunters and their dogs every fall, but I had to retire him two winters ago after a bear wandered into our backyard and he decided to take it on alone. A forty-five-pound dog and a five-hundred-pound black bear aren't an even match, no matter what the dog thinks. Most people don't notice at first that Rambo has only three legs, but with a twenty-five percent handicap, I'm not about to put him back in the field. After he started running deer last winter out of boredom, we had to start keeping him tied. Around here, a dog with a reputation for harassing deer can be shot on sight.

"Do we have any cookies?" Iris calls from the kitchen. She's waiting patiently at the table with her back straight and her hands folded while her sister scavenges crumbs on the floor. Iris's teacher must love her, but wait till she meets Mari. Not for the first time, I wonder how two such different people can come from the same set of parents. If Mari is fire, Iris is water. A follower and not a leader; a quiet, overly sensitive child who prefers reading to running and loves her imaginary friends as much as I once did mine, and takes the slightest rebuke far too much to heart. I hate that I caused her that moment of panic. Iris the Largehearted has already forgiven and forgotten, but I haven't. I never forget.

I go into the pantry and take a bag of cookies from the top shelf. No doubt my little Viking raider will one day attempt the climb, but Iris the Obedient would never think to. I put four cookies on a plate and pour two glasses of milk and head for the bathroom. Turn on the tap and splash a handful of water on my face. Seeing my expression in the mirror, I realize I've got to hold it together. As soon as Stephen gets home, I'll confess everything. Meanwhile, I can't let my girls see that anything is wrong.

After they finish their milk and cookies I send them to their room so I can follow the news without their listening in. Mari is too young to understand the import of terms like "prison escape" or "manhunt" or "armed and dangerous," but Iris might.

CNN is showing a long shot of a helicopter skimming the trees. We're so close to the search area, I could practically go outside and stand on our front porch and see the same helicopter. A warning from the state police scrolling across the bottom of the screen urges everyone to stay inside. Pictures of the murdered guards, pictures of the empty prison van, interviews with the grieving families. A recent photograph of my father. Prison life has not been kind. Photos of my mother as a girl and as a hollow-cheeked woman. Pictures of our cabin. Pictures of twelve-year-old me. No mention of Helena Pelletier yet, but give it time.

Iris and Mari come pattering down the hallway. I mute the set.

"We want to play outside," Iris says.

"'Side," Mari echoes. "Out."

I consider. There's no logical reason to make the girls stay inside. Their play yard is surrounded by a six-foot-high chain-link fence, and I can see the entire area from the kitchen window. Stephen had the fence installed after the bear incident. "Girls in, animals out," he said with satisfaction when the contractors finished, dusting his hands on the seat of his pants as if he'd set the posts himself. As if keeping your children safe was that simple.

"Okay," I say. "But just for a few minutes."

I open the back door and turn them loose, then take a box of mac and cheese from the cupboard and pull a head of lettuce and a cucumber from the fridge. Stephen texted an hour ago to say he's running late and he'll grab a bite to eat on the road, so it's boxed macaroni and cheese for the girls and a salad for me. I **really** don't like to cook. People might think that's strange considering the way I make my living, but a person has to work with what they have. Blueberries and strawberries grew on our ridge. I learned how to make jelly and jam. End of story. There aren't a lot of jobs that list ice fishing or beaver skinning as qualifications. I'd go so far as to say I hate to cook, but I can still hear my father's gentle scolding: "**Hate** is a strong word, Helena."

I dump the box of noodles into the pot of salted water boiling on the stove and move to the window to check on the girls. The quantity of Barbies and My Little Ponies and Disney princesses littering the play yard makes me ill. How will Iris and Mari develop qualities like patience and self-control if Stephen gives them everything they want? When I was a child, I didn't have so much as a ball. I made my own toys. Pulling apart horsetails and fitting the sections together again was every bit as educational as those toys where babies are supposed to match shapes to holes. And after a meal of young cattail spikes, we were left with a pile of what my mother always said looked like plastic knitting needles on your plate, but to me, they looked like swords. I'd stick them in the sand outside our back door like the palisades of a fort, where my pinecone warriors had many epic battles.

Before I dropped off the supermarket tabloid grid, people used to ask me what was the most incredible/amazing/unexpected thing I discovered after I joined civilization. As if their world was so much better than mine. Or that it was indeed civilized. I could easily make a case against the legitimate use of that word to describe the world I discovered at the age of twelve: war, pollution, greed, crime, starving children, racial hatred, ethnic violence—and that's just for starters. Is it the Internet? (Incomprehensible.) Fast food? (A taste easily acquired.) Airplanes? (Please—my knowledge of technology was solid through the 1950s, and do people really think airplanes never flew over our cabin? Or that we thought they were some kind of giant silver bird when they did?) Space travel? (I'll admit I'm still having trouble with that one. The idea that twelve men have walked on the moon is inconceivable to me, even though I've seen the footage.)

I always wanted to turn the question around. Can you tell the difference between a grass and a rush and a sedge? Do you know which wild plants are safe to eat and how to fix them? Can you hit a deer in that patch of brown hide low behind its shoulder so it drops where it stands and you don't have to spend the rest of the day tracking it? Can you set a snare for a rabbit? Can you skin and clean the rabbit after you catch it? Can you roast it over an open fire so the meat is done in the middle while the outside is deliciously black and crusty? For that matter, can you build a fire without matches in the first place?

But I'm a quick study. It didn't take me long to figure out that, to most people, my skill set was seriously undervalued. And in all honesty, their world offered some pretty amazing technological marvels. Indoor plumbing ranks high on the list. Even now when I wash dishes or run a bath for the girls, I like to hold my hands under the stream, though I'm careful to do it only when Stephen isn't around. There aren't many men who'd be willing to put up with my staying alone overnight in the bush on foraging expeditions, or going bear hunting, or eating cattails. I don't want to push it.

Here's the true answer: the most amazing discovery I made after my mother and I were recovered is electricity. It's hard to see now how we managed all those years without it. I look at people blithely charging their tablets and cell phones and toasting bread and microwaving popcorn and watching television and reading e-books late into the night and a part of me still marvels. No one who's grown up with electricity gives a thought to how they'd get along without it except on the rare occasion when a storm knocks out the power and sends them scrambling for flashlights and candles.

Imagine never having power. No small appliances. No refrigerator. No washer or dryer. No power tools. We got up when it got light and went to bed when it got dark. Sixteen-hour days in the summer, eight-hour days in the winter. With electricity, we could have listened to music, cooled ourselves with fans, heated the coldest corners of the rooms. Pumped water from the marsh. I could easily live without television and computers. I'd even give up my cell phone. But if there's one thing I'd miss if I had to do without it now, it's electricity, hands down.

A shriek comes from the play yard. I crane my

neck. I can't always tell from the pitch of my daughters' screams if their emergencies are trivial or real. A genuine emergency would involve buckets of blood pouring from one or both girls, or a black bear nosing around outside the fence. Trivial would be Iris waving her hands and screaming like she's eaten rat poison while Mari claps her hands and laughs. "Bee! Bee!" Another word she has no trouble saying.

I know. It's hard to believe that a woman who was raised under what were arguably the ultimate wilderness survival conditions has produced a daughter who is afraid of bugs, but there it is. I've given up bringing Iris with me in the field. All she does is complain about the dirt and the smells. I'm doing better so far with Mari. A parent isn't supposed to favor one child over the other, but sometimes it's hard not to.

I stand at the window until the bee wisely retreats to calmer airspace and the girls settle down. I imagine their grandfather watching from across the yard behind the tree line. One girl fair, the other girl dark. I know which one he'd choose.

I open the window and call the girls inside.

# 3

I give Mari and Iris their baths as soon as the dishes are cleared and put them to bed over their objections. We all know it's too early. No doubt they'll giggle and talk for hours before they fall asleep, but as long as they stay in their beds and out of the living room, I don't care.

I make it back to the living room in time to catch the six o'clock news. Two hours since my father escaped, and no reported sightings as yet, which really doesn't surprise me. I still don't think he's anywhere near the wildlife refuge. The same terrain that makes the refuge difficult to search makes it a hard place to escape into. That said, my father never does anything without a purpose. There's a reason he escaped where he did. I just have to figure out what it is.

Before I had my grandparents' house razed, I used to wander the rooms looking for insight into my father. I wanted to know how a person goes from child to child molester. The trial transcripts offer a few details: My grandfather Holbrook was a full-blooded Ojibwa who was given his non-Native name when he was sent away as a child to Indian boarding school. My grandmother's people were Finns who lived in the northwestern part of the U.P. and worked in the copper mines. My grandparents met and married when they were in their late thirties, and my father was born five years later. The defense painted my father's parents as perfectionists who were too old and rigid to adapt to the needs of their rambunctious little boy and punished him for the least infraction. I found a cedar spanking stick in the woodshed with the handle end worn smooth, so I know this part is true. In a cubby beneath a loose board in his bedroom closet I found a shoe box with a pair of handcuffs, a nest of blonde hairs I assumed were from his mother's hairbrush with a tube of lipstick and a pearl earring tucked inside like bird's eggs, and a pair of white cotton underpants I assumed were also hers. I can imagine what the prosecution would have done with that.

The rest of the transcripts don't offer much. My father's parents kicked him out of the house after he dropped out of school in the tenth grade. He cut pulpwood for a while, then joined the Army, where he was dishonorably discharged after a little more than a year because he couldn't get along with the other soldiers and wouldn't listen to his commanders. The defense said none of this was my father's fault. He was a bright young man who was acting out only because he was looking for the love and acceptance his parents never gave him. I'm not so sure. My father may have been wise in the ways of the wilderness, but I honestly can't recall a single instance when he sat down and read one of the **Geographics.** Sometimes I wondered if he knew how. He didn't even bother looking at the pictures.

Nothing pointed to the father I knew until I found his trout-fishing gear in a gunnysack hanging from the rafters in the basement. My father used to tell stories about fishing the Fox River when he was a boy. He knew all the best places to fish. Once he even guided a **Michigan Out of Doors** television crew. Since I found his gear, I've fished both the East Branch and the main stream of the Fox many times. My father's rod has a nice, fast action. With a four- or five-weight floating line, sometimes a six if I'm nymph or streamer fishing, I usually come home with my creel full. I don't know if I'm as good a trout fisherman as my father, but I like to think so.

I think about my father's fishing stories as the news report plays on and on. If I murdered two men to get out of prison knowing my escape would generate one of the biggest manhunts in Michigan's history, I wouldn't go floundering around blindly in the marsh. I'd go to one of the few places on Earth where I was happy.

IT'S A QUARTER TO NINE. I'm sitting on our front porch waiting for Stephen and slapping mosquitoes. I have no idea how he's going to react to the news that the escaped prisoner is my father, but I know it won't be pretty. My mild-mannered nature-photographer husband rarely loses his temper, which is one of the things that attracted me to him in the first place, but everyone has their limits.

Rambo is stretched out on the porch boards beside me. I drove down to the Plott family breeders in North Carolina eight years ago to get him when he was a puppy. This was long before Stephen and the girls came along. He's definitely a one-person dog. Not that he wouldn't protect Stephen or the girls if the occasion called for it. Plott hounds are utterly fearless, so much so that fans of the breed call them the ninja warriors of the canine world, the world's toughest dog. But if push came to shove and my entire family was in danger, Rambo would look out for me first. People who like to romanticize animals would call it love, or loyalty, or devotion, but it's just his nature. Plotts are bred to stay on game for days at a time, to sacrifice themselves before they run from a fight. He can't help what he is.

Rambo woofs and lifts his ears. I cock my head. I can discern crickets, cicadas, the shush of the wind through the jack pines, a rustling in the needles beneath that's probably a mouse or a shrew, the "who cooks for you, who cooks for you" of a barred owl calling from the far side of the meadow between our place and the neighbors', the cackles and squawks from the pair of night herons that nest in the wetland behind our house, and the Dopplered whoosh of a car whizzing past our place on the highway, but to his canine supersenses, the night is rich with sounds and smells. He whines under his breath and his front paws twitch, but other than that, he doesn't move. He won't unless I tell him to. I've trained him to both voice commands and hand signals. I put my hand on his head and he rests it again on my knee. Not everything roaming around in the dark needs to be investigated and chased down.

Of course I'm talking about my father. I know what he did to my mother was wrong. And killing two guards to escape from prison is unforgivable. But a part of me—a part no bigger than a single grain of pollen on a single flower on a single stem of marsh grass, the part of me that will forever be the little pigtailed girl who idolized her father—is happy my father is free. He's spent the past thirteen years in prison. He was thirty-five when he took my mother, fifty when we left the marsh, fifty-two when he was captured and convicted two years later. This November, he'll be sixty-six. Michigan isn't a death penalty state, but when I think about my father spending the next ten, twenty, possibly even thirty years in prison if he lives to be as old as his own father, I think maybe it should be.

After we left the marsh, everyone expected me to hate my father for what he did to my mother, and I did. I do. But I also felt sorry for him. He wanted a wife. No woman in her right mind would have willingly joined him on that ridge. When you look at the situation from his point of view, what else was he supposed to do? He was mentally ill, supremely flawed, so steeped in his Native American wilderness man persona that he couldn't have resisted taking my mother if he'd wanted to. Psychiatrists for both the defense and the prosecution even agreed on his diagnosis, antisocial personality disorder, though the defense argued mitigating factors, like the traumatic brain injury he suffered from being whacked on the head repeatedly as a boy.

But I was a child. I loved my father. The Jacob Holbrook I knew was smart, funny, patient, and kind. He took care of me, fed and clothed me, taught me everything I needed to know not only to survive in the marsh, but to thrive. Besides, we're talking about the events that resulted in my existence, so I can't very well say I'm sorry, can I?

The last time I saw my father, he was shuffling out of the Marquette County courtroom in handcuffs and leg shackles on his way to being locked up with a thousand other men. I didn't attend his trial—my testimony was considered unreliable because of my age and upbringing, and unnecessary because my mother was able to supply the prosecution with more than enough evidence to put my father away for a dozen lifetimes—but my mother's parents brought me over from Newberry the day my father was sentenced. I think they were hoping that if I saw my father get his just deserts for what he did to their daughter, I'd come to hate him as much as they did. That was also the day I met my paternal grandparents. Imagine my surprise when I discovered that the mother of the man I'd always thought of as Ojibwa was blonde and white.

Since that day I've driven past the Marquette Branch Prison at least a hundred times, every time we take Mari to see her specialist, or bring the girls shopping, or when we go to Marquette to see a movie. The prison isn't visible from the highway. All passersby see is a winding drive bracketed by two old stone walls; it looks like the entrance to an old-money estate that leads through the trees to a rocky escarpment overlooking the bay. The sandstone administration buildings are on the state's historic registry and date to the prison's opening in 1889. The maximum security section where my father was housed is made up of six level-five single-cell housing units surrounded by a twenty-foot-thick stone wall topped with a ten-foot wire fence. The perimeter is monitored by eight gun towers, five equipped with cameras to observe activity inside the housing units as well. Or so says Wikipedia. I've never been inside. I checked out the prison once using Google Earth's satellite view. There were no prisoners in the yard.

And now the prison population has been reduced by one. Which means that in a few short minutes, I'm going to have to tell my husband the truth, the whole truth, and nothing but the truth about who I am and the circumstances surrounding my birth, so help me God.

As if on cue, Rambo barks a warning. Seconds later headlights sweep the yard. The yard light kicks on as an SUV pulls into the driveway. It's not Stephen's Cherokee; this vehicle has a light bar on top and the state police logo on the side. For a fraction of a second I let myself believe I can answer the officers' questions and get rid of them before Stephen gets home. Then the Cherokee turns in immediately after. The interior lights of both vehicles come on at the same time. I watch Stephen's puzzlement turn to panic when he sees the officers' uniforms. He runs to me across the yard.

"Helena! Are you all right? The girls? What's wrong? Are you okay?"

"We're fine." I signal Rambo to stay and descend the porch steps to meet him as the officers approach.

"Helena Pelletier?" the lead officer asks. He's young, somewhere around my age. His partner looks even younger. I wonder how many people they've questioned. How many lives their questions have ruined. I nod and grope for Stephen's hand. "We'd like to ask you a few questions about your father, Jacob Holbrook."

Stephen's head whips around. "Your fath—

Helena, what's going on? I don't understand. The escaped prisoner is **your father**?"

I nod again. A gesture I hope Stephen will take as both apology and confession. **Yes, Jacob Holbrook is my father. Yes, I've been lying to you from the day we met. Yes, the blood of this evil man flows through my and your daughters' veins. I'm sorry. Sorry you had to find out like this. Sorry I didn't tell you before now. Sorry. Sorry. Sorry.**

It's dark. Stephen's face is in shadow. I can't tell what he's thinking as he looks slowly from me to the officers, to me, and back to the officers again.

"Come inside," he says at last. Not to me, but to them. He drops my hand and leads the officers across our front porch and into our house. And just like that, the walls of my carefully constructed second life come tumbling down.

# 4

The Michigan State Police officers sit on our living room sofa, one at each end, like a pair of blue bookends: same uniforms, same height, same hair, hats placed respectfully on the middle cushion, and knees splayed because Stephen is not a tall man and the sofa sits low. They seem bigger than they did in our yard, more intimidating, as if the authority their uniforms give them somehow also makes them physically larger. Or maybe the room only feels smaller with them in it because we so rarely have visitors. Stephen offered to make coffee when he invited them in. The officers declined, which I was glad about. I certainly wouldn't want them to linger.

Stephen is perched on the armchair next to the

sofa, a songbird ready to take flight. His right leg is jigging and his expression says clearly that he'd rather be anywhere but here. I'm sitting in the only remaining chair on the opposite side of the room. That the physical distance between me and my husband is as great as the room will allow isn't lost on me. Nor is the fact that since he welcomed the officers into our home, Stephen has been making an obvious and concerted effort to look anywhere but at me.

"When was the last time you saw your father?" the lead officer asks as soon as we're settled.

"I haven't spoken to my father since the day I left the marsh."

The officer raises an eyebrow. I can imagine what he's thinking. I live fifty miles from the prison where my father was incarcerated for thirteen years and I've never gone to visit him?

"So, thirteen years." He takes a pen and notepad from his shirt pocket and makes like he's going to write the number down.

"Fifteen," I correct. After my mother and I left the marsh, my father roamed the Upper Peninsula wilderness for two years before he was captured. The officer knows this as well as I do. He's establishing a baseline, asking a question he already knows the answer to so he can tell going forward when I'm lying and when I'm telling the truth. Not that I have any reason to lie, but he doesn't yet know that. I understand he has to treat me as a suspect until proven otherwise. Prisoners don't generally escape from a maximum security prison unless they have help, whether someone on the inside or someone on the outside. Like me.

"Right. So you haven't spoken to your father in fifteen years."

"You can check the visitors' logs if you don't believe me," I say, though I have no doubt they already have. "Phone records. Whatever. I'm telling the truth."

This is not to say I haven't thought about visiting my father in prison many times. The first time the police caught my father, I desperately wanted to see him. Newberry is a small town, and the jail where he was held until his arraignment was only a few blocks from my school; I could have walked over after classes or ridden my bike anytime I wanted. No one would have denied me a few minutes with my father. But I was afraid. I was fourteen. It had been two years. I'd changed, and maybe he had, too. I worried my father would refuse to see me. That he'd be angry with me since it was my fault he'd been caught.

After he was convicted, no one was going to drive a hundred miles from Newberry to Marquette and a hundred back so I could visit my father in prison, even if I'd had the courage to ask. Later, after I changed my last name and got my own transportation, I still couldn't visit because I would have had to show my ID and leave my name on the visitors' list, and I couldn't let my new life intersect with the old. Anyway, it wasn't like I felt a constant longing to see him. The idea of going to see him surfaced only once in a while, usually when Stephen was playing with the girls and something about their interaction reminded me of those long-ago days when we were together.

The last time I seriously considered reaching out was two years ago, when my mother died. It was a tough time. I couldn't acknowledge my mother's death without taking the chance that someone would connect the dots and figure out who I was. I was in a witness protection program of my own design; if I was going to make my new life stick, I had to cut all ties with the old. Still, I was my mother's only child, and staying away from her funeral felt like a betrayal. The idea that I could never see or talk to her again also stung me. I didn't want the same thing to happen with my father. Maybe I could have passed myself off as a prison groupie or a journalist if anybody wondered why I suddenly showed up to see him. But my father would have had to go along with my plan in order to make it work, and there was no way to know in advance if he'd be willing to do that or if he'd refuse.

"Do you have any idea where he might be heading?" the officer asks. "What he's planning?"

"None." **Other than the obvious desire to put as much distance between himself and the people who are looking for him as possible,** I'm tempted to say, but I know better than to antagonize men with guns. Briefly I consider asking for an update on the search, but the fact that they're asking for my help tells me all I need to know.

"Do you think he'll try to contact Helena?" Stephen asks. "Is my family in danger?"

"If there's somewhere you can go for a few days, that's probably a good idea."

Stephen's face blanches.

"I don't think he'll come here," I say quickly. "My father hated his parents. He has no reason to come back to the place where he grew up. He just wants to get away."

"Wait. You're saying your father **lived** here? In our house?"

"No, no. Not this house. This was his parents' property, but after I inherited it I had the original house torn down."

"His parents' property . . ." Stephen shakes

his head. The officers look at him pityingly, like they see this kind of thing all the time. **Women,** their expressions seem to say. **Can't trust 'em.** I feel sorry for Stephen as well. It's a lot to take in. I wish I could have broken the news in private, in my own time and way, instead of being forced into making a spectacle out of his ignorance and confusion.

Stephen watches me intently as the questions continue, no doubt waiting for the other shoe to drop: Where was I when my father escaped? Was anyone with me? Did I ever send my father a package when he was in prison? Not even a jar of jelly or a card on his birthday?

Stephen's eyes bore into mine as the interrogation goes on and on. Accusing me. Judging me. My hands sweat. My mouth forms the appropriate answers to the officers' questions, but all I can think about is how this is hitting Stephen, how my silence put him and my daughters at risk. How all of the sacrifices I made to keep my secret are worth nothing now that my secret is out.

At last, footsteps down the hall. Iris pokes her head around the corner. Her eyes get big when she sees the policemen in her living room. "Daddy?" she says uncertainly. "Are you coming to kiss me good night?"

"Of course, Pumpkin," Stephen says without

a hint of the tension we're both feeling. "Go back to bed. I'll be right there." He turns to the officers. "Are we done?"

"For now." The lead officer gives me a look like he thinks I know more than I'm telling, then makes a show of handing me his card. "If you think of anything that will help us find your father, anything at all, give me a call."

"I WANTED TO TELL YOU," I say as soon as the door closes behind them.

Stephen looks at me for a long time, then slowly shakes his head. "Then why didn't you?"

There could not be a fairer question. I wish I knew how to answer. Certainly I didn't set out to lie to him. When we met seven years ago at the Paradise blueberry festival and Stephen asked me out for a burger after he bought all my remaining stock, I couldn't very well say, "I'd love to go out with you. I'm Helena Eriksson, and by the way, remember that guy who kidnapped a Newberry girl back in the late eighties and kept her prisoner in the swamp for a dozen years? The one they called The Marsh King? Yeah, he's my dad." I was twenty-one. By then I'd enjoyed three blissful years of anonymity. No whispers behind my back, no gossip or pointed fingers, just me and my dog, minding our own business, hunting and fishing and foraging. I wasn't about to break my silence for a dark-haired, dark-eyed stranger with a suspicious fondness for cattail-blueberry jelly.

But there were other times I could have brought it up. Maybe not on our first date, or our second, or our third, but sometime after the getting-to-know-you train was moving down the tracks and before we stood at the rail of the Pictured Rocks tour boat, knowing without having to say it that we were now a couple. Definitely before Stephen got down on one knee on a rocky Lake Superior beach. But by then I had so very much to lose, and I could no longer see what I had to gain.

Stephen shakes his head again. "I give you all the space in the world, and this is how you . . . Do I say anything when you go bear hunting? When you stay in the woods by yourself overnight? When you disappeared for two weeks when Mari was a baby because you needed time alone? I mean, whose wife goes **bear hunting**? I would have **worked** with you on this, Helena. Why couldn't you trust me?"

It would take a thousand words to begin to answer him fully, but I come up with only two. "I'm sorry." And even to my ears, the words sound lame. But they're true. I **am** sorry. I'd apologize every day for the rest of my life if it would help.

"You lied to me. Now you've put our family in danger." Stephen brushes past me and goes into the kitchen. The side door bangs. I can hear him shifting things around in the garage. He comes back with a suitcase in each hand.

"Pack whatever you need for yourself and for the girls. We're going to my parents'."

"Now?"

Stephen's parents live in Green Bay. It's a four-hour drive, never mind the multiple bathroom stops you have to make when you're traveling with two small children. If we leave now, we won't get to his parents' until at least three a.m.

"What else are we supposed to do? We can't stay here. Not with a murderous psychopath on the loose." He doesn't say **a murderous psychopath who also happens to be your father,** but he may as well have.

"He's not coming here," I say again—not so much because I believe it, but because Stephen has to. I can't stand the idea of his thinking I would willfully and knowingly do anything that would jeopardize my family.

"Do you **know** that? Can you promise your father won't come after you or the girls?"

I open my mouth, then shut it. Of course I

can't promise. As much as I might think I know what my father will or won't do, the truth is, I don't. He murdered two men to escape from prison, and I never anticipated that.

Stephen's hands clench into fists. I get ready. Stephen has never hit me, but there's always a first time. Certainly my father never hesitated to hit my mother for less. Stephen's chest swells. He draws a deep breath. Lets it out. Takes another, then lets that out, too. Picks up the girls' pink princess suitcase and turns on his heel and stomps off down the hall. Dresser drawers bang open and closed. "Daddy?" Iris says plaintively. "Are you mad at Mommy?"

I grab the other suitcase and head for the master bedroom. Pack everything Stephen will need to stay at his parents' as long as he has to and carry the case into the living room and put it by the front door. I want to tell him that I understand how he feels. That I wish things could have been different. That it's shattering me to see him drawing away. But when he comes back with the girls' suitcase and walks past me to carry both cases to the car like we're strangers, I don't.

We button the girls' sweaters over their pajamas without speaking. Stephen slings Mari over his shoulder and carries her to the car. I follow, leading Iris by the hand. "Be a good girl," I tell her as I lift her into her booster seat and buckle her in. "Listen to your father. Do what he says." Iris blinks and rubs her eyes like she's trying not to cry. I pat her head and tuck the well-loved stuffed animal she calls Purple Bear beside her, then go around to stand by the driver's side door.

Stephen's eyebrows go up when he sees me. He rolls the window down.

"Aren't you going to get Rambo?" he asks.

"I'm not coming," I say.

"Helena. Don't do this."

I know what he's thinking. It's no secret I dread going to his parents' under the best of conditions—never mind showing up with the girls in the middle of the night because my father is an escaped prisoner. It's not only the effort of having to pretend to be interested in what interests them even though we have absolutely nothing in common; it's the gauntlet of rules and manners I have to navigate. I've come a long way from the socially inept twelve-year-old I once was, but whenever I'm around them, Stephen's parents make me feel like I haven't.

"It's not that. I have to stay here. The police need my help."

This is only partially correct. Stephen would never accept the real reason I have to stay behind. The truth is, sometime between the officers' first question and when the door closed behind them, I realized that if anyone is going to catch my father and return him to prison, it's me. No one is my father's equal when it comes to navigating the wilderness, but I'm close. I lived with him for twelve years. He trained me, taught me everything he knows. I know how he thinks. What he'll do. Where he'll go.

If Stephen knew what I was planning, he'd remind me that my father is armed and dangerous. My father killed two prison guards, and the police are convinced he's ready to kill again. But if there's one person who is not in danger from my father, it's me.

Stephen's eyes narrow. I can't tell if he knows I'm not being entirely honest. I'm not sure it would make a difference if he did.

At last he shrugs. "Call me," he says wearily. The window goes up.

The yard light kicks on as Stephen backs into the turnaround and starts down the driveway. Iris cranes her neck to watch out the back window. I lift my hand. Iris returns my wave. Stephen does not.

I stand in the yard until the Cherokee's taillights fade into the distance, then walk back to the house and sit down on the porch steps. The night feels empty, cold, and suddenly I realize that in the six years since I got married, I've never spent the night at my house by myself. A lump forms in my throat. I swallow it down. I have no right to self-pity. I did this to myself. I just lost my family, and it's my fault.

I know how this works. I've been down this road before, after my mother sank into a depression so deep that she wouldn't come out of her room for days and sometimes weeks at a time and my grandparents sued her for custody of me. If Stephen doesn't come back, if he decides my sin of omission is too big to forgive and he wants a divorce, I'll never see my girls again. Stand me and my dysfunctional childhood and idiosyncrasies and quirks alongside Stephen's one-hundred-percent normal middle-class upbringing and conventional family values and there's no way I'll measure up. I have so many strikes against me, I may as well not go to bat. There's not a judge on Earth who'd decide in my favor. Even I wouldn't award myself custody.

Rambo plops down beside me and puts his head in my lap. I gather him in my arms and bury my face in his fur. I think about all of the years and all of the chances I had to come clean about who I am. In hindsight, I think I'd convinced myself that if I didn't say my father's name, I could pretend he didn't exist. But he does. And now, in my heart, I realize I always knew that one day, there'd be an accounting.

Rambo whines and pulls away. I let him go off into the night and stand up and go inside the house to get ready. There's only one way to fix this. One way to get my family back. I **have** to capture my father. It's the only way to prove to Stephen that nothing and no one is more important to me than my family.

# 5

## The Cabin

A long time passed after the Marsh King dragged the terrified princess beneath the slime. At last the stork saw a green stalk shooting up out of the deep, marshy ground. As it reached the surface of the marsh, a leaf spread out, and unfolded itself broader and broader, and close to it came forth a bud.

One morning when the stork was flying over, he saw that the power of the sun's rays had caused the bud to open, and in the cup of the flower lay a charming child—a little maiden, looking as if she had just come out of a bath.

"The wife of the Viking has no children, and how often she has wished

**for a little one," the stork thought. "People always say the stork brings the babies; I will do so in earnest this time."**

**The stork lifted the little girl out of the flower-cup and flew to the castle. He picked a hole with his beak in the bladder skin covering the window, and laid the beautiful child in the bosom of the Viking's wife.**

—HANS CHRISTIAN ANDERSEN,
**The Marsh King's Daughter**

I had no idea when I was growing up that there was anything wrong with my family. Children usually don't. Whatever their situation, that's what's normal to them. Daughters of abusers fall in with abusive men as adults because that's what they're used to. It feels familiar. Natural. Even if they don't like the circumstances in which they were brought up.

But I loved my life in the marsh, and I was devastated when it all fell apart. I was the **reason** everything fell apart, of course, but I didn't fully understand the role I played in that until much later. And if I had known then what I do now, things would have been very different. I wouldn't have adored my father. I would have been much more understanding of my mother. I suspect, though, that I still would have loved hunting and fishing.

The papers called my father The Marsh King after the ogre in the fairy tale. I understand why they gave him that name, as anyone who's familiar with the fairy tale will as well. But my father was no monster. I want to make that absolutely clear. I realize that much of what he said and did was wrong. But at the end of the day, he was only doing the best he could with what he had, same as any other parent. And he never abused me, at least not in a sexual way, which is what a lot of people assume.

I also understand why the papers called our place a farmhouse. It looks like an old farmhouse in the pictures: two stories, weathered clapboard siding, double-hung casement windows so crusted with dirt that it was impossible to see in or out, wood-shingled roof. The outbuildings contribute to the illusion—a three-sided slab-wood utility shed, a woodshed, an outhouse.

We called our place the cabin. I can't tell you who built our cabin, or when, or why, but I can guarantee it wasn't farmers. The cabin sits on a narrow, densely forested ridge of maple and beech and alder that juts out of the marsh like an overweight woman lying on her side: one small hump for her head, a slightly bigger hump for her shoulders, a third for her massive hips and thighs. Our ridge was part of the Tahquamenon River basin, 129 square miles of wetland that drain into the Tahquamenon River, though I didn't learn that until later. The Ojibwa call the river **Adikamegong-ziibi,** "river where the whitefish are found," but all we caught were muskies, walleye, perch, and pike.

Our ridge was far enough from the main branch of the Tahquamenon that it couldn't be seen by fishermen or canoeists. The swamp maples that grew around the cabin make it nearly invisible from the air as well. You might think the smoke from our woodstove would have given away our location, but it never did. If anyone happened to notice during the years we lived there, they must have assumed the smoke came from a fisherman's dinner or a hunting cabin. At any rate, my father is nothing if not cautious. I'm sure he waited months after he took my mother before he risked a fire.

My mother told me that for the first fourteen months of her captivity, my father kept her shackled to the heavy iron ring set in a corner post of the woodshed. I'm not sure I believe her. I've seen the handcuffs, of course, and used them myself when the need arose. But why would my father go to all the trouble of keeping her chained in the woodshed when there was no place for her to go? Nothing but grasses as far as the eye could see, broken only by the occasional beaver or muskrat lodge, or another solitary ridge. Too thick to push a canoe through, too insubstantial to walk on.

The marsh kept us safe during the spring, summer, and fall. In winter, bears, wolves, and coyotes occasionally crossed the ice. One winter, as I was pulling on my boots to go to the outhouse before I went to bed—because believe me, you do **not** want to leave your bed to go to the outhouse in the middle of the night in the winter—I heard a noise on the porch. I assumed it was a raccoon. The night was unseasonably warm, the temperature almost above freezing, the kind of bright, full-moon midwinter night that stretches the shadows and fools the hibernators into thinking it's spring. I stepped onto the porch and saw a dark shape almost as tall as me. Still thinking coon, I yelled and slapped it on the rump. Coons can make a real mess if you let them, and guess whose job it would've been to clean it up.

But it wasn't a raccoon. It was a black bear, and not a young one, either. The bear turned around and looked at me and chuffed. If I close my eyes, I can still smell its warm fish breath, feel my bangs flutter as it exhales in my face. "Jacob!" I yelled. The bear stared at me and I stared back until my father came with his rifle and shot it.

We ate bear for the rest of that winter. The carcass strung up in the utility shed looked like a person without its skin. My mother complained that the meat was greasy and tasted like fish, but what would you expect? "You are what you eat," as my father says. We spread the hide in front of the fireplace in the living room and nailed it to the floor so it would stay flat. The room smelled like rotten meat until the skin side dried, but I liked sitting on my bearskin rug with my toes stretched toward the fire and a bowl of bear meat stew in my lap.

My father has a better story. Years ago, long before my mother and me, when he was still a teenager, he was hiking through the woods north of his parents' place on Nawakwa Lake near Grand Marais to check his snare line. The snow was extra deep that year, and another six inches had fallen overnight, so the trail and the markers he used to navigate it had gotten buried. He wandered off the path before he realized it, and all of a sudden, his foot broke through the snow and he fell into a big hole. Snow and sticks and leaves fell down with him, but he wasn't hurt because he landed on something warm and soft. As soon as he realized where he was and what had happened, he scrambled up and out, but not before he saw that he was standing on a tiny wee bear cub no bigger than his hand. The cub's neck was broken.

Every time my father told that story, I wished his story belonged to me.

I WAS BORN two and a half years into my mother's captivity. She was three weeks shy of seventeen. She and I weren't a bit alike, neither in looks nor in temperament, but I can imagine what it must have been like for her to be pregnant with me.

**You're going to have a baby,** my father would have announced one late autumn day as he stomped the muck from his boots on our back porch and strode into the overheated kitchen. He had to tell my mother what was going on because she was too young and naive to understand the significance of the changes to her body. Or possibly she did know, but was in denial. A lot depends on how good the health classes at the Newberry Middle School were and how closely she paid attention.

My mother would have turned to face him from where she was cooking at the stove. She was always cooking, or heating water for cooking and washing, or hauling water to heat for washing and cooking.

In my imagination's first version, disbelief spreads across her face as her hands fly to her belly. **A baby?** she whispers. She doesn't smile. In my experience she rarely did.

In the second, she tosses her head defiantly and spits out, **I know.**

As much as I prefer the second version, I'm going with the first. In all the years we lived together as a family, I never once saw my mother talk back to my father. Sometimes I wish she would have. Think about what it was like for me. I was an infant, a toddler, a growing girl, and all I knew of motherhood aside from the perky, aproned housewives in the **National Geographic** advertisements was a sullen young woman who shuffled through her chores with her head down and her eyes rimmed red in secret misery. My mother never laughed, barely talked, seldom hugged or kissed me.

I'm sure she was terrified at the idea of having a baby in that cabin. I know I would have been. Maybe she hoped my father would realize a cabin in the marsh was no place for her to give birth, bring her to town, and leave her on the hospital steps like a foundling.

He didn't. The jeans and Hello Kitty T-shirt

my mother had been wearing since he snatched her became a problem. Eventually my father must have noticed that her shirt no longer covered her stomach and she couldn't zip her jeans, so he let her borrow one of his flannel shirts and a pair of suspenders.

I imagine my mother growing thinner as her belly swelled. During the early years at the cabin, she lost a lot of weight. The first time I saw her newspaper photo, I was shocked at how fat she used to be.

And then, when my mother was five months pregnant and really starting to show, an extraordinary thing happened. My father took her shopping. It seems that in all of the preparation for my mother's abduction and their life at the cabin, my father forgot to purchase clothing for the future me.

His predicament still makes me smile. Imagine, this resourceful wilderness man who could kidnap a young girl and keep her hidden for more than fourteen years overlooked the inevitable consequence of taking her as his wife. I picture my father examining his options with his head tipped to the side as he stroked his beard in that thoughtful way he has, but in the end, there weren't many. And so, true to character, he selected the most practical and began making preparations for a trip to the Soo, the only city within a hundred and fifty–mile radius of our cabin that had a Kmart.

Taking my mother shopping wasn't as dangerous as it sounds. Other kidnappers have done it. People stop looking. Memories fade. As long as the victim doesn't make eye contact or identify herself, the risk is small.

My father cut my mother's hair as short as a boy's and dyed it black. The fact that he had black hair dye at the cabin was a key point the prosecution later used to prove that my father acted with knowledge and malice aforethought. How did he know he would need hair dye? Or that my mother would be a blonde? At any rate, anyone looking at them would have seen a father shopping with his daughter. If they also happened to notice that my mother was pregnant, what of it? Certainly the average person wouldn't have guessed that the man holding tightly to the young girl's elbow was not her father, but the father of her child. I asked my mother later why she didn't tell anyone who she was or ask for help, and she said it was because she felt like she was invisible. Think of it: she was only sixteen, and by then my father had spent more than a year convincing her that no one was looking for her. That nobody cared. And so as they walked up and down the baby aisles filling their cart and no one paid any attention, it must have seemed to her like it was true.

My father bought two of everything I'd need in every size from infant to adult. One to wash and one to wear, my mother later told me. Boy clothes, because they'd work no matter which sex I turned out to be, and what use would I have at the cabin for a dress? Much later, after the police cleared the crime scene and reporters swarmed our ridge, someone took a picture of the row of shoes lined up in graduated sizes along my bedroom wall. I'm told the picture trended on Twitter and Facebook. People seemed to see the photo as a commentary on my father's evil nature, photographic proof that he intended to keep my mother and me prisoners for life. To me, the shoes just marked my growth the same way other people measure their kids against a wall.

In addition, my father bought my mother two long-sleeved shirts, two short-sleeved T-shirts, two pairs of shorts, two pairs of jeans, six pairs of underwear and a bigger bra, a flannel nightgown, and a hat, scarf, mittens, boots, and winter jacket. My father snatched my mother on the tenth of August; the only coat she'd worn the previous winter was his. My mother told me he didn't ask what colors she liked or whether she wanted a scarf that was solid or striped; he simply picked out everything for her. I can believe that, as my father liked to be in control.

Even at Kmart prices, the trip must have cost a fortune. I have no idea where he got the money. It's possible he sold some beaver skins. Possibly he shot a wolf. Wolf hunting was illegal in the Upper Peninsula when I was a child, but there was always a thriving market for skins, especially among Native Americans. He may have stolen the money, or he could have used a credit card. There was a lot about my father I didn't know.

I'VE THOUGHT a lot about the day I was born. I've read accounts of girls who were kidnapped and held captive, and they helped me understand some of what my mother went through.

She should have been in school, crushing on a boy or hanging with her girlfriends. Going to band practice and football games and whatever else kids her age were doing. Instead, she was about to have a baby with no one to help except the man who took her from her family and raped her more times than she could count.

My mother labored on the old wood-spindled bed in my parents' bedroom. Covering the bed were the thinnest sheets my father could find;

he knew by the time I arrived, he would have to throw everything away. My father was as solicitous in my mother's most difficult moment as he was capable of being, which meant that occasionally he offered her something to eat or brought her a glass of water. Aside from that, my mother was on her own. It wasn't cruelty on my father's part, though he can be cruel. It was just that until it was time for her to give birth, there wasn't a lot he could do.

At last my head crowned. I was a big baby. My mother tore enough to let me out, and it was over. Except it wasn't. One minute passed. Five. Ten. My father realized they had a problem. My mother's placenta had not detached. I don't know how he knew this, but he did. My father told her to hang on to the spindles in the headboard and to get ready, because it was going to hurt. My mother told me she couldn't imagine anything hurting worse than what she'd gone through, but my father was right. My mother passed out.

She also said my father damaged her when he reached inside to work the placenta loose, and that's why she never had more children. I wouldn't know. I don't have brothers and sisters, so this could be true. I do know that when the placenta doesn't detach, you have to act quickly if you're going to save the mother, and you don't have a lot of options. Especially when doctors and hospitals are out of the picture.

During the days that followed, my mother was out of her mind with fever as the inevitable infection took hold. My father kept me quiet with a rag soaked in sugar water between the times he laid me at my mother's breast. Sometimes my mother was conscious. Most of the time she was not. Whenever she was awake, my father made her drink willow bark tea, and that broke her fever.

I can see now that the reason my mother was indifferent toward me is because she never bonded with me. She was too young, too sick in the days immediately after I was born, too scared and lonely and collapsed in on herself from her own pain and misery to see me. Sometimes when a baby is born in similar circumstances, she gives her mother a reason to keep going. This wasn't true of me. Thank God I had my father.

# 6

I fetch my rucksack from the hall closet and pack it with extra ammunition and a couple of granola bars and bottles of water, then toss my father's fishing gear in the back of my pickup along with my tent and sleeping bag. The camping and fishing equipment will provide decent cover if anyone questions where I'm going or what I'm doing. I won't be anywhere near the search area, but you never know. A lot of people are looking for my father.

I load my rifle and hang it on the rack over the cab window. Technically you're not supposed to drive with a loaded weapon in your vehicle, but everybody does it. Regardless, I'm not about to join the hunt for my father without it. My weapon of choice these days is a Ruger

American. I've shot at least a half-dozen Rugers over the years; they're ridiculously accurate and they sell for a lot less than the competition. For bear, I also carry a .44 Magnum. An adult black bear is a tough animal with thick muscles and bones, and not many hunters can bring down a black bear with a single shot. A wounded bear doesn't bleed out the way a deer does, either. Bear bleed between their layer of fat and fur, and if the caliber is too small, the bear's fat can plug the hole while their fur soaks up the blood like a sponge, so the bear won't even leave a blood trail. An injured bear will run till it's too weak to keep going, which can be as far as fifteen or twenty miles. Another reason I only hunt bear with dogs.

I load the Magnum and put it in the glove box. My heart hammers and my palms are wet. I get nervous before any hunt, but we're talking about my father. The man I loved as a child. Who took care of me for twelve years in the best way he knew. The father I haven't spoken to in fifteen years. The man I escaped from so long ago but whose own escape just destroyed my family.

I'm too wired to sleep, so I pour a glass of wine and carry it into the living room. I set the glass on the coffee table without the requisite coaster and slouch into a corner of the sofa, put my feet on the table. Stephen has a fit when the girls put their feet on the furniture. My father, on the other hand, wouldn't have cared about anything as inconsequential as scuffs on a table. I've heard it said that when it comes to picking a husband, a girl chooses a man like her father—but if this is the rule, I'm the exception. Stephen's not from the Upper Peninsula. He doesn't fish or hunt. He could no more break out of prison than he could drive a race car or perform brain surgery. At the time I married him, I thought I was choosing wisely. Most of the time I still do.

I drain the glass in one long swallow. The last time I messed up on this scale was when I left the marsh. I knew two weeks after my mother and I were recovered that the new life I'd envisioned for myself wasn't going to work out as I'd hoped. I blame the media. I don't think anyone can grasp the magnitude of the news feeding frenzy that nearly swallowed me whole unless they were at the center of it. The world was riveted by what had happened to my mother, but the person it couldn't get enough of was me. The wild child who grew up in primitive isolation. The offspring of the innocent and her captor. The Marsh King's daughter. People I didn't know sent me things I didn't want: bicycles and stuffed animals and MP3 players and laptops. One anonymous donor offered to pay for my college education.

It didn't take my grandparents long to realize that the family tragedy had turned into a gold mine, and they were more than ready to cash in. "Don't talk to the media," they admonished my mother and me, meaning the hordes of reporters who left messages on my grandparents' answering machine and camped out in news vans across the street. If we kept quiet, I gathered, one day we could sell our story for a lot of money. I wasn't sure how long we weren't supposed to talk, or how stories were bought and sold, or even why we'd want a lot of money in the first place. But if this was what my grandparents wanted, I'd do as they asked. Back then I was still eager to please.

**People** magazine turned out to be the highest bidder. To this day I don't know what they paid. Certainly my mother and I never saw any money from the sale. All I know is that right before it was time to leave for the big welcome-home party my grandparents threw for my mother and me, my grandfather sat us down and told us that a reporter from **People** magazine was going to interview us at the party while a photographer took pictures, and we should tell her whatever she wanted to know.

The party was held at the Pentland Township

Hall. Judging by the name I imagined something on the order of a Viking keep: high vaulted ceilings, thick stone walls, slitted windows, straw-covered floor. I pictured chickens and dogs and goats wandering about, a milk cow tied to an iron ring in the corner, a wooden table running the length of the room for the peasants, and private rooms upstairs for the lords and ladies. But this hall turned out to be a big white wooden building with its name on a sign in the front so no one would miss it. Inside there was a dance floor and a small stage on the main level and a dining room and a kitchen in the basement. Not nearly as grand as I had dreamed, but easily the biggest building I had ever seen.

We were the last to arrive. This was mid-April, so beneath the fluffy goose-down jacket somebody had sent me I wore a red sweater trimmed with what looked like white fur but wasn't and a pair of blue jeans, along with the steel-toed work boots I was wearing when we left the marsh. My grandparents wanted me to wear a yellow-checked dress that belonged to my mother and a pair of tights to hide the tattoos on my legs. The zigzag bands around my calves were the first tattoos my father gave me. In addition to these and a double row of dots across my cheeks, my father tattooed on my right bicep a small deer similar to the ones you see in cave drawings to commemorate my first major kill, and in the middle of my upper back a bear to represent the one I faced down on our porch when I was a child. My spirit animal is **mukwa,** the bear. After Stephen and I started feeling comfortable with each other, he asked about my tattoos. I told him I got them as part of a tribal initiation ceremony when I was growing up, the daughter of Baptist missionaries on a remote South Pacific island. I've noticed that the more outlandish the story you tell, the more inclined people are to believe it. I also told him my parents were tragically murdered on the same island while they were attempting to settle a dispute between warring native tribes in case he ever got the idea that one day he would like to meet them. I suppose now that my secret is out I could tell the truth about my tattoos, but the truth is, I've gotten used to telling stories.

The dress my grandparents wanted me to wear to the party reminded me of the kitchen curtains in our cabin, only brighter, and with no rips or holes. I liked the way the material was so loose and floaty; it felt like I wasn't wearing anything at all. But while I looked like a girl as I stood in front of my grandmother's tall bedroom mirror, I still sat with my knees spread like a boy, so my grandmother decided it would be better if I stuck with jeans. My mother wore the blue dress and matching hair ribbon from her "Have you seen me?" posters, though my grandmother fussed that the dress was both too tight and too short. Looking back, I'm not sure which was worse: that my grandparents expected my twenty-eight-year-old mother to play the role of the fourteen-year-old daughter they'd lost, or that my mother was willing to go along with it.

As we walked up a wooden ramp that looked like a drawbridge to a castle, my muscles were strung so tight with anticipation, they were practically humming. I felt like I was about to take a shot at a rare wild turkey preening and spreading his tail feathers for a female, and if I so much as twitched I'd scare him off. I'd already met more people than I could have imagined, but this was family.

"They're here!" someone shouted when they saw us. The music stopped. There was a moment of silence, and then the room exploded with the sound of a hundred people whistling and cheering and clapping. My mother was swept into a river of blonde aunts and uncles and cousins. Relatives swarmed over me like ants. Men shook my hand. Women pulled me into their bosoms, then held me at arm's length and pinched my cheeks like they couldn't believe I was really there. Boys and girls peeked out from behind them as wary as foxes. I used to study the street scenes in the **Geographics** and try to imagine what it would be like to be surrounded by people. Now I knew. It's noisy. Crowded, hot, and smelly. I loved every second of it.

The **People** reporter pushed a path for us through the crowd and down the stairs. I think she thought I was frightened by the commotion and the noise. She didn't yet know this was where I wanted to be. That I had left the marsh by choice.

"Are you hungry?" the reporter asked.

I was. My grandmother wouldn't let me eat before we came because she said there would be plenty of food to eat later at the party, and she was right about that. The reporter led me to a long table next to the kitchen that was set with more food than I'd seen in my life. More than my father and mother and I could have eaten in a year, possibly two years.

She handed me a plate that was thin as paper. "Dig in."

I didn't see a shovel. What's more, I couldn't see anything that needed digging. But since I'd left the marsh, I'd learned that whenever I didn't know what to do, the best thing was to copy other people. So as the reporter started down the length of the table putting food on her plate, I did the same. Some of the dishes were labeled.

I could read the names—**Meatless Lasagna, Macaroni & Cheese, Cheesy Potatoes, Ambrosia Salad, Green Bean Casserole**—but I had no idea what they meant, or if I'd like how they tasted. I put a spoonful of everything on my plate anyway. My grandmother told me I had to eat a few bites from every dish or the women who brought the food would get their feelings hurt. I wasn't sure how everything was going to fit on one plate. I wondered if I was allowed to take two. But then I saw a woman drop both her plate and the food on it in a big metal can and walk away, so I figured when my plate got full, that's what I'd do. It seemed an odd custom. In the marsh we never threw food away.

When we came to the end of the long table, I spotted another off to the side full of pies and cookies and cakes. On it was a cake with thick brown frosting and rainbow sprinkles, and not just a few. Twelve tiny candles arching over the words **Welcome Home, Helena** written in yellow frosting meant this cake was for me. I dropped my macaroni-potato-ambrosia-casserole in the metal can, picked up an empty plate, and slid the entire cake onto it. The **People** reporter smiled while the photographer took pictures, so I knew I'd done the right thing. Since I'd left the marsh, I'd been doing a lot of things wrong. To this day I can taste that first mouthful: so light and fluffy, it was like biting into a chocolate-flavored cloud.

While I ate, the reporter asked questions. How did I learn to read? What did I like best about living in the marsh? Did it hurt when I got my tattoos? Did my father touch me in ways I didn't like? I know now this last question meant did my father touch me in a sexual way, which he absolutely did not. I only answered yes because my father used to whack me on my head or backside when I needed punishing the same as he did to my mother, and of course I didn't like that.

After I finished eating, the reporter and the photographer and I went upstairs to the bathroom so I could wash off the makeup my grandparents put on my face to hide my tattoos. (Why was it called a bathroom, I remember thinking, when there was no place to take a bath? And why were there doors labeled MEN and WOMEN, but no door for children? And why did men and women need their own bathrooms in the first place?) The reporter said that people would like to see my tattoos, and I agreed.

When I finished, through the open doors to the parking lot I saw a group of boys playing with a ball. I knew that's what it was called because my mother had named it for me from the **Geographics.** But I hadn't yet seen a ball in real life. I was particularly fascinated by the way the ball jumped back into the boys' hands after they smacked it against the pavement, like it was alive, like it was inhabited by a spirit being.

"Want to play?" one of the boys asked.

I did. And I'm sure I could have caught the ball if I had known he was going to throw it at me. But I didn't, so the ball whacked me in the stomach hard enough to make me go **oof**—though it didn't really hurt—and then it rolled away. The boys laughed, and not in a good way.

What happened next has gotten blown all out of proportion. I only took off my sweater because my grandparents warned me the sweater needed to be "dry-cleaned," and that cost a lot of money, so I shouldn't get the sweater dirty. And I only pulled my knife because I wanted to throw it from behind my back and stick it in the wooden post that held their basketball hoop to show the boys that I was as skilled with my knife as they were with their ball. I can't help that one of the boys tried to grab my knife away from me, or that he sliced his palm open in the process. What kind of idiot grabs a knife by its blade, anyway?

The rest of "The Incident," as my grandparents forever after referred to it, was a blur of boys screaming and grown-ups shouting and my grandmother crying that ended with my sitting in the back of a police car in handcuffs with no idea why or what went wrong. Later I found out the boys thought I was going to hurt them, which was as ridiculous as it sounds. If I had wanted to slit someone's throat, I would have.

Naturally **People** magazine published the most sensational pictures. The photograph of me with my bare chest and facial tattoos and the sun glinting off my knife blade like a Yanomami warrior graced the cover. I'm told mine was one of their best-selling issues (number three, after the one about the World Trade Center and the Princess Diana tribute), so I guess they got what they paid for.

In hindsight I can see where we were all more than a little naive. My grandparents, for thinking they could cash in on what had happened to their daughter without repercussions; my mother, for thinking she could step back into her old life as if she'd never left; me, for thinking I could fit in. After that, the kids I went to school with fell into two camps: those who feared me and those who admired and feared me.

I stand up and stretch. Carry my glass to the kitchen and rinse it in the sink, then go into the bedroom and set my phone alarm and lie down fully dressed on top of the covers so I can head out as soon as it gets light in the morning.

This won't be the first time I've hunted my father, but I'm going to do everything in my power to make sure it will be the last.

# 7

The alarm goes off at five. I roll over and grab my phone off the nightstand and check my messages. Nothing from Stephen.

I thread my knife onto my belt and go to the kitchen to start a pot of coffee. Growing up, the only hot drink we had besides my father's foul-tasting medicinal teas was chicory. Digging the taproots, then washing, drying, and grinding them was a lot of work to make what I now know is essentially a second-class substitute for coffee. I've noticed you can buy ground chicory in grocery stores. I can't imagine why anyone would want to.

Outside it's just starting to get light. I fill a thermos and grab my truck keys from the hook by the door. I'm torn about leaving Stephen a note. Normally I would. Stephen likes to know where I am and how long I'll be gone, and I'm okay with that as long as he also understands that my plans could change and I might not be able to let him know when they do, since cell reception is spotty to nonexistent over much of the U.P. I always think it's ironic that in an area where you might conceivably truly need to use a cell phone, you so often can't. But in the end, I decide not to. I'll be home long before Stephen gets back. If he comes back.

Rambo scents out the window as I pull out of the driveway. It's 5:23. Forty-three degrees and dropping, which after the Indian summer weather we had yesterday only proves what everybody says: if you don't like the weather in Michigan, just wait a few minutes. Winds are steady out of the southwest at fifteen miles an hour. There's a thirty percent chance of rain later this morning, increasing to fifty percent this afternoon, which is the part of the forecast that worries me. Not even the best tracker can read sign after it's washed away.

I turn on the radio long enough to confirm that the hunt for my father is still going strong, then turn it off. The maples along the highway I pass are halfway to yellow. Here and there a swamp maple blazes bloodred. Overhead the clouds are dark as bruises. Traffic is light because it's a Tuesday. Also because the roadblock on M-77 at Seney has slowed traffic coming north to Grand Marais to a trickle.

I figure after my father laid down his decoy trail yesterday, he cut a wide circle and doubled back to the river and walked through the night in order to put as much distance between himself and the refuge as possible. He followed the Driggs River north because that's easier than striking out cross-country, and following it south would have led him deeper into the refuge. Also because wading through the river culvert under M-28 would be a convenient way to cross the highway without being seen. I picture him making his way carefully through the dark, weaving between trees and wading creeks as he avoids the old logging roads that would make travel easier but would leave him vulnerable to the helicopter's searchlight.

Then as soon as it started to get light, he holed up for the day in someone's empty cabin. I've broken into a cabin more than once myself when I got caught out after the weather turned. As long as you leave a note explaining why you broke in and a few dollars for the food you ate and any damage you caused, nobody cares. My challenge now is to find that cabin. Even if the rain holds off, as soon as it gets dark, my father will be on the move. I can't follow his trail if I can't see it, so if I don't find him before nightfall, by morning he'll have such a long lead, I never will.

Ultimately, I believe my father is heading for Canada. In theory he could roam the Upper Peninsula wilderness for the rest of his life, constantly on the move, never lighting a fire, moving strictly at night, never making a phone call or spending any money, hunting and fishing and eating and drinking whatever he finds in whatever cabins he breaks into like the North Pond Hermit did in Maine for almost thirty years. But it will be a whole lot easier if he just leaves the country. Obviously he can't cross at a manned border crossing, but there's a long stretch of border between Canada and northern Minnesota that's only lightly monitored. Most of the roads and railroad crossings have buried sensors to let authorities know when someone's trying to sneak through, but all my father has to do is pick a remote, deeply forested section and walk across. After that, he can keep going as far north as he likes, maybe settle near an isolated native community, take another wife if he's so inclined, and finish out his days in peace and obscurity. My father can pass as First Nations when he wants to.

Five miles south of our place I turn west onto a sandy two-track that will eventually come out at the Fox River campground. The entire peninsula is crisscrossed with old logging trails like this one. Some are as broad as a two-lane highway. Most are narrow and overgrown. If you know your way around the back roads as well as I do, you can drive from one end of the peninsula to the other without hitting pavement. If my father is heading toward the Fox River, as I suspect, there are three roads he'll have to cross. Taking into account the time he escaped and how far he could travel before he had to go to ground, this middle road is my best guess. There are a couple of cabins down this road I want to check. No doubt the searchers would be investigating these cabins as well if my father hadn't led them into the wildlife refuge. I imagine they'll get around to it eventually. Or maybe not. My mother stayed missing for close to fifteen years.

The irony of my mother's kidnapping is that it happened in a place where kidnappings never happened. The towns in the middle of Michigan's Upper Peninsula barely qualify for the descriptor. Seney, McMillan, Shingleton, and Dollarville are little more than highway intersections marked by a welcome sign, a church, a gas station, and a bar or two. Seney also has a restaurant with a motel and a laundromat. Seney marks the beginning of the "Seney

Stretch" if you're traveling west on M-28 or the end of it if you're traveling east. Twenty-five miles of straight-as-an-arrow, flat-as-a-pancake, mind-numbingly boring highway between Seney and Shingleton that crosses the remains of the Great Manistique Swamp. Travelers stop at the towns on either end to top off their gas tanks, or to grab some chips and a Coke to break up the ride, or to use the bathroom one last time before they head out because this is all they're going to see of civilization for the next half hour. Some say the Seney Stretch is really fifty miles long, but it only feels that way.

Until my mother's abduction, the children of Luce County weren't kept under lock and key. Possibly not even after, because old habits die hard, and because no one ever really thinks that bad things are going to happen to them. Especially after they've already happened to somebody else. **The Newberry News** reported every crime, no matter how small. And they were all small: a CD wallet taken from the front seat of an unlocked car, a mailbox vandalized, a bicycle stolen. No one could have dreamed the theft of a child.

Also ironic is the fact that during the years my grandmother and grandfather were desperately trying to find out what had happened to their daughter, she was less than fifty miles away. The

Upper Peninsula is a big place. Twenty-nine percent of the land area of the state of Michigan, three percent of the population. One-third state and national forest.

The newspaper's microfiche archives show the progress of the search.

Day One: Missing. Presumed to have wandered off and expected shortly to be found.

Day Two: Still missing. State police search and rescue dogs brought in.

Day Three: Expanded search, including a Coast Guard helicopter from St. Ignace assisted by Department of Natural Resources officers on the ground and assorted small aircraft.

And so on.

It wasn't until a full week after she went missing that my mother's best friend admitted they were playing in some empty buildings by the railroad tracks when they were approached by a man who said he was looking for his dog. This is also the first time the word **abducted** appears. By then, of course, it was too late.

From my mother's newspaper photo, I can see what drew my father's eye: blonde, chubby, pigtailed. Still, there must have been plenty of chubby blonde fourteen-year-olds my father could have taken. I've often wondered why he chose her. Did he stalk her in the days and weeks before he grabbed her? Was he secretly in love with her? Or was my mother's abduction merely the unfortunate convergence of time and place? I tend to believe the latter. Certainly I can't recall ever seeing anything pass between my father and mother that remotely resembled affection. Was keeping us supplied with food and clothing evidence of my father's love for us? In my weaker moments, I like to think so.

Before we were recovered, no one knew if my mother was dead or alive. The story **The Newberry News** published every year on the anniversary of her kidnapping grew progressively shorter. The last four years the headline and the single paragraph of text that accompanied it were exactly the same: "Local Girl Still Missing." No one knew anything about my father beyond my mother's girlfriend's description: a small, slender man with "darkish" skin and long, black hair, wearing work boots and jeans and a red plaid shirt. Considering the ethnicity of the area at the time was roughly evenly split between Native Americans and Finns and Swedes, and every other male over the age of sixteen tramped around in work boots and flannel, her description was next to useless. Except for those annual two column-inches and the twin holes in my grandparents' hearts, my mother was forgotten.

And then one day, fourteen years, seven months, and twenty-two days after my father kidnapped my mother, she returned, setting off the most extensive manhunt that Upper Peninsula residents had ever seen—until today.

I'M DRIVING approximately as fast as a man can walk. Not only because this road is the kind where if I drive too close to the edge and I'm not paying attention, the deep sand will pull my truck in up to its axles before I realize what's happening and there's no way I'm getting out without a tow truck, but also because I'm looking for footprints. I can't really track a person on foot from a vehicle, of course, and the odds that my father left a visible trail as he traveled this road—**if he traveled this road**—are extremely small, but still. When it comes to my father, I can't be too careful.

I've driven this road many times. There's a place about a quarter mile ahead as the road curves where the shoulder is solid enough to pull off and park. From there, if I walk another quarter mile north and west, then make my way down a steep incline, I come to the biggest patch of blackberries I've ever seen. Blackberries like a lot of water, and a creek runs along the bottom of the gully, so the berries grow especially big. When I'm lucky, I can gather enough to make a year's worth of jam from a single picking.

Strawberries are a different story. The thing people have to understand about wild strawberries is that the berries are nothing like the California behemoths they buy in grocery stores. Not much bigger than the tip of an adult's little finger on average, but with a flavor that more than makes up for their tiny size. Every once in a while, I might come across a berry that's as big as the end of my thumb (and when I do, that berry goes into my mouth and not into my berry pail), but that's about as big as wild strawberries ever get. Obviously it takes a great many wild strawberries to make a decent quantity of jam, which is why I have to charge a premium for mine.

Anyway, today I'm not looking for berries.

My phone vibrates in my pocket. I pull it out. A text from Stephen:

**Home in half an hour. Girls at my parents. Don't worry. We'll get through this. Love S**

I stop in the middle of the road and stare at the screen. Stephen coming back is just about the last thing I expected. He must have turned around and started for home as soon as he dropped off the girls. My marriage isn't over. Stephen is giving me another chance. **He's coming home.**

The implications are almost overwhelming. Stephen isn't giving up on me. He knows who I am and he doesn't care. **We'll get through this. Love S.** I think about all of the times I said or did something off and tried to cover for my ignorance as if my gaffe was a joke. Now I realize I didn't have to pretend. I put myself in this box. Stephen loves me for who I am.

**Home in half an hour.** Of course I won't be there when he arrives, but that's probably just as well. I'm glad now that I didn't leave him a note. If Stephen had any idea where I am or what I'm doing, he'd lose his mind. Let him think I went out for breakfast, or I'm picking up a few things at the store, or I went down to the police station to help them follow up on a lead, and I'll be right back. Which, if all goes according to plan, I will be.

I read the text one last time and put the phone in my pocket. Everyone knows how spotty cell reception in the U.P. can be.

# 8

## The Cabin

The Viking's wife was above measure delighted when she found the beautiful little child lying on her bosom. She kissed it and caressed it, but it cried terribly, and struck out with its arms and legs and did not seem to be pleased at all. At last it cried itself to sleep, and as it lay there so still and quiet, it was a most beautiful sight to see.

When the Viking's wife awoke early the following morning, she was terribly alarmed to find that the infant had vanished. She sprang from her couch and searched all round the room. At last, she saw, in that part of the bed where her

**feet had been, not the child, but a great, ugly frog.**

**At the same moment the sun rose and threw its beams through the window till it rested on the couch where the great frog lay. Suddenly it appeared as if the frog's broad mouth contracted, and became small and red. The limbs moved and stretched out and extended themselves till they took a beautiful shape; and behold, there was the pretty child lying before her, and the ugly frog was gone.**

**"How is this?" she cried, "Have I had a wicked dream? Is it not my own lovely cherub that lies there." Then she kissed it and fondled it; but the child struggled and fought, and bit as if she had been a little wild cat.**

—HANS CHRISTIAN ANDERSEN,
**The Marsh King's Daughter**

My father liked to tell the story of how he found our cabin. He was bow hunting north of Newberry when the deer he shot jumped at the last second and was only wounded. He trailed it to the edge of the marsh, then watched the panicked deer swim out to deep water and drown. As he turned to leave, the sun caught a glint of the metal flashing along the edge of our cabin's roof. My father used to say that if this had been another time of year, or another time of day, or if the cloud cover had been different that day, he never would have discovered it, and I'm sure that this is true.

He marked the spot and came back later in his canoe. As soon as he saw the cabin, he says he knew the Great Spirit had led him there so he'd have a place to raise his family. I know now this means that we were squatting. At the time, it didn't seem to matter. Certainly during the years we lived there, nobody cared. There are a lot of abandoned properties like that all over the U.P. People get the idea they'd like to have a place to get away from it all, so they buy a piece of property on a backwoods road surrounded by state land and build a cabin. Maybe it works for a while and they like having a place they can go to when they feel like roughing it until life gets in the way: kids, jobs, aging parents. A year goes by without their going to their cabin, and then another, and the next thing you know, paying taxes on a piece of property they're not using starts to look pretty unattractive. Nobody's going to buy forty acres of swamp and a rustic cabin except some other poor fool who wants to get away from it all, so in most cases, the owners let the property go to the state for back taxes.

After the police cleared the crime scene and the media attention died down, the state quietly took ours off the tax rolls. Some people thought the cabin should be torn down because of what happened there, but in the end, no one wanted to take on the cost.

You can visit the cabin if you want, though it might take a few tries to find the tributary that leads to our ridge. Souvenir hunters have long ago stripped the place bare. To this day you can buy items on eBay that are supposed to have belonged to me, though I can tell you with one hundred percent certainty that most of the things people are selling did not. But aside from a hole in the kitchen wall where a porcupine has chewed through, the cabin, the utility shed, the woodshed, the sweat lodge, and the outhouse are all as I remember them.

The last time I went back was two years ago, after my mother died. Ever since I'd had my girls, I'd been thinking about what it was like for me growing up, and I wanted to see how the reality matched my memories. The porch was covered in leaf litter and pine needles, so I broke a branch off a pine to sweep it clean. I set up my tent under the apple trees and filled a couple of milk jugs with marsh water, then sat down on an upended piece of firewood munching a granola bar and listening to the chickadees chatter. The marsh gets quiet right before dusk after the daytime insects and animals have gone silent and the nighttime creatures haven't yet come out. I used to sit on the cabin's porch steps every evening after supper paging through the **Geographics** or practicing the square knots and half hitches my father taught me while I waited for the stars to appear: **Ningaabi-Anang, Waaban-anang,** and **Odjiig-anang,** Evening Star, Morning Star, and Big Dipper, the three main stars of the Ojibwa people. When the wind was quiet and the pond was still, you could see the stars reflected perfectly in the water. After I left the marsh, I spent a lot of time on my grandparents' porch looking up.

I stayed at the cabin for two weeks. I fished, hunted, snared. Cooked my meals over a fire in the yard because someone had taken our woodstove. On the thirteenth day, when I found a mud puddle swarming with tadpoles and thought about how I'd love to show them to Mari and Iris, I knew it was time to go home. I loaded my things into my canoe and paddled back to my truck, taking a good long look at everything along the way because I knew this would be the last time I'd be back.

I realize two weeks probably seems like a long time for a young mother to stay away from her family. At the time, I would have been hard-pressed to explain why I needed to get away. I'd made a new life for myself. I loved my family. I wasn't unhappy. I think it was just that I'd been hiding who I was for so long and trying so hard to fit in, I needed to reconnect with the person I used to be.

It was a good life, until it wasn't.

MY MOTHER NEVER TALKED much about the years before my own memories kick in. I imagine an endless round of washing and nursing. "One to wash and one to wear" sounds good in theory, but I know from my own girls that babies can go through three or four outfit changes a day. Not to mention diapers. I overheard my mother telling my grandmother once how she struggled to control my diaper rash. I don't recall being particularly uncomfortable as an infant, but if my mother said my entire bottom was covered in nasty, red, oozing, bleeding sores, I have to believe her. It couldn't have been easy. Scraping the solids from my diapers into the outhouse, then rinsing the diapers by hand in a bucket. Heating water to wash them on the woodstove. Stringing lines across the kitchen to dry them when it was rainy and hanging my diapers in the yard when it wasn't. Indians never bothered to keep their infants diapered, and if my mother was smart, after the weather warmed up enough to let me run around with my bottom half naked, she'd have done the same.

There was no fresh water on our ridge. The people who built our cabin had evidently tried to dig a well, because there was a deep hole in our yard that my father kept covered with a heavy wooden lid where he occasionally shut me inside as a punishment, but the well came up dry. Maybe that's why they abandoned the cabin. We got our water from the marsh, in a rocky area shaped like a semicircle that we kept clear of vegetation. The pool it formed was deep enough to dip a bucket into without stirring up the sediment on the bottom. My father used to joke that by the time he carried the buckets up the hill, his arms were six inches longer than when he started. When I was little I believed him. When I got old enough to carry my share of buckets I understood the joke.

Cutting, hauling, and splitting the firewood my mother needed to keep me clean and dry was my father's job. I loved watching him split wood. He'd braid his long hair to keep it out of the way and take off his shirt, even in cold weather, and the muscles rippling beneath his skin were like a summer wind shivering across the Indian grass. My job was to stand the logs on end so my father could move down the row without stopping: **thwack, thwack, thwack, thwack, thwack, thwack.** One blow per log, each log split cleanly in two as he gave the ax head that last-second twist that sends the two halves flying. People who don't know how to split wood tend to bring the ax head straight down, as if weight and momentum alone would get the job done. But that only buries the head in the dense green wood as solidly as a chisel, and have fun getting it back out. One year the organizers of the blueberry festival in Paradise, Michigan, where I sell my jams and jellies brought in a traveling carnival with a sideshow. You know that game where you swing a mallet onto a platform that sends a weight up a pole and if it rings the bell at the top, you win a prize? I cleaned up on that one.

Our woodlot was on the low end of our ridge. After my father cut and limbed the trees and cut the logs to firewood length, we'd haul the wood up to our cabin. My father liked eight- and ten-inch-diameter trees best—not too big to handle, large enough that the chunks he left unsplit would hold the fire overnight. The maples near our cabin he let grow big for our sugar bush.

The average maple or beech tree of that size produces about a cord of firewood, and we needed between twenty and thirty cords every year depending on the severity of any given winter, so cutting and stacking firewood was a year-round job. A full woodshed was like money in the bank, my father liked to say, though ours wasn't always full. In the winter, he cut on a nearby ridge to make our woodlot last. He'd skid the logs across the ice using a cant hook or a pair of log dogs and a rope looped over his shoulder. The giant paper companies that log pulpwood throughout the U.P. like to say that trees are a renewable resource, but by the time we left the cabin, the trees on the lower end of our ridge were nearly gone.

Considering all of the effort we put into gathering firewood, you might think that life in the cabin during the winter was cozy. It was not. Surrounded by ice and snow five feet deep or more was like living in a freezer. From November to April, our cabin was never truly warm. Sometimes the outside temperature during the day never climbed above zero. Frequently the overnight low hit thirty and forty below. At those temperatures, you can't draw a breath without gasping when your capillaries constrict as the cold air hits your lungs, while the hairs inside your nose crinkle when the moisture in your nasal passages freezes. If you've never lived in the far north, I promise you have no idea how incredibly difficult it is to counteract that kind of deep and all-pervasive cold. Imagine the cold as a malignant fog, pushing down and in on you from all sides, rising up from the frozen ground, working its way through every minute crack and chink in the floor and the walls of your cabin; **Kabibona'kan,** Winter Maker, coming to devour you, stealing the warmth from your bones until your blood turns to ice and your heart freezes and all you have to fight against him is the fire in your woodstove.

Often I'd wake after a storm to find my blankets dusted with snow that had blown through the gaps around the windows where the boards had shrunk. I'd shake off the snow and gather the blankets around me and hurry down the stairs to sit by the woodstove with my hands wrapped around a mug of hot chicory until I was ready to brave the chill. We didn't bathe during the winter—we simply couldn't—which is one of the reasons my father later built the sauna. I know that probably sounds terrible to most people, but there wasn't much point to washing our bodies when we couldn't wash our clothes. Anyway, it was just the three of us, so if we stank, we didn't notice because we all smelled the same.

I DON'T REMEMBER MUCH from my toddler years. Impressions. Sounds. Smells. More déjà vu sensations than actual memories. Of course there are no baby pictures. But life in the marsh followed a regular pattern, so it's not difficult to fill in the gaps. December through March is ice, snow, and cold. In April, the crows come back and the peepers hatch. By May the marsh is all green grass and flowers, though you can still find patches of snow in the shadow of a boulder or on the north side of a log. June is bug month. Mosquitoes, blackflies, horseflies, deerflies, no-see-ums—if an insect flies and it bites, we've got it. July and August are everything people who live in more southern latitudes associate with summer, with a bonus: we're so far north, daylight lasts past ten o'clock. September brings the first frost, and we often see a September snowfall—just a light dusting because the leaves haven't finished turning, but a portent of things to come. This is also the month the crows take off and the Canada geese flock. October and November the marsh shuts down, and by mid-December, we're locked in the deep freeze again.

Now picture a toddler running around through all of that: rolling and sliding in the snow, splashing in the water, hopping around the yard pretending she's a rabbit or flapping her arms like she's a duck or a goose, her eyes, ears, neck, and hands puffy with bug bites despite the homemade insect repellent her mother slathers on her according to her father's recipe (ground goldenseal rootstock mixed with bear grease), and that pretty much covers my early years.

My first true memory is of my fifth birthday. At five I was a pudgy, four-foot-tall version of my mother, but with my father's coloring. My father liked long hair, so mine had never been cut. It reached almost to my waist. Most of the time, I wore it in pigtails or a single braid like my father's. My favorite outfit was a pair of overalls and a red plaid flannel shirt that nearly matched one of his. My other shirt that year was green. My tan leather work boots were identical to the ones my father wore, only without the steel toe, and smaller. When I wore this outfit I felt as though I could one day become every bit the man my father was. I copied his mannerisms, his speech patterns, his walk. It wasn't worship, but it was close. I was unabashedly, absolutely, and utterly in love with my father.

I knew this was the day I turned five, but I

wasn't expecting anything out of the ordinary. My mother surprised me, however, by baking a cake. Somewhere in the stacks of cans and bags of rice and flour in the storage room, my mother found a boxed cake mix. Chocolate with rainbow sprinkles, of all things, as if my father knew that one day, he'd have a child. I wasn't inclined toward doing anything in the kitchen I didn't have to, but the picture on the front of the box looked intriguing. I couldn't imagine how this bag of dusty brown powder would turn into a cake with tiny multicolored candles and swirly brown frosting, but my mother promised it would.

"What does 'Preheat oven to 350 degrees' mean?" I asked as I read from the directions on the back. I'd been reading since I was three. "And what are we going to do about an oven?" I'd seen pictures in the ads for kitchen appliances in the **Geographics,** and I knew we didn't have one.

"We don't need an oven," my mother replied. "We'll bake the cake the same way we bake biscuits."

This worried me. The baking powder biscuits my mother made in our cast-iron frying pan on top of our box stove were sometimes burned and always hard. I once lost a baby tooth biting into one. Her lack of cooking skills was a constant sore point with my father, but it didn't bother me. You can't miss what you've never known. In hindsight it's easy to see where he could have prevented the problem by kidnapping someone a little older, but who am I to second-guess my father? He made his bed, as the saying goes.

My mother dipped a rag in the bucket of bear grease we kept in a mice-proof cupboard and rubbed it over the inside of our frying pan, then set the pan to heat on top of the stove.

"'Mix in two eggs and one-fourth C cooking oil,'" I continued. "Cooking oil?"

"Bear grease," my mother said. "And the **C** means **cup.** Do we have any eggs?"

"One." Wild ducks breed in the spring. Luckily I was born the end of March.

My mother cracked the egg into the powder, added the grease she melted in a tin cup on top of the stove along with an equal amount of water, and whipped up the batter. "'Three minutes with an electric mixer at high speed, or three hundred strokes.'" When her arm got tired, I took a turn. She let me add the sprinkles, though by the time the batter was ready I'd eaten half. They were sweet, which was always nice, but the texture as I pushed them around in my mouth with my tongue made me think of mouse droppings. She added another dollop of grease to the pan so the batter wouldn't stick, poured the batter in, and covered the pan with a cast-iron lid.

Ten minutes later, after admonishing me twice not to peek or the cake wouldn't bake and then lifting the lid to check on its progress herself, she discovered that the edges of the cake were turning black while the middle was still goopy. She opened the firebox and stirred the embers so the heat distributed more evenly and added another log to the fire, and that did the trick. The final product looked nothing like the picture, but we polished it off all the same.

Maybe a cake made with duck eggs and bear grease doesn't sound like much to you, but it was the first time I tasted chocolate, and it was heaven to me.

THE CAKE BY ITSELF would have been more than enough. But the day wasn't over. In a rare demonstration of what I assume only in hindsight was motherly affection, my mother made me a doll. She stuffed one of my old baby sleepers with dried cattail rushes, poked five twigs into each sleeve for fingers and tied them in place with a piece of string, and fashioned a head by drawing a lopsided smiley face with a lump of charcoal on one of my father's old socks. And yes, the doll was as ugly as it sounds.

"What is it?" I asked when she laid it on the table in front of me as I licked the last cake crumbs from my plate.

"It's a doll," she said shyly. "I made it. For you."

"A doll." I was pretty sure this was the first time I'd heard the word. "What's it for?"

"You . . . play with it. Give it a name. Pretend it's a baby and you're its mother."

I didn't know what to say to this. I was very good at pretending, but imagining myself as the mother of this lifeless lump was beyond me. Thankfully my father found the concept just as ridiculous. He burst out laughing, and that made me feel better.

"Come, Helena." He pushed back from the table and held out his hand. "I have a present for you, too."

My father led me into my parents' bedroom. He lifted me onto their high bed. My legs dangled off the edge. Normally I wasn't allowed in their room, so I swung my feet in happy anticipation as my father got down on his hands and knees. He reached under the bed and pulled out a brown leather case with a brown handle and shiny gold trim. I could tell the case was heavy because he grunted as he lifted it, and when he plopped it down on the bed next to me, the bed bounced and jiggled like it did when I jumped on it, though I wasn't supposed to. My father selected the smallest key from his key ring and inserted it into the lock. The latch sprang open—**thwang.** He lifted the lid and turned the case so I could see inside.

I gasped.

The case was full of knives. Long ones. Short ones. Skinny ones. Fat ones. Knives with wooden handles. Knives with carved bone handles. Folding knives. Curved knives that looked like swords. Later my father taught me their names and the differences between them and how to use each one for hunting or combat or self-defense, but at the time all I knew was that I itched to touch them. I wanted to run my fingers over every one. Feel the coldness of the metal, the smoothness of the wood, the sharpness of each blade.

"Go ahead," he said. "Pick one. You're a big girl now. Old enough to carry a knife of your own."

Instantly my insides burned as hot as the fire in our woodstove. I'd wanted a knife for as long as I could remember. I had no idea such treasure lay beneath my parents' bed. Or that my father would one day share a piece of his treasure with me. I glanced toward the doorway. My mother's arms were crossed over her chest and she was frowning, so I could tell she didn't like the idea.

When I helped her in the kitchen, I wasn't allowed to touch anything sharp. I looked again to my father, and suddenly, in a burst of insight, I realized I didn't have to listen to my mother. Not anymore. Not when my father said I was old enough to have my own knife.

I turned back to the case. Looked over each knife carefully twice. "That one." I pointed to a knife with a gold-colored hilt and a shiny dark wood handle. I especially liked the raised leaf design on the knife's leather sheath. It wasn't a small knife, because even though my father said I was a big girl I knew I would grow bigger still, and I wanted a knife I could grow into, not one I'd grow out of, like the pile of discarded shirts and overalls in a corner of my bedroom.

"Excellent choice." My father held out what I now know is an eight-inch double-sided Bowie knife like a king presenting a knight with a sword. I started to reach for it, then stopped. My father had this game he liked to play where he pretended to give me something and when I tried to take it, he snatched it away. I didn't think I could bear it if he was playing now. He smiled and nodded encouragingly as I hesitated. This was also sometimes part of the game.

But I wanted that knife. I **needed** that knife. Quickly, I grabbed it before he could react. I closed my fist around it and hid the knife behind my back. I'd fight him for it if I had to.

My father laughed. "It's okay, Helena. Really. The knife is yours."

Slowly I brought the knife out from behind me, and when his smile got bigger and his hands stayed by his sides, I knew that this beautiful knife was indeed mine. I slid the knife from its cover, turned it over in my hands, held it up to the light, laid it across my knees. The weight of the knife, the size and the shape and the feel told me I'd made the right choice. I ran my thumb along one edge to test its sharpness like I'd seen my father do. The knife drew blood. It didn't hurt. I stuck my thumb in my mouth and looked again toward the doorway. My mother was gone.

My father locked the case and slid it back under the bed. "Get your coat. We'll go check the snare line."

How I loved him—and his invitation made me love him all the more. My father checked his snare line every morning. It was now late afternoon. That he would go out a second time just so I could try out my new knife made my heart explode. I would kill for this man. I would die for him. And I knew he would do the same for me.

Quickly I put on my winter gear before he

changed his mind, then slipped my knife in my coat pocket. The knife bumped against my leg as I walked. Our snare line ran the length of our ridge. The snow on either side of the trail was almost as tall as me, so I matched my father's footsteps closely. We wouldn't go far. Already the sky and trees and snow were turning evening blue. **Ningaabi-Anang** glittered low in the west. I offered a prayer to the Great Spirit to **please please please** send a rabbit before we had to turn back.

But **Gitche Manitou** tested my patience, as the gods sometimes do. The first two snares we came to were empty. In the third, the rabbit was already dead. My father slipped the noose from the rabbit's neck, reset the snare, and dropped the stiffened rabbit in his sack. He pointed toward the darkening sky. "What do you think, Helena? Shall we keep going, or turn back?"

By now the Evening Star had been joined by many others. It was cold and getting colder, and the wind was blowing like it was going to snow. My cheeks ached and my teeth chattered and my eyes watered and I couldn't feel my nose. "Keep going."

My father turned without a word and continued down the trail. I stumbled after him. My overalls were wet and stiff and I couldn't feel my feet. But when we came to the next snare, I forgot all about my frozen toes. This rabbit was alive.

"Quickly." My father pulled off his gloves and blew on his hands to warm them.

Sometimes when a rabbit was caught in a snare by its hind leg as this one was, my father picked it up and swung its head against a tree. Other times, he slit its throat. I knelt in the snow. The rabbit was limp from fear and cold, but it was definitely breathing. I slid my knife from its sheath. "Thank you," I whispered to the sky and the stars, and drew my blade swiftly across the rabbit's neck.

Blood spurted from the wound, sprayed my mouth, my face, my hands, my coat. I yelped and scrambled to my feet. I knew right away what I did wrong. In my eagerness to make my first kill, I had forgotten to stay to the side. I scooped up a handful of snow and rubbed it over the front of my jacket and laughed.

My father laughed with me. "Leave it. Your mother will take care of it when we get back."

He knelt beside the rabbit and dipped two fingers in its blood. Gently, he pulled me toward him. **"Manajiwin,"** he said. "Respect." He lifted my chin and drew his fingers across each cheek.

He started down the trail. I picked up my

rabbit and slung it over my shoulder and followed him back to the cabin. My skin crinkled as the wind dried my stripes. I grinned. I was a hunter. A warrior. A person worthy of respect and honor. A wilderness man like my father.

My mother wanted to wash my face as soon as she saw me, but my father wouldn't let her. She roasted my rabbit for dinner after she cleaned the blood from my coat and served it with a side of boiled arrowroot tubers and a salad of fresh dandelion greens that we forced in wooden boxes in our root cellar. It was the best meal I'd ever eaten.

Years later the state sold my father's extensive knife collection to help pay for his court costs. But I still have mine.

# 9

The knife my father gave me on my fifth birthday is a cold-steel Natchez Bowie that currently retails for close to seven hundred dollars. It's the perfect fighting knife, flawlessly balanced and perfectly shaped for strength, reach, and leverage, with a razor-sharp edge that cuts like a machete and pierces like a dagger.

The knife he used to escape from prison was made of toilet paper. I was surprised when I heard it. Given his proclivity and his expertise, I would have thought he'd opt for a metal knife. He certainly had the time to make one. I think he decided to go with toilet paper because he could appreciate the irony of crafting a deadly weapon from innocent materials. Prison inmates can be incredibly creative when it comes to making shivs—sharpening plastic spoons and broken-off toothbrushes against the cement walls or floors of their cells and studding them with disposable razor blades, sawing metal knives from steel bed frames over the course of many months using dental floss. But I had no idea that you could kill a person with toilet paper.

On YouTube, there's a video that shows how to make one. First, you roll the paper tightly into a cone shape, using toothpaste as a binding agent similar to the glue in papier-mâché. Then you mold your shiv until it's just the way you want it, building up layers of toilet paper on one end and squeezing for a custom-fit grip. Once you're satisfied with the result, you let your shiv dry and harden, sharpen it in the usual way, and you have a lethal weapon. Plus, it's biodegradable. Drop it in a toilet when you're done with it, and after it softens, you can flush it away.

My father left his at the crime scene. The knife had accomplished its purpose, and it's not as though he needed to create a scenario of plausible deniability. According to the news reports, my father's shiv has a six-inch double-sided blade with a hilt and a handle colored brown by I don't want to know what. That part doesn't surprise me. Bowies always were one of his favorites.

Aside from the details the police released yesterday about the knife, all that's known for sure is that two guards are dead, one stabbed and the other shot, and my father and both guards' weapons are missing. There are no witnesses. Either no one saw the prison transport van crash into a ditch in the middle of the Seney Stretch or no one is willing to own up to having seen anything as long as my father is out and about.

Knowing my father as I do, I can fill in the gaps. No doubt he's been planning his escape for a long time. Possibly years, the same way he planned my mother's abduction. One of the first things he would have done was to establish himself as a model prisoner so he could get on good terms with the guards who drove him between the prison and his court appointments. Most prison escapes involve at least some element of human error—the guards don't bother to double lock the prisoner's handcuffs because they don't see the prisoner as a threat, or a handcuff key hidden in the prisoner's body or clothes is missed during a search for the same reason. Prisoners who are known as troublemakers call for extra security measures, so my father would have made sure he wasn't one of them.

It's a hundred miles from the Marquette Branch Prison to the Luce County courthouse where my father was arraigned, so they logged a lot of driving time. Psychopaths like my father can be very charismatic. I imagine him chatting with the guards, figuring out what interested them, engaging them little by little. Just like he tricked my mother into trusting him by telling her he was looking for his dog. Just like he played on my interests when I was a child to turn me against my mother so subtly and thoroughly, it took years of therapy for me to accept the idea that she cared.

I don't know how he got the knife out of his cell and into the prison van. He could have hidden it in the seam of his jumpsuit up high near his groin where the officers would be less likely to pat him down. Or he could have concealed it in the spine of a book. This is where a smaller knife would have been considerably more practical. But one thing people have to understand about my father is that he never does anything halfway. Another thing they have to understand is that he's a patient man. I'm sure he let any number of escape opportunities go by until all of the conditions were right. Maybe one day the weather was bad, or the guards were unusually grouchy or unusually attentive, or the knife wasn't quite finished to his satisfaction. It's not like he was in a hurry.

Yesterday, the stars aligned. My father successfully smuggled the knife out of his cell and hid it in the crack of the seat in the back of the prison van. He waited until the return trip to make his move because the guards would be tired from a long day on the road and because it would be harder for searchers to follow if he escaped shortly before sundown. Also because they'd be traveling due west on the way back, and everyone knows how distracting it can be to drive straight into a sunset.

My father slouched in the backseat while he pretended to doze. He knew the route well enough to follow it with his eyes closed, but my father never leaves anything to chance, and so every couple of minutes he cracked open an eye to track their progress. They passed the turnoff to Engadine, drove past Four Corners and up a hill and through the tiny town of McMillan, past a handful of houses and the old McGinnis farm and down the hill to King's Creek. Up another hill and past the abandoned pottery studio and cabin built by a hippie couple in the 1970s, past the Danaher Road, down one more small hill and up another and then down to the marshy area west of the Fox River Bridge at last. Seeing the marshland made my father's pulse race, but he was careful to hide it.

They drove through Seney without stopping. Maybe the driver asked the other guard if he needed the bathroom; maybe he kept going assuming his partner would speak up if he did. My father wasn't granted that luxury. This time he didn't care. He shifted in the backseat, slid forward ever so slightly, faked a snore to cover his movement. He reached into the crack of the seat and slid the knife from its hiding place. Cupped it between his handcuffed hands with the blade pointing toward him so he could strike from above, and slid forward even farther.

Ten miles west of Seney, right after they passed the Driggs River Road that parallels the river and leads into the heart of the wildlife refuge, my father lunged forward. Possibly he roared like an attacking soldier, possibly he was quiet as an assassin. Either way, he plunged the knife into the passenger guard's chest, driving the blade deep into his flesh and penetrating the right ventricle and cutting the septum so the guard died not from blood loss but from the blood pooling around his heart, compressing it and causing it to stop.

The guard was too surprised to yell, and by the time he realized he was dying, my father had grabbed his gun and shot the driver. The van veered into the ditch, and that was that. My father confirmed both guards were dead, patted them down for the handcuff key, climbed into the front seat, and clambered out. He looked up and down the highway to be sure there were no witnesses before he stepped out of the cover of the van and headed directly south, trampling the stretch of grass between the road and the trees so the searchers would know which way he was heading.

After a mile or so, he waded into the Driggs River. He walked down the river a short distance and came out again on the same side because the river was too deep to cross without swimming, and because he didn't want to make it too hard for the searchers to follow until he convinced them the wildlife refuge was his destination. He left a bent fern here, a broken branch there, a partial footprint, laying down a trail that was just challenging enough for the searchers to think they were smarter than he was and they'd catch up to him before nightfall. Then at the moment of his choosing, he evaporated into the marsh like the morning mist and disappeared.

That's how I figure he did it. Or at least, that's how I would have done it.

WE'RE A MILE from the first cabin I want to check when Rambo whines in the particular way he has that tells me he needs to be let out. I don't want to stop, but when he starts digging at the armrest and turning circles on the seat I have to pull over. I've noticed lately that when he has to go, he really has to go. I don't know if his problem is age or a lack of exercise. Plotts live between twelve and sixteen years, so at eight, he's getting up there.

I reach inside the glove box and stick the Magnum in the front of my jeans. As soon as I open the passenger door, Rambo is through it like a shot. I walk the edges of the road more slowly, looking for signs that a person has been through. Nothing as obvious as a piece of orange cloth stuck to a branch. More along the lines of a footprint from a laceless tennis shoe. My father used to tell my mother and me that if anyone ever showed up unexpectedly on our ridge, we should wade out into the marsh grass and roll around in the muck and stay still until he told us it was safe to come back. I'm sure by now my father's prison jumpsuit is similarly camouflaged.

Judging by the lack of trees and the density of the underbrush along the road, I'd say it's been ten years since this area was clear-cut. The only things growing now are blueberries and tag alders. The brush piles the loggers left behind along with the ready food source make this prime bear country. No doubt Rambo thinks this is why we've come.

I cross the road and walk back along the other side. My father taught me to track when I was little. He'd lay out a trail for me while I was off playing or exploring, and then it would be up to me to find it and follow it while my father walked beside me and showed me all the signs I'd missed. Other times we'd walk wherever our feet took us and he'd point out interesting things as we went along. Drifts of scat. A red squirrel's distinctive tracks. The entrance to a wood rat's den littered with feathers and owl pellets. My father would point to a pile of droppings and ask, "Opossum or porcupine?" It's not easy to tell the difference.

Eventually I realized that tracking is like reading. The signs are words. Connect them into sentences and they tell a story about an incident in the life of the animal that passed through. For example, I might come upon a depression where a deer has bedded down. It might be on a little island sticking up out of the marsh or similar high ground so the deer can keep an eye on his surroundings. The first thing I do is look at how worn the depression is, and that tells me how much the bed is used. If the bed is worn all the way to the dirt, it's a primary bed, which means the deer is most likely coming back. Next I look at the direction the bed is facing. Most of the time a buck will bed down with the wind to his back. Knowing what wind the buck is using with that particular bed lets me pick a day when that particular wind is blowing so I can come back and shoot it. Stories like that.

Sometimes my father would pretend to be the prey. He'd sneak away from the cabin while I waited blindfolded in the kitchen in a chair facing away from the window so I wouldn't be tempted to peek. After I counted to one thousand, my mother would take off my blindfold and I'd take up the chase. With all of the footsteps crisscrossing the sand outside our back door, it wasn't easy figuring out which ones were his. I'd crouch on my heels on the bottom step and study all of the prints carefully until I was sure which were the most recent, because if I started down the wrong trail, I'd never find him, and depending on how far he'd walked and how long he had to stay hidden and what kind of mood he was in that day, that could lead to more contemplation time in the well than I cared to spend.

Occasionally my father would jump off the porch into a pile of leaves or onto a rock to make the game more challenging. Sometimes he'd take off his shoes and tiptoe away in his socks or his bare feet. Once he tricked me by wearing a pair of shoes that belonged to my mother. We both had a good laugh about that. Since I left the marsh, I've noticed a lot of parents let their children beat them at games in order to build their children's self-esteem. My father never made it easy for me to track him, and I wouldn't have wanted him to. How else was I going to learn? As for my self-esteem, the times I was able to hunt down and kill my father kept me grinning for days. I didn't really kill him, of course, but depending on where he was hiding, the game always ended with a bullet shot into the ground near his feet or into a tree trunk or a branch next to his head. After I won three times in a row, my father stopped playing. Much later my teacher read to the class a short story called "The Most Dangerous Game," and it sounded a lot like the one my father and I used to play. I wondered if that was where he got the idea. I wanted to tell the class I knew what it was like to be both hunter and hunted, but by then I'd learned that the less I said about my life in the marsh, the better.

A COP CAR IS PARKED at the side of the road. Or more accurately, an Alger County Sheriff's patrol car, one of the new ones they featured recently on the news: white with a black stripe and a black and orange logo on the side, push bars in front, light bar on top. A car so pristine and shiny, it looks like this is the first time it's been taken out.

I slow. There are two ways I can play this. I can drive past like I have no idea why a cop car might be sitting at the side of the road in the middle of nowhere. Let the officer flag me down, then let the fishing gear in the back of my truck do the talking. Maybe the officer will recognize my name and make the connection to my father when he checks my plates and ID. Maybe not. Either way, the worst the officer can do is send me packing with a warning to go home and stay safe.

Or I can tell the officer I cut my fishing trip short and am on my way home because I heard about the escaped prisoner on the news. Option number two gives me a chance to ask how the search is going, which could be useful. Or perhaps I can keep the officer talking long enough to pick up some helpful police radio chatter.

Then I realize both options are moot. The patrol car is empty.

I pull over and stop. Except for an occasional burst of static from the car's radio, the woods are quiet. I take the Ruger from the rack over the window and the Magnum from the glove box. Scan the area for movement, then squat on my heels to study the prints in the road. One set. Male, judging by the shoe size. One seventy-five to two hundred pounds, judging by the depth.

Proceeding with extreme caution, judging by the spacing.

I follow the prints to where they disappear into the vegetation at the side of the road. Broken ferns and crushed grasses tell me the officer was running. I study the trail he made for a long time and decide that the officer was running toward something he thought warranted investigation, not away.

I sling the Ruger over my shoulder and hold the Magnum with both hands in front of me. My footsteps are virtually silent, thanks to the moccasins I wear when I'm in the bush. Thanks to my father's training.

The trail leads through a stand of mixed birch and aspen to the top of a steep ravine. I walk to the edge and look down. At the bottom of the ravine is a body.

# 10

## The Cabin

**Soon it became clear to the Viking's wife how matters stood with the child; it was under the influence of a powerful sorcerer. By day it was charming in appearance as an angel of light, but with a temper wicked and wild; while at night, in the form of an ugly frog, it was quiet and mournful, with eyes full of sorrow.**

**Here were two natures, changing inwardly and outwardly with the absence and return of sunlight. And so it happened that by day the child, with the actual form of its mother, possessed the fierce disposition of its father; at night, on the contrary, its outward appearance plainly showed its descent on the father's**

**side, while inwardly it had the heart and mind of its mother.**

—HANS CHRISTIAN ANDERSEN,
**The Marsh King's Daughter**

The **National Geographics** were my picture books, my early readers, my history and science and world culture textbooks rolled into one. Even after I learned to read, I could spend hours paging through the pictures. My favorite was of a naked Aboriginal baby somewhere in the outback of Australia. She had stringy, reddish-brown hair, reddish-brown skin, and was sitting on dirt almost the same color as she was, chewing on a strip of bark and grinning like a baby Buddha. She looked so fat and happy, anyone could see that in that place and at that moment, she had everything she could ever want or need. When I looked at her picture, I liked to imagine this baby was me.

After the Aboriginal baby, I liked the pictures of the Yanomami tribe in the rain forest in Brazil. Mothers with straight-cut bangs and tattooed faces naked from the waist up nursing babies or carrying toddlers on their hips, their cheeks and noses pierced with sticks decorated with tufts of yellow feathers. Boys wearing string loincloths that didn't cover their boy parts and carrying over their shoulders dead monkeys and brightly colored birds they had shot with their very own bows and arrows. Boys and girls swinging from vines as thick as their arms and dropping into a river that the article said was home to black caiman, green anaconda, and red-bellied piranha. I liked to pretend that these wild, brave boys and girls were my brothers and sisters. On hot days I'd take off all my clothes and paint myself with marsh muck and run around the ridge with a piece of string tied around my waist, brandishing the bow and arrows I made from willow saplings that were too springy and green to take down so much as a rabbit but were good enough for pretending. I hung the doll my mother made from the handcuffs in the woodshed and used it for target practice. Most of the time the arrows only bounced off, but once in a while I could get one to stick. My mother didn't like seeing me without my clothes on, but my father didn't mind.

I tore these pictures from the magazines and hid them between my mattress and the box spring. My mother hardly ever came up to my room, and my father never did, but I wasn't taking any chances. The other magazine I kept beneath my bed was the one with the article about the first Viking settlement in the New World. I loved everything about the Vikings. The artist's drawings of what their settlement life must have been like looked a lot like mine, only with sod houses and more people. On the nights my father built a fire, I'd sit as close to the fireplace as I could stand and pore over the pictures of the artifacts they'd found, including human bones, until my father decided it was time for the three of us to go to bed.

I loved to read, but only on rainy days or at night by the fire. I especially loved my book of poems. The descriptions of morning mist and yellow leaves and frozen swamps really spoke to me. Even the poet's name was appropriate: Frost. I used to wonder if he made it up, like how I called myself "Helga the Fearless" when I played Viking. I was genuinely sorry when my father cut the cover off the book and put the pages in the outhouse. My mother said we had real toilet paper once, but if this was true we must have run out a long time before this, because I don't remember. The **Geographics** were far too stiff and glossy for anybody's liking, but they got the job done.

If I had realized sooner that the book of poems wasn't going to be around forever, I would have worked harder to memorize more. To this day

I can recall snippets: **The woods are lovely, dark and deep . . . To the midnight sky a sunset glow . . . Two roads diverged in a yellow wood, and I took the road less traveled on.** Or is it **by**?

Iris taught herself to read before she started school. I like to think she gets that from me.

I REALIZE some people will find aspects of my childhood offensive. For instance, people who don't hunt might be upset to learn that I was six years old when my father taught me to shoot. Then again, my mother had no objections to that. In the U.P., hunting is practically a religion. Schools close on the first day of hunting season so teachers and students alike can bag their buck, while the handful of businesses that stay open operate with a skeleton crew. Everyone old enough to pick up a rifle heads out to deer camp to hunt and drink and play euchre and cribbage in a two-week-long "Who'll get the biggest buck this year?" celebration. Toll booth operators at the Mackinac Bridge post a running tally of the number of deer that cross from the Upper to the Lower Peninsula on the tops of cars or in the backs of pickups. Most are taken at bait piles using carrots and apples that gas stations and grocery stores sell to hunters in fifty-pound sacks. You can probably guess what I think about that.

We heard their gunshots every year, day after day, sunup till sundown during those two frenetic weeks in November, just as we occasionally heard the distant whine of a chain saw that was not my father's. My father explained that this was the white man's "hunting season" and that white men were only allowed to shoot deer during these two weeks. I felt sorry for the white men. I wondered who would make such a rule and if the people who made it would punish those who broke it by shutting them inside a well like my father did to me when I disobeyed him. I worried about what would happen to us if the white men found out we shot deer whenever we wanted. My father said that because he was Native American, the white men's hunting rules didn't apply to him, and that made me feel better.

My father shot two deer every winter, one in the middle of December after the deer settled down from all the commotion and another in the early spring. We could have lived perfectly well on fish and vegetables, but my father believed it was better to eat a variety. Aside from the black bear who came calling and ended up as our living room rug, the only game animals we shot were deer. We had only one rifle, and we had to be careful with ammunition. Rabbits we snared. We also ate the hindquarters and backstraps of the muskrats and beavers my father trapped. Squirrels and chipmunks I killed with my throwing knife. The first time I pinned a chipmunk, I cooked it over a fire in the yard and ate it because not being wasteful is the Indian way. But there was so little meat on those tiny bones, after that, I didn't bother.

My father promised that as soon as I could pick off ten cans from the line he set up on our split-rail fence without missing a shot, he would take me deer hunting. That my father would use some of our precious ammunition to teach me to shoot showed how important it was. I think he was surprised at how quickly I learned, but I wasn't. The first time I picked up my father's rifle it felt natural, like an extension of my eyes and arms. At eight pounds, the Remington 770 was on the heavy side for a six-year-old, but I was big for my age, and thanks to carrying water buckets I was very strong.

Weeks passed after I met my father's requirement, and nothing happened. We fished, we trapped, we snared, while my father's Remington remained securely locked in the storage room. My father carried the key on a ring that jangled constantly from his belt. I don't know what the others were for. Certainly we never locked the cabin. I think he just liked the sound and the weight and the feel. As though carrying a lot of keys meant you were important.

The first time I saw the storage room, I thought we had enough food for an army. But my father explained that every can we used could never be replaced, so we needed to make our supply last. My mother was allowed to open one can a day. Sometimes she let me pick. Creamed corn one day, green beans another, Campbell's Cream of Tomato soup the next, though I didn't learn until later that the "cream" part of the name comes from using milk to thin the soup, not water. Sometimes when I was bored I'd count how many cans were left. I used to think that when all of the cans were gone, we would leave.

Each time I asked my father when we were going deer hunting, he told me a good hunter needed to be patient. He also said that every time I asked would push the day back by one week. I was only six, so it took me a while to grasp the concept. When I did, I stopped asking.

When my father unlocked the storage room early one morning the following spring and came out with his rifle over his shoulder and his pockets jingling with ammunition, I knew this was the day at last. I put on my winter gear without being told and followed him outside. My breath made white clouds as we hiked over the frozen marsh. My mother hated going outside when it was cold out, but I loved exploring the marsh in winter. It was as if the land had magically expanded and I could walk wherever I wanted. Here and there, frozen cattail heads poked out of the snow to remind me I was walking on water. I thought about the frogs and fish sleeping below. I closed my mouth and blew two streams from my nose like a Spanish bull. When my nose got drippy, I leaned over and blew the snot into the snow.

The snow squeaked as we walked. Snow makes different sounds at different temperatures, and the squeak from our footsteps meant that it was very cold. A good day for hunting, because the deer would be huddled together for warmth and wouldn't be foraging and moving around. A bad day because our noisy footsteps would make it harder for us to get close.

A crow cawed. My father gave the crow's Indian name, **aandeg,** and pointed to a distant tree. My eyesight was sharp, but the crow's black body melted so cleverly into the branches that if **aandeg** hadn't given away his location by cawing, I'm not sure I would have seen him. My heart warmed with admiration for my father. My father knew everything about the **Anishinaabe,** the Original People, and about the marsh: how to find the best places to cut ice-fishing holes, what time of day the fish would bite, how to test the thickness of the ice so we didn't fall through. He could have been a medicine man or a shaman.

When we came to the snow-covered mound I recognized as the beaver lodge where my father set his traps, my father crouched behind it so the sound of his voice wouldn't carry. "We'll take our shot from here," he said quietly. "Use the lodge for cover."

Slowly I raised my head. I could see the cedar trees surrounding the ridge, but no deer beneath them. Disappointment stung my eyes. I started to stand, but my father pulled me back down. He put his finger to his lips and pointed. I squinted and looked harder. At last I saw the faint puffs of white smoke from the deer's breath. Snow-covered deer lying on snowy ground under snow-covered cedar branches weren't easy to spot, but I found them. My father handed me his rifle, and when I sighted through the scope, I could see the deer clearly. I panned the herd. One animal lying apart from the others was bigger than the rest. The buck.

I pulled off my mittens and dropped them in the snow, then clicked off the safety and slid my finger through the trigger. I could feel my father watching. In my head I heard his instructions: **Keep your elbows down. Put your sup-**

**port hand farther forward on the forestock; it will give you better control. Watch carefully. Always follow up on any deer you take a shot at. Never assume you missed completely.** I held my breath and squeezed. The gun exploded against my shoulder. It hurt, but no more than when my father hit me. I kept my eyes on my buck as the herd scattered. A heart or a lung shot will make the deer jump and run off at full speed. A gut-shot deer holds its tail down and hunches its back as it runs away. My deer did neither. My shot was clean.

"Come." My father got to his feet and stepped to the side so I could take the lead. I broke trail through snow higher than my knees until we came to the carcass. The buck's eyes were open. Blood ran down its neck. Its tongue hung out the side of its mouth. My buck didn't have horns, but this time of year, I didn't expect him to. His belly was huge, and that's what was important.

Then the buck's belly moved. Not a lot. Just a ripple or a shiver, like when my father and mother rolled around under the bedcovers. At first I thought the deer wasn't dead. Then I remembered that anaconda swallow their prey whole while it's still alive and you can sometimes see the prey moving inside. But deer didn't eat meat. It was a puzzle.

"Hold the legs." My father rolled my buck

onto its back. I moved to the rear and took one leg in each hand to keep the buck steady. My father slid his knife carefully through the white belly fur and opened the buck's stomach. As the slit widened, a tiny hoof appeared, and then another, and then I understood that the deer I had shot wasn't a buck at all. My father lifted the fawn from the doe's belly and laid it in the snow. The fawn must have been close to being born, because when my father cut the birth sack, the fawn thrashed and kicked like it wanted to stand.

My father pressed the fawn into the snow and exposed its neck. I pulled out my knife, remembering to stay to the side so the blood sprayed away from me and not toward. As my father field-dressed the doe, I followed his instructions with the fawn: "Find the sternum. Feel for the place where the breastbone ends and the belly begins. Okay, now cut the belly from the sternum to the crotch. Take it slow. You want your knife to penetrate the hide and the membrane beneath it, but not to pierce the guts. Good. Now pull the guts out like this, starting from the crotch and working your way up, cutting the membranes that link the innards to the spine as you go. Now cut the skin around the anus and pull the colon out of the body cavity. Good. Okay. That's it, you're done."

We cleaned our hands and knives in the snow. I dried my hands on my jacket and pulled on my mittens and looked down proudly at my gutted fawn. The fawn was too small for more than one or two meals, but the hide looked big enough for my mother to make me a pair of spotted mittens.

My father heaped the steaming entrails into a pile as **aandeg** and his friends waited noisily in the trees for us to leave. He lifted my doe easily across his shoulders. I did the same with my fawn. The fawn was so small and light, as I followed my father back to our cabin, it felt like nothing at all.

OVER THE NEXT SEVERAL WEEKS, my mother worked on my mittens. There was a lot of stretching and rubbing and pulling involved. Native women used to chew the skins to soften them, but my mother's teeth weren't that good. My mother rubbed the fawn's hide back and forth, back and forth over the top knob of one of our wooden kitchen chairs, going over and over a small section until it was soft and then moving on to the next.

My father tanned the skin with the hair on because a fawn's spots don't go all the way down. He used the fawn's brains for tanning. We could have tanned our hides the Indian way by weighting them down with rocks in a cold stream and letting the force of the water and time loosen the hair. But we weren't going to eat the brains anyway, and this way they didn't go to waste. Each animal's brain is just the right size to tan its hide, my father said, which told me the Great Spirit really knows what he's doing. After you scraped off every bit of flesh from the hide, you cooked the deer's brains with an equal amount of water and mashed them into an oily liquid. Then you spread your hide on the ground or on the floor with the skin side up and slopped half the brain mixture on. The trick was making sure the hide had just the right amount of moisture after it finished soaking. If the hide was too dry, the brains wouldn't penetrate the skin. But if it was too wet, there wouldn't be any place for the brains to go. When you finished, you rolled up the hide and left it overnight in a place where animals couldn't get to it, and the next day, you unrolled it and did the same thing again. Once the brains finished working and you scraped off all the hair and washed the hide, the next step was to soften the skin, which was where my mother came in.

I realize I haven't said much till now about my mother. It's hard to know what I should say. Aside from wondering what she was going to fix for dinner when I came home hungry from my wanderings, growing up I honestly didn't give her much thought. She was just there, hovering in the background, doing the job nature assigned to her by way of procreation by keeping me clothed and fed. I know she didn't get the life she deserved or wanted, but I don't think living in the marsh was as bad as she liked to claim. There had to have been times when she was happy. I'm not talking random, fleeting moments, like when the family of baby skunks that crossed our yard every evening during the spring made her smile. I'm talking times when she was well and truly happy. When she could step outside of herself and look down objectively as if from above and think, **Yes, I like this. Right here, right now. This is good.**

I believe she felt this way when she worked in her garden. Even as a child, I could see that whenever my mother was hoeing or weeding or harvesting, her shoulders seemed less stooped. Sometimes I'd catch her singing: **I'm gonna always love you girl . . . Please don't go girl.** I thought she was singing about me. After we left the marsh and I saw the posters of the four dark-haired boys in white T-shirts and ripped jeans plastered all over her time-capsule-of-a-bedroom walls, I learned the song was performed by a group called a "boy band"

and that the band claimed to be the new kids on the block, though by then they were neither kids nor new. More astonishing than learning the origin of what I had always thought of as my song was the discovery that my mother had once hung her favorite pictures on her walls.

My mother's obsession with vegetables bordered on the fanatic. I never understood how she could find passion in peas and potatoes. Every spring, as soon as the ground began to thaw and long before the snow had finished melting, she would bundle up in her hat, scarf, and mittens and head outside, shovel in hand, to begin turning the soil. As if exposing the frozen underside of each laboriously hand-carved spadeful to the strengthening sun would hurry the process.

My mother's garden was small, not more than fifteen feet on each side and surrounded by a six-foot-high chicken-wire fence, but it produced abundantly thanks to the vegetable scraps we threw year-round in her compost pile. I don't know how my mother knew that decomposing vegetable matter would eventually turn the ridge's sandy soil into something approximating loam, just as I'm not sure how she knew to let some of each crop go to seed every fall so she could plant them again the next spring—or for that matter, how she figured out that some of the carrots had to be left in the ground over winter to grow again the next year because carrots need two seasons to complete the process. I don't think my father taught her; he was more hunter than gatherer. I don't think she learned from her parents, either. Certainly during the years I lived with my grandparents they never showed any interest in gardening, and why should they? All they had to do was drive down to the Supervalu or the IGA to buy fresh vegetables by the cart if they wanted. Perhaps she read about it in the **Geographics.**

My mother grew lettuce, carrots, peas, squash, corn, cabbage, and tomatoes. I don't know why she bothered with tomatoes. Our growing season was so short that by the time the first tomatoes started turning red we had to pick off all the fruits no matter how small and green they were so they didn't get turned to mush by the first frost. My mother wrapped each tomato individually in paper and spread them over the floor of our root cellar to ripen, where nine out of ten immediately started to rot. Corn was also a lost cause. Raccoons have an almost uncanny ability to time their nighttime raids to when the ears are a day or two away from being ripe, and there's not a fence in the world that can keep them out.

One summer a groundhog burrowed under the chicken wire and wiped out my mother's entire carrot crop. The way she carried on, you'd have thought someone died. I knew this meant that we would never again enjoy carrots, but there were other root crops we could eat. For instance, arrowroot tubers. The Indians call arrowroot **wapatoo.** My father told me the Indian method of harvesting **wapatoo** is to wade barefoot into the mud and pull the tubers from the connecting roots with your toes. I couldn't always tell when my father was serious and when he was joking, so I never tried it. We used an old four-tined rake like farmers use for pitching hay. My father would strap on his waders and step out into the deep muck near the shore and drag the rake back and forth. My job was to collect the tubers that floated to the surface. The water was so cold, I could barely stand it, but what doesn't kill you makes you stronger, my father liked to say. My father taught me to swim when I was a toddler by tying a rope around my waist and tossing me in.

After I learned the truth about my father and mother, I used to wonder why my mother didn't run away. If she hated living in the marsh as much as she later claimed, why didn't she leave? She could have walked across the marsh when it was frozen while my father and I were running the snare line. Strapped on my father's waders and slogged her way out while we were fishing in his canoe. Stolen his canoe and paddled away while we were hunting. I understand she was a child when my father brought her to the cabin, so some of these options might not have occurred to her right away. But she had fourteen years to figure something out.

Now that I've read accounts of girls who were kidnapped and held captive, I understand more of the psychological factors that were at work. Something breaks in the mind and the will of a person who's been stripped of autonomy. As much as we might like to think we'd fight like bobcats if we were in a similar situation, odds are we'd give in. Most likely sooner rather than later. When a person is in a position where the more they fight the worse they're punished, it doesn't take them long to learn to do exactly what their captor wants. This is not Stockholm syndrome; psychologists call it learned helplessness. If a kidnapped person believes her captor will withhold punishment or even give her a reward such as a blanket or a scrap of food if she does what he wants, she'll do it, no matter how disgusting or degrading it might be. If the kidnapper is willing to inflict pain, the process goes a lot faster. After a while, as much as she wants to, the captive won't even try to escape.

It's like when you catch a mouse or a shrew and you put it in a metal washtub to see what it will do. At first, it hugs the edges of the tub and runs around and around in a circle looking for a way out. After a few days, it gets used to being in the tub and will even come into the middle for food and water, though that goes against its natural instincts. After a few more days, you can make a way out for it by tying a piece of cloth or a rope to one of the handles and draping both ends over the sides, but the mouse will just keep running in circles because that's all it knows. Eventually, it dies. Some creatures just don't do well in captivity. If it wasn't for me, my mother and I would still be living on that ridge.

One other thing stands out about my mother: she always wore long pants and long sleeves when she was working in her garden. Never the shorts and T-shirts my father bought for her. Not even on the hottest days. So different from the Yanomami mothers.

# 11

I stand at the top of the ravine looking down. The sides are steep, the vegetation sparse. I can clearly see the body at the bottom. The dead officer—buzz-cut brown hair, ruddy cheeks, sunburned neck—looks to be somewhere in his early forties. Reasonably fit, maybe a hundred and eighty pounds—smack-dab in the middle of the weight range I predicted based on his footprints. His head is turned toward me, eyes open in surprise, like he can't quite comprehend the enormity of the bullet hole in his back.

I think about the dead prison guards, about their families. About the grief that will consume them long after my father is once again behind bars. I think about this man's family. How they're going about their day as if it were normal. How they have no idea that their husband and father and brother is gone. I think about how I'd feel if something happened to Stephen.

I scan the area moving only my eyes, looking for activity at the periphery of my vision that would indicate my father is nearby. But when a jay shrieks from the other side of the ravine and a woodpecker starts drilling, I know my father is gone.

I make my way down the hill. There's no doubt that the officer is dead, but I roll him over anyway, intending to put two fingers to his neck to confirm. When he flops onto his back, I yank my hand away like I've been burned. His shirt has been ripped open. Written in blood on his ruined chest is this: **For H.**

I shudder, force my breathing to slow. I flash back to the last time my father left a similar message. The Lake Superior agate I found on my bedroom windowsill two years after I left the marsh was a big one, about the size of a baby's fist: a rich, deep red surrounded by orange and white concentric bands with a cluster of quartz crystals in the center. The kind that would be worth a lot of money after it was cut and polished. When I turned it over, I saw four letters written in black marker on the bottom: **For H.**

At first I assumed the agate was a prank. By this time I had beaten all of the boys at school who felt compelled to challenge me after the knife incident at my welcome home party, but there were still a handful who couldn't let it go who had moved on to stupid stuff like putting dead animals in my locker, and some clever guy had once sprayed the words **The Marsh King's Daughter** across the front of my grandparents' house in red paint.

All I did with the agate was put it in a shoe box and put the shoe box under my bed. I didn't say anything to my mother or my grandparents because I didn't know what to think. I hoped the agate was from my father, yet I didn't. I didn't want to see him, yet I did. I loved my father, but at the same time, I blamed him for my deep unhappiness and for my struggle to fit in. There was so much about the outside world he should have taught me that I didn't know. What did it matter if I could hunt and fish as well as any man and better than most? To my classmates I was a freak—a know-nothing who thought color television had only recently been invented, had never seen a computer or a cell phone, had no idea that Alaska and Hawaii were now states. I think things would have been different if I had been a blonde. If I had looked like my mother, my grandparents might have loved me. But I was a carbon copy of my father, a daily reminder of what he'd done to their daughter. I thought when I left the marsh that my mother's parents would be thrilled to get their long-lost daughter back with a bonus. But I was his.

When a second agate appeared on my windowsill tucked inside a sweetgrass basket, I knew the gifts were from my father. My father could make anything out of natural materials: woven baskets, birch-bark boxes decorated with porcupine quills, miniature snowshoes made from willow twigs and rawhide, tiny birch-bark canoes with carved wooden seats and paddles. The mantel above the fireplace at the cabin was lined with his creations. I used to walk its length admiring the things he'd made, hands clasped behind my back because I was allowed to look, but not to touch. My father did most of his craft work during the winter, as there were a lot of empty hours to fill. He tried to teach me more than once, but for some reason when it came to artwork I was all thumbs. A person can't be good at everything, my father said after I'd mangled yet another attempt at working with porcupine quills—but as far as I could see, that wasn't true of him.

I knew why my father was leaving me presents. The gifts were his way of telling me that he was close by. That he was watching me, and he would never leave me, even though I'd left him. I knew I shouldn't keep them. I'd seen enough television cop shows to know that withholding evidence made me an accessory to my father's crimes. But I liked that this was our secret. My father trusted me to keep quiet. Keeping quiet was something I could do.

The gifts kept coming. Not every day. Not even every week. Sometimes so much time went by between presents, I was sure my father had moved on and forgotten all about me. Then I'd find another. Each went into the box beneath my bed. Whenever I was feeling lonely, I'd take out the box and finger each gift and think about my father.

Then one morning I found a knife. I snatched it off the windowsill before my mother woke up and I hid it in my shoe box. I could hardly believe my father had given this knife to me. My father and I used to sit on my parents' bed at the cabin with the knife case open between us while he told each knife's story. This small silver knife shaped like a dagger with the initials **G.L.M.** etched into the base of the blade was my second favorite, after the knife I chose for myself on my fifth birthday. Whenever I asked my father who G.L.M. was, all he would say was that it was a mystery. I used to make up my own stories. The knife belonged to the man my father murdered. He won it in a bar fight, or in a knife-throwing competition. He stole it when he picked somebody's pocket. I had no idea if picking pockets was among my father's many skills, but it served the story.

Later, after my grandmother drove my mother to her therapist and my grandfather finished lunch and went back to his shop, I took out the box and spread my treasures over my bed. Sometimes when I played with my collection I sorted the items into piles according to kind. Other times I arranged them in the order I received them, or from the most-liked to the least, though of course I loved them all. My mother's appointments normally lasted an hour and sometimes more, so I figured I had forty-five minutes before I had to put them away. I still resisted the idea of carving up a day into hours and minutes, but I could see that there were times when it was useful to know exactly how long a person was going to be gone and when they'd be back.

I was sitting on my bed, pretending my father was sitting beside me at last, telling this knife's true story, when my mother and grandmother came into the room. They shouldn't have been able to sneak up on me. All I can think is that I was so caught up in my father's story, I didn't hear the car pull in. Later I found out my mother's therapy session hadn't gone well, and that's why they came home early. That part didn't surprise me. I was supposed to be seeing the same therapist, but I'd stopped going six months before this because the therapist kept pushing me to finish school no matter how miserable I was so I could enroll at Northern Michigan University in Marquette and get a degree in biology or botany and get a job somewhere one day doing field research. I couldn't see how sitting in a classroom could possibly teach me more about the marsh than I already knew. I didn't need a book to tell me the difference between a swamp and a marsh and a bog and a fen.

The first thing my grandmother spotted when she came into the room was the knife. She came over to the bed and glared down at me and held out her hand.

"What are you doing with that? Give that to me."

"It's mine." I tossed the knife into the shoe box along with the rest of my things and shoved the box under my bed.

"Did you steal it?"

We both knew I couldn't have purchased the knife on my own. My grandparents never let me have any money, not even the money people sent after I left the marsh that was supposed to be for me. They said the money had been put into something called a "trust" and that meant they couldn't touch it. After I turned eighteen, the lawyer I hired to get it for me told me there was no trust and never had been, which went a long way toward explaining the Ford F-350 my grandparents drove, as well as the Lincoln Town Car. I can't help thinking that if my grandparents had been less concerned about making money from what had happened to my mother and more concerned about helping her get over it, things would have gone a lot better for her.

My grandmother got down on her hands and knees and pulled the box out from under the bed, which wasn't easy because she was a large woman and her knees were bad. She dumped the contents on my bed and grabbed the knife and started waving it around and yelling like I wasn't sitting two feet away and couldn't hear her perfectly well even if she had whispered. I still hate when people yell. Say what you will about my father; he never raised his voice.

The knife was so distinctive, as soon as she saw it, my mother knew right away that it used to belong to my father. She clapped her hand over her mouth and started backing out of the room like the knife was a cobra and it was going to attack her. At least she didn't scream. My mother still tended to freak whenever anything reminded her of my father or someone said his name, though by this time it had been two years. Maybe her therapist really was helping.

My grandmother took the shoe box to the police. The police found my prints on the knife along with a set that matched the ones they'd taken from the cabin. They still didn't know my father's name, but the prints proved he was in the area. The detective promised my grandparents it was only a matter of time before they'd catch my father, and he was right about that. Inquiries about an Indian with a big knife collection led to a remote logging camp north of Tahquamenon Falls, where my father was living with a couple of First Nations men. Back then it wasn't uncommon for a jobber to hire Indians from Canada to cut the junk wood nobody else wanted. They'd set them up on the job site in a trailer or a camper and bring them gas for their generator and groceries once a week and pay them under the table.

I've watched the body cam footage of the FBI raid many times on YouTube. It's like an episode of **Cops** or **Law & Order** starring your very own father, though the uncut version runs a little long. There's a lot of whispering and odd camera angles as the team sets up behind a log pile and under the skidder and behind the tool trailer and even inside the outhouse because they weren't taking any chances. Then there's a long stretch of nothing while they wait for my father and the men he was living with to come back from the day's cutting. The look on my father's face as the team swarms out with their weapons drawn, shouting for him to "Get down! Get down!" still makes me laugh. But it goes by so fast, you have to be ready to hit pause or you'll miss it. I'm sure the jobber was more than a little surprised when he found out he was harboring the top man on the FBI's Most Wanted list.

In theory, my father should have remained a free man forever the first time he was on the run, because back then no one knew who he was. My mother and I always assumed Jacob was his real name, because why would we think otherwise? But that's all we knew. I always thought the police artist did a decent job of capturing my father's likeness, but my father must have had one of those faces that looked like a lot of other men's, because even though you couldn't turn on the television or pick up a newspaper or drive down the highway without seeing his picture, in the end nothing came of it. You might think my father's parents would have recognized their son and come forward to identify him, but they must have found it difficult to step up and admit that their child was a kidnapper and a murderer.

People say my father got tired of being on the run and that's why he reached out to me. I think he got lonely. He missed our life in the marsh. Missed me. Or, I **liked** to think so.

For a long time, I blamed myself for my father's capture. My father trusted me, and I let him down. I should have been more careful, hidden the things he gave me in a safer place, fought harder to keep my collection out of the hands of the people who wanted to use it to hurt him.

Later, after I understood the extent of my father's crimes and their impact on my mother, it didn't bother me as much that he was going to spend the rest of his life in prison, even though I was the one who'd sent him there. I was genuinely sorry that he would never again be allowed to roam the marsh or hunt or fish. But he had his chance to flee the area. He could have gone west to Montana or north into Canada and no one would ever have called him to account. Leaving me the presents that led to his capture was his mistake, not mine.

I PULL OUT the officer's shirttail and wipe away the words my father wrote on his chest, then roll the officer's body back onto his stomach the way I found him. I realize I'm tampering with a crime scene, but I'm not about to leave the message my father left for me on the dead officer's chest, considering the police are already looking at me as a possible accomplice. As I climb back up the hill, I feel like I'm going to throw up. My father killed this man because of me. He left the body for me to find the way a cat leaves a dead mouse for its master on the porch.

**For H.** The words are gone, but the message is burned into my brain. My father's ability to manipulate any situation to his advantage is almost beyond comprehension. Not only did he anticipate that I would come looking for him along this road, when he saw the cop car and concluded correctly that the driver was a lone searcher who had the right instincts at the wrong time, he drew him out and led him into the ravine for the sole purpose of staging this scene for me to find. I picture him darting across the road in front of the patrol car, letting the officer get a glimpse of the man everyone is seeking so he'd pull over and park. Maybe he stumbled so the officer would think he was wounded and therefore not a threat, then staggered like he was at the limit of his endurance as he led the officer into the bush, letting the man's head swell with visions of the acclaim he would get for capturing the prisoner single-handedly before my father circled around and shot the officer in the back.

I wonder what else my father has in store for me.

Back at the road, I go straight to my truck. I open the passenger door and slip my hand inside and clip on Rambo's leash. He whines and pulls. He smells the blood in the air, feels the tension coming off of me. I let him lead me to the bottom of the ravine to get a snoutful of my father's scent and start back up the hill. I should call in the murder. Let the authorities take up the search for my father while I go home to my husband. But the message my father left on the man he murdered is for me.

I think about my mother, gone and forgotten by most. I think about my daughters. I think about my husband, alone and waiting for me. The killing has to stop. I **will** find my father. I **will** capture him. I **will** return him to prison and make him pay for everything he's done.

# 12

## The Cabin

**She was, indeed, wild and savage even in those hard, uncultivated times. They had named her Helga, which was rather too soft a name for a child with a temper like hers, although her form was still beautiful.**

**It was a pleasure to her to splash about with her white hands in the warm blood of the horse which had been slain for sacrifice. In one of her wild moods she bit off the head of the black cock which the priest was about to slay.**

**To her foster-father she said one day, "If thine enemy were to pull down thine house about thy ears, and thou shouldest be sleeping in unconscious security, I**

**would not wake thee; even if I had the power I would never do it, for my ears still tingle with the blow that thou gavest me years ago. I have never forgotten it."**

**But the Viking treated her words as a joke; he was, like everyone else, bewitched with her beauty, and knew nothing of the change in the form and temper of Helga at night.**

—HANS CHRISTIAN ANDERSEN,
**The Marsh King's Daughter**

I was eight the first time I saw my father's sadistic side. At the time I didn't understand that what he did to me was wrong, or that normal fathers don't treat their offspring the way my father sometimes treated me. I don't like making my father out to be worse than people already think he is. But I'm trying to be honest in telling about how things were for me when I was growing up, and that has to include both the good parts and the bad.

My father claimed he chose to live in the marsh because he killed a man. He was never accused, and his involvement in the death of the mentally challenged man whose badly decomposed body was found in an empty cabin north of Hulbert, Michigan, was never proven. Sometimes when he told the story, he said he beat the man to death. Other times he said he slit the man's throat because he didn't like the way the man drooled and stuttered. Most of the time he was alone when the murder occurred, but in one version his younger brother helped him get rid of the body—even though I later learned my father was an only child. It's hard to know if anything my father said about the murder was true, or if the tale was just something he made up to pass the time on a long winter's evening. My father told a lot of stories.

My father saved his best stories for our **madoodiswan,** our sweat lodge. My mother called the sweat lodge a sauna. My father tore down our front porch the summer I was eight to build it. We didn't need both a front and a back porch, my father said, and while the cabin looked odd without it, I had to agree.

My father built our sweat lodge because he was tired of bathing standing up. Also because while I could still sit down in the blue enamel washtub I'd been using since I was a baby, it wouldn't be long before I would have to do the same. My mother never took baths, so her needs didn't matter. (My mother never took off her clothes in front of my father and me and only wiped herself down with a wet cloth when she needed cleaning, though I saw her swimming in the marsh in her underwear when she thought no one was around.)

This was around late August or early September. I can't be more specific than that because I didn't always keep track. Late summer is a good time to tackle an outdoor construction project because the weather is still warm but most of the bugs are gone. My mother was one of those people bugs seemed attracted to. Often she was so covered with bites, she wept with frustration. I've read about pioneers in Siberia and Alaska being driven mad by mosquitoes, but generally speaking mosquitoes don't bother me. Blackflies are a lot worse. Blackflies like to go for the back of your neck or behind your ears, and their bites stay itchy and sore for weeks. A single bite near the corner of your eye can make your whole eyelid swell shut. You can imagine what happens when you get two. Sometimes when we were cutting firewood in the woodlot during June, the blackflies would be so thick, we couldn't take a breath without swallowing a few. My father used to joke that this only meant we were getting extra protein, but I didn't like it, even if there was now one less fly to bite me. Horseflies take out a chunk. Deerflies will bite if you let them, but they're so predictable as they buzz around your head that if you time it right you can clap your hands together when they pass in front of your face, and that's that. No-see-ums are as tiny as the period at the end of a sentence, but with a bite all out of proportion to their size. If you're sleeping in a tent and something keeps biting you that feels like a mosquito but you can't see anything, that will be no-see-ums. There's nothing you can do against them except burrow into your sleeping bag and pull the covers over your head and stay like that until the morning. People worry about the chemicals in insect repellent causing cancer, but if we'd had bug spray when we lived in the marsh, you can bet we would have used it.

Our sweat lodge was a family project. Picture a hot day with all of us pitching in and doing our part. Sweat rolled down my father's back and dripped off the end of my nose as we worked. When I lent him the handkerchief I kept in my back pocket to wipe his face and neck, my father joked that it was such a good lodge, it was already making us sweat. My mother sorted and stacked the lumber: floorboards in one pile, floor joists in another, support beams in a third. The joists and beams would become the corner posts and uprights of our sweat lodge, while the floorboards would cover the sides. The porch roof my father took down in one piece. We only needed half, but my father explained that we could stack the firewood for our sweat lodge under the parts that stuck out to protect it from the weather. Our **madoodiswan** would have a bench along the back wall where we could sit and a circle of stones from the porch's foundation where my father would build the fire. We burned maple and beech in our kitchen stove, but in the sweat lodge we would burn cedar and pine because we needed a hot, quick fire. It was hard for me to see how sitting in a tiny hot room would make us clean, but if my father said this was how the sweat lodge worked, I believed him.

My job was to straighten the nails he pulled. I liked the way the nails screeched before they let go, like an animal caught in a trap. I balanced the nails on a flat stone with the kinked side pointing up the way my father showed me and tap-tap-tapped with a hammer until the nails were as straight as I could make them. I especially liked the nails with square sides. My father said these nails were made by hand, and this meant our cabin was very old. I wondered how the other nails were made.

I wondered about the people who built our cabin. What would they think if they could see us tearing part of it down? Why did they build the cabin on this ridge instead of the one where the deer liked to gather? Why did they build the cabin with two porches instead of one? I thought I knew some of the answers. I thought they built our cabin with two porches so they could sit on the front porch and watch the sun come up and then sit on the back porch and watch the sun go down. And I thought the reason they built here instead of the ridge with the deer was so the deer would feel safe until the people who built our cabin were ready to hike over and shoot one.

Lately I'd been wondering about a lot of things. Where did my father get the blue pry bar he used to pull nails? Did he bring it with him, or was it already at the cabin? Why didn't I have brothers and sisters? How would we cut firewood when my father ran out of gas for his chain saw? Why didn't our cabin have a stove like the pictures in the **Geographics**? My mother said her family had a big white stove with four burners on top and an oven for baking when she was little, so why didn't we? Most of the time I kept my wonderings to myself. My father didn't like it when I asked too many questions.

My father told me to whack the nails with the hammer instead of tapping them to make the job go faster. Not that we were in a hurry, but he would like to use the **madoodiswan** this winter and not have to wait until the next. He smiled when he said this so I knew he was joking. I also knew he really did want me to work faster, so I swung the hammer harder. I wondered if I could straighten a nail with a single blow. I sorted through the pile looking for a nail that was only slightly bent.

Later, I wondered what made me miss the nail so badly. It's possible I glanced away when a squirrel dropped a pinecone. Or I could have been distracted by a red-winged blackbird calling. Possibly I blinked when the wind blew a bit of sawdust into my eye. Whatever the reason, when the hammer smashed my thumb, I yelped so loudly, both my father and mother came running. In seconds my thumb turned fat and purple. My father poked my thumb and turned it this way and that and said it wasn't broken. My mother went into the cabin and came out with a strip of cloth and tied it around my thumb. I wasn't sure what that was supposed to do.

I spent the rest of the afternoon on the big rock in our backyard paging one-handed through the **Geographics.** When the sun sat like an orange ball on top of the marsh grass, my mother went inside to dish up the rabbit stew I'd been smelling for hours. She called out that supper was ready, and my father put down his tools and quiet settled over the marsh once again.

There were three chairs at our kitchen table. I wondered if the people who built our cabin were also a family of three. No one said anything while we ate because my father didn't like it when we talked with our mouths full.

When my father finished eating, he pushed back his chair and came around the table to stand beside me. "Let me see your thumb."

I laid my hand on the table with my fingers spread.

He untied the strip of cloth. "Hurts?"

I nodded. In truth, my thumb didn't hurt anymore unless I touched it, but I liked being the center of my father's attention.

"It's not broken, but it could have been. You understand that, don't you, Helena?"

I nodded again.

"You have to be more careful. You know there's no room in the marsh for mistakes."

I nodded a third time and tried to make my expression as serious as his. My father had told me many times to be careful. If I hurt myself, I'd just have to deal with the consequences, because we weren't going to leave the marsh no matter what. "I'm sorry," I said in a small voice, because now I really was. I hated when my father was unhappy with me.

"Saying sorry isn't enough. Accidents always have consequences. I'm not sure how I can teach you to remember that."

My stomach got hard when he said this, like

I'd swallowed a stone. I hoped I wouldn't have to spend another night in the well. Before I could tell my father that I was truly, **truly** sorry, and I **would** remember to be more careful, and I would never hit my thumb with a hammer ever, **ever** again, he balled his hand into a fist and smashed it down on my thumb. The room exploded with stars. White-hot pain shot up my arm.

I woke up on the floor. My father was kneeling beside me. He picked me up and sat me down in my chair and handed me my spoon. My hand shook as I took it. My thumb hurt worse than when I smashed it with the hammer. I blinked back tears. My father didn't like it when I cried.

"Eat."

I felt like I was going to throw up. I dipped my spoon into my bowl and took a bite. The stew stayed down. My father patted my head. "Again." I took another bite, and another. My father stood beside me until all of my stew was gone.

I understand now that what my father did was wrong. Still, I don't think my father wanted to hurt me. He only did what he believed he had to do to teach me a lesson I needed to learn.

What I didn't understand until much later was how my mother could watch the whole episode from across the table, as small and useless as the rabbit she had served for dinner, without lifting a finger to help me. It was a long time before I could forgive her for that.

IN OUR NEW SWEAT LODGE that winter, my father told a story. I was sitting between my father and mother on the narrow bench. My mother was wearing her Hello Kitty T-shirt and underpants. Except for the polished Lake Superior agate my father wore constantly on a leather thong around his neck, my father and I were properly naked. I liked when my father took off his clothes because then I could see all of his tattoos. My father tattooed himself the Indian way, using fish-bone needles and soot. My father had promised that when I was nine, he'd start tattooing me.

"One winter, a newly married couple moved with their entire village to new hunting grounds," my father's story began. I snuggled closer. I knew this would be a scary story. Scary stories were the only kind my father told. "There they had a child. One day as they were gazing at their son in his cradleboard, the child spoke. 'Where is that **Manitou**?' the baby asked."

My father paused his story and looked at me.

"**Manitou** is the Sky Spirit," I answered.

"Very good," he said, and continued. "'They say he is very powerful,' the baby said. 'Someday I am going to visit him.' 'Hush,' said the baby's mother. 'You must not talk like that.' After that, the couple fell asleep with the baby in his cradleboard between them. In the middle of the night, the mother discovered that her baby was gone. She woke her husband. The husband made a fire, and the couple looked all over the wigwam, but they couldn't find their baby. They searched the neighbor's wigwam as well, then lit birchbark torches and searched the snow for tracks. At last they found a row of tiny tracks leading to the lake. They followed the tracks until they found the cradleboard. The tracks leading from the cradle to the lake were far bigger than human feet would make. The horrified parents realized their child had turned into a **wendigo,** the terrible ice monster who eats people."

My father dipped a cup into the water bucket and drizzled the water slowly over the tin plate balanced on top of the fire. The drops sizzled and danced. Steam filled the room. Water ran down my face and dripped off my chin.

"Sometime later, a **wendigo** attacked the village," my father's story continued. "The **wendigo** was very thin and terrible. It smelled of death and decay. Its bones pushed against its skin, and its skin was gray like death. Its lips were tattered and bloody, and its eyes sat deep in their sockets. This **wendigo** was very large. A **wendigo** is never satisfied after killing and eating. He searches constantly for new victims. Every time he eats another person, he grows bigger, so he can never be full."

From outside there came a noise. **Scritch-scritch, scritch-scritch.** It sounded like a branch brushing against the side of the sweat lodge, except that our **madoodiswan** sat in the middle of our clearing and there were no branches close enough to touch. My father cocked his head. We waited. The sound didn't come again.

He leaned forward. The glow from the fire threw the top of his face into shadow as it lit his chin from below.

"As the **wendigo** approached the village, the little people who protect the **manitou** ran out to meet it. One threw a rock at the **wendigo.** The rock became a bolt of lightning that struck the **wendigo** in the forehead. The **wendigo** fell down dead with a noise like that of a big tree falling. As the **wendigo** lay in the snow, he looked like a big Indian. But when the people started to chop him up, they saw that he was really a huge block of ice. They melted the pieces and found in the middle a tiny infant with a hole in his head where the rock had hit him. This was the baby who had turned into a **wendigo.** If the

**manidog** hadn't killed it, the **wendigo** would have eaten up the entire village."

I shivered. In the flickering firelight I saw the baby with the hole in its forehead, its parents weeping over the terrible fate that befell their too-curious child. Water dripped through the cracks in the roof and drew an icy path down my neck.

From outside the noise came again. **Scritch scritch scritch.** I heard breathing—**uh, uh, uh**—as if whatever was outside had arrived on our ridge after a long run. My father stood up. His head almost touched the ceiling. His fire-shadow was even bigger. Surely my shaman of a father was a match for whatever was outside. He stepped around the fire pit and opened the door. I shut my eyes and shrank back against my mother as the cold rushed in.

"Open your eyes, Helena," my father commanded in a terrible voice. "See! Here is your **wendigo**!"

I squeezed my eyes shut tighter and drew my feet up onto the bench. The **wendigo** was in the room—I could feel it. I heard the **wendigo** panting. Smelled its horrible, foul breath. Something cold and wet touched my foot. I shrieked.

My father laughed. He sat down beside me and pulled me onto his lap. "Open your eyes, **Bangii-Agawaateyaa**," he said, using the pet name he had given me, which meant "Little Shadow." And so I did.

Wonder of wonders, it was not a **wendigo** that found its way into our sweat lodge. **It was a dog.** I knew this was a dog because I'd seen pictures in the **Geographics.** Also because its coat was short and speckled and nothing like the fur of a coyote or a wolf. Its ears hung down, and its tail lashed from side to side as it pushed its nose against my toes.

"Sit," my father commanded. I wasn't sure why, as I was already sitting. Then I realized my father was talking to the dog. Not only that, but the dog understood what my father said and obeyed him. The dog plopped down on its haunches and looked up at my father with its head tipped to the side as if to say, **All right. I did as I was told. What next?**

My mother stretched out her hand and scratched the dog behind its ears. It was the bravest thing I'd ever seen her do. The dog whined and scooted closer to my mother. She stood up and wrapped a towel around her shoulders. "Come," she said to the dog. The dog trotted after her. I'd never seen anything like it. All I could think was that my mother had somehow stolen a piece of my father's shaman magic.

My mother wanted the dog to spend the

night with us in the cabin. My father laughed and said that animals belonged outside. He tied a rope around the dog's neck and led it to the woodshed.

Long after my mother and father stopped making the bedsprings squeak, I stood at my bedroom window, looking out over the yard. The moon reflecting off the snow turned the night as bright as day. Through the gaps in the woodshed I could see the dog moving around. I tapped the window with my fingernail. The dog stopped pacing and looked up at me.

I wrapped my blanket around my shoulders and tiptoed down the stairs. Outside, the night was cold and still. I sat down on the steps and pulled on my boots, then crossed the yard to the woodshed. The dog was tied to the iron ring in the back. I stood in the doorway and whispered the Indian name my father had given it. The dog's tail thumped. I thought about my father's story about how Dog came to the Ojibwa people. How the giant who sheltered the hunters who got lost in the forest gave them his pet Dog to protect them from the **wendigo** on their return. How Dog allowed the men to pet it, and took food from their hands, and played with their children.

I went inside and sat down on the dried cattail rushes my mother spread on the floor for bedding. I whispered the Indian name my father had given the dog a second time: "Rambo." Again the dog's tail thumped. I scooted closer and stretched out my hand. The dog stretched forward as well and sniffed my fingers. I edged closer still and put my hand on its head. If my mother was brave enough to touch the dog, then so was I. The dog wriggled out from beneath my hand. Before I could pull back, its tongue came out and licked my fingers. The tongue was raspy and soft. I put my hand on its head, and the dog licked my face.

When I woke up, daylight poured through the slats in the woodshed. It was so cold, I could see my breath. Rambo curled against me. I pulled up a corner of my blanket and laid the blanket over the sleeping dog. Rambo sighed.

IT HURTS ME PHYSICALLY to think about how much I loved that dog. For the rest of that fall and on into the winter until it got too cold, I slept beside Rambo in the woodshed. The sides of the woodshed were slatted and open to the weather, so I made a shelter out of firewood and hung my blankets over the sides and top, similar to the forts Stephen and the girls build with pillows and couch cushions in our living room.

Rambo had been trained to basic commands

like "come" and "sit" and "stay," but I didn't know this. So as I gradually learned Rambo's vocabulary, I thought that he was learning mine. Whenever Rambo would break off in the middle of following a rabbit trail or gnawing on a deer antler or worrying a chipmunk and come or sit at my command, I felt as powerful as a shaman.

My father hated my dog. At the time, I couldn't understand why. Indians and dogs were supposed to be friends. Yet whenever Rambo tried to follow my father, my father would kick him away or yell at him or hit him with a stick. When he wasn't beating Rambo, all he did was complain about how Rambo was one more mouth to feed. I couldn't see where this should be a problem. My father said Rambo was a bear dog who got lost during a hunt. Bear season is in August. This was the middle of November, which meant that Rambo had been feeding himself perfectly well for months. I only gave him the food scraps we didn't want. Why should my father care if Rambo ate the bones and entrails we were only going to throw away?

Now I know that my father hated my dog because my father is a narcissist. A narcissist is only happy as long as the world runs the way he wants it to. My father's plan for our life in the marsh didn't include a dog; therefore he couldn't see a dog as anything but a problem.

I also think he saw Rambo as a threat. He let me keep Rambo initially as a display of generosity, but when in time I grew to love my dog as purely as I loved my father, he was jealous because he thought my affections were divided. But my affections **weren't** divided; they were **multiplied.** My love for my dog didn't diminish my love for my father. It's possible to love more than one person. Rambo taught me that.

I think Rambo was the reason why the next spring, my father disappeared. One day he was with us at the cabin, and then he wasn't. My mother and I had no idea where my father had gone or why he left, but we had no reason to think that this time was any different from the other occasions when he'd disappear for hours or even a day or, every once in a while, overnight, so we held to our regular routine as much as possible. My mother hauled water and kept the fire going while I chopped wood and checked the snare line. Most of the time the snares came up empty. Rabbits breed in the spring, so they spend most of their time in their nests and are harder to catch. I would have tried to shoot a deer, except that my father had taken the rifle. Mostly we ate the vegetables that were left in the root cellar. I thought many times about using my father's ax to chop down the door to the storage room so we could get at the supplies. But then I thought about what he would do to me when he came back and saw it, so I didn't. When Rambo dug up a nest of rabbits to get at the babies, we ate those, too.

And then two weeks later, as abruptly as he'd disappeared, my father returned, whistling as he strode up the ridge with his rifle over his shoulder and a marsh marigold poking out of his gunnysack as if he had never left. He had a bag of salt for my mother and a Lake Superior agate that was almost identical to the one he wore: a gift for me. He never said where he had been or what he had been doing, and we didn't ask. We were just glad he came back.

In the weeks that followed, we went about our chores as if nothing had changed. But it had. Because for the first time in my life, I could imagine a world without my father.

# 13

I'm driving down the road, head swiveling like a barn owl's as I watch for signs of my father. I don't know what I'm looking for. Certainly I don't expect to come around a bend and see my father standing in the middle of the road waving for me to stop. I guess I'll know it when I see it.

Rambo's leash is tied to the grab handle above the passenger door. I generally don't tie him up when he rides with me in the truck, but Rambo is as antsy as I feel, nose twitching, muscles trembling. Every once in a while, he lifts his head and whines like he's caught a whiff of my father. Every time he does this my hands clench and my stomach gets tight.

I've been thinking a lot about Stephen as I

drive. About our argument last night. About how he came back this morning. How he wants to support me in spite of everything I've done to him. I think about the roles we play in our relationship, me as protector and Stephen as nurturer, and how I used to think this was a problem.

And of course I think about the day we met at the blueberry festival, a day I'm sure the gods arranged. After I set out my jars and hung my sign off the front of my table, I watched Stephen set up his tent directly across from mine. To be honest, I was more impressed with his display than I was with his photos. I understand that lighthouse pictures are popular with tourists because, with more than three thousand miles of coastline, Michigan has more lighthouses than any other state, but still it's hard for me to see why anyone would want to hang a picture of one on their wall.

I never would have gone into his tent except that when I left my table to use a porta-john and walked past, I happened to look inside and see a photograph of a bear. I've seen a lot of bear pictures and postcards in the souvenir shops when I make my rounds, but there was something about this bear that grabbed my attention. Whether it was the lighting when he took the photo or the angle he chose is hard to say. All I know is that there was something about the glint in the bear's eye and the set of its jaw that caught my eye.

I stopped. Stephen smiled, and I went inside. On the opposite side of the wire framework on which he'd hung his lighthouse photos were the pictures that captured my heart: herons and bitterns, eagles and minks, otters and beavers and martins. All animals from my childhood, all photographed in such a way as to show off their unique characteristics and personalities, as if Stephen could see into their souls. I bought the bear photo, Stephen bought all my remaining jam and jelly, and the rest, as they say, is history.

I know what I saw in Stephen. I'm still not sure what he saw in me, but I try not to think about it too much. Stephen is the only person on the face of the Earth who chose me. Who loves me not because he has to, but because he wants to. My gift from the universe for surviving my past.

I think again about all of the years and all of the chances I had to come clean about who I am but didn't. The sacrifices I made to keep my secret. Staying away from my father. Wanting to introduce the newborn Iris to my mother but not being able to. The times when I said or did something outside the norm and Stephen looked at me as if I'd lost my mind and I wasn't able to offer an explanation. Things would have been a lot easier if I'd told the truth.

Ten minutes later, I pull over and park. Rambo puts his paws on the window ledge and presses his nose against the glass like he thinks I'm going to let him out, but this time, it's me who has to go. I walk a short way into the underbrush and unzip my jeans. There's hardly any traffic on this road, but you never know. My father and I never worried about privacy when we were hunting or fishing and needed to answer nature's call, but out here people are a lot more sensitive.

I'm almost finished when Rambo barks the sharp staccato warning that means he's spotted something. I zip my jeans and grab the Magnum and drop to my belly with the gun in both hands in front of me and peer through the underbrush.

Nothing. I belly-crawl using the wind as cover to a spot where I can see the truck from another angle, thinking there'll be a pair of legs crouched on the other side, but everything is quiet. I count slowly to twenty, and when nothing changes, I stand up. Rambo sees me and starts barking and scratching to get out. I walk over to the truck and crack the passenger door enough to slip my hand through, then grab him by his collar and untie his leash from the grab handle. If I let Rambo have his way in this condition, I won't see him again for days. Maybe never. There's a reason the first Rambo showed up on our ridge.

As soon as he hits the ground, Rambo drags me over to a stump not twenty feet from where I was occupied, barking and running circles around it like he's treed a squirrel or a raccoon. Only there is no squirrel. Instead, in the exact middle of the stump is a Lake Superior agate.

# 14

## The Cabin

**The wife of the Viking lived in constant pain and sorrow about the child. Her heart clung to the little creature, but she could not explain to her husband the circumstances in which it was placed. If she were to tell him, he would very likely, as was the custom at that time, expose the poor child in the public highway, and let anyone take it away who would.**

**The good wife of the Viking could not let that happen, and she therefore resolved that the Viking should never see the child excepting by daylight. After a while, the foster-mother began to love the poor frog, with its gentle eyes and**

**its deep sighs, even better than the little beauty who bit and fought with all around her.**

—HANS CHRISTIAN ANDERSEN,
**The Marsh King's Daughter**

My childhood came to an end the day my father tried to drown my mother. It was my fault. The incident began innocently enough, and while the outcome wasn't anything I could have foreseen, I can't change the facts. It's not the sort of thing you get over quickly. To this day whenever the radio plays that song about the wreck of the **Edmund Fitzgerald,** or I hear a news report about a ferry tipping over or a cruise ship capsizing or a mother pushing a car full of toddlers into a lake, it makes me want to throw up.

"I saw a patch of strawberries on the next ridge," I told my mother one late June morning. It was the summer I was eleven, after she had complained that the berries I'd picked for her on our ridge weren't going to be nearly enough to make the quantity of jam she wanted.

The thing you need to know in order to understand what happened next is that when I told my mother I'd seen a patch of strawberries growing on "the next ridge," she knew exactly which ridge I was talking about. White people tend to name geographic features for themselves, or for other important people, but we followed the Native tradition and named our surroundings according to how we used them, or for their proximity to our own. **The next ridge. The cedars where the deer like to gather. The bog where the arrowroot grows. The place where Jacob shot the eagle. The rock where Helena cut her head.** Like the Ojibwa word for the Tahquamenon River, **Adikamegong-ziibi,** "river where the whitefish are found." I still think the Native way makes more sense.

"Will you pick them for me?" my mother asked. "If I stop stirring now, this batch won't set."

And this is why my mother's near-drowning was my fault: I wanted to say yes. There was nothing I loved better than taking out my father's canoe, except possibly deer hunting or beaver trapping. Normally I would have jumped at the chance. In hindsight I wish I had. But at eleven I was just getting to that age where I was driven much of the time by the need to assert myself. So I shook my head. "I'm going fishing."

My mother looked at me for a long time, like there was more she wanted to say but couldn't.

At last she sighed and moved the pot to the back of the stove. She picked up one of the willow twig baskets my father had woven the previous winter and went outside.

As soon as the screen door banged behind her, I drizzled some of the hot strawberry syrup over a plateful of yesterday's biscuits, poured myself a cup of chicory, and carried my breakfast to the back porch. The day was already warm. In the U.P., winter lasts forever and the spring drags on and on until, suddenly, you wake up one morning in the middle of June—and just like that, it's summer. I unbuckled my overall straps and took off my shirt, then rolled up my pant legs as high as they would go. I seriously considered using my knife to cut off the legs and make the overalls into shorts, but this was the biggest pair of overalls I owned, and I was going to need those pant legs next winter.

I had almost finished eating and was about to go back into the kitchen to sneak a second helping when my father came over the side of the hill with a water bucket in each hand. He set the buckets on the porch and sat down beside me. I gave him the last biscuit, tossed what was left of my chicory into the dirt, and dipped my cup into one of the buckets. The water was cool and clear. Sometimes mosquito larvae got scooped up with the water. We'd find them swimming in our buckets, twisting and turning in on themselves like fish on dry land. When that happened we dipped our cups around them or flicked them out with a finger. We probably should have boiled the water before we drank it, but you try passing up a nice, cool drink of marsh water on a hot summer day. Anyway, we were never sick. After we left the marsh, my mother and I spent the next two years coughing and sneezing. That was one benefit of our isolation that people never think about: no germs. I always think it's funny when people say they caught a cold because they went outside without a hat or a jacket. According to that logic, you should catch a fever in the summer if you get too hot.

"Where's your mother going?" My father's voice was thick with biscuit and syrup as he chewed. I wanted to ask why he was allowed to talk with his mouth full while my mother and I couldn't, but I didn't want to spoil the mood. There wasn't a lot of physical contact in my family, and I liked sitting next to my father on the top step with our hips and knees pressed together like Siamese twins.

"To pick strawberries," I told him proudly, pleased that thanks to me, this year we would have plenty of strawberry jam. "I found a patch on the next ridge."

By this time my mother was almost to the woodlot. Our woodlot was on the low end of our ridge. At the bottom of the woodlot was the V-shaped depression where my father kept his canoe.

My father's eyes narrowed. He jumped off the porch and took off running down the hill. I'd never seen him move so fast. I still had no idea what was about to happen, why my mother's taking the canoe could possibly be a problem. I honestly thought my father only wanted to go with her to help, though he always said that picking berries was a job for women and children.

He caught up to her as she was pushing off and splashed into the water. But instead of getting into the canoe as I expected, he grabbed my mother by the hair, yanked her out of the canoe, and dragged her screaming all the way up the hill to our back porch, where he jammed her head into one of the water buckets and held it there while she flailed and clawed. When she went limp, I thought she was dead. The look on her face when he pulled her head out—hair dripping, eyes wild as she choked and coughed and sputtered—said she'd thought so, too.

My father tossed her to the side and strode off. After a while my mother pushed herself to her knees and crawled across the porch boards into the cabin. I sat on the big rock in the yard and stared at the trail of water she'd left behind until it dried. I had always been afraid of my father, but until that moment it had been more of a respectful awe. A fear of displeasing him, not because I was afraid of being punished, but because I didn't want to disappoint him. But watching my father almost drown my mother terrified me—especially since I didn't understand why he wanted to kill her or what she'd done wrong. I didn't know then that my mother was his prisoner, or that she might indeed have been trying to run away. If I had been her, that near-drowning would have made me more determined than ever to escape my captor. But one thing I've learned since I left the marsh is that everybody's different. What one person **must** do another one **can't.**

Anyway, that's why I have a problem with drowning.

BEFORE MY FATHER TRIED to drown my mother, I used to enjoy trapping beaver. There was a beaver pond about a half mile up the Tahquamenon River from our cabin. My father trapped beaver in December and January when the pelts were prime. He'd walk the edges of the pond looking for places where the beaver had come out for fresh air and sunlight, and set both leg traps and snares. I assume the pond is still there, but who knows? Sometimes the Department of Natural Resources will blow up a beaver dam if they think it's interfering with the way a river ought to run, or if the dam is somehow making problems for people. Property damage caused by beavers runs into the millions of dollars every year, and the DNR takes its management responsibilities seriously. Timber loss, crop loss, damage to roads and septic systems from flooding, even the destruction of ornamental landscape plantings in suburban gardens are all considered legitimate reasons for taking out a beaver dam. Never mind the needs of the beavers.

Our pond was made when beavers dammed one of the Tahquamenon's smaller unnamed tributaries. The largest beaver dam on record is more than half a mile long. That's twice the length of the Hoover Dam, in case you were trying to picture it, which is pretty impressive when you consider that an adult male beaver is roughly the size and weight of a two-year-old child. Our dam was nowhere near that long. I used to walk along the top throwing rocks and sticks into the pond, or fishing largemouth bass, or sitting with my legs dangling over the dry side munching an apple. I liked the idea that the habitat I was exploring had been created by the animals that lived in it. Sometimes I'd tear apart a section of the dam to see how long it would take the beavers to fix it.

In addition to beavers, our pond was home to many species of fish, water insects, and birds, including ducks, blue herons, kingfishers, mergansers, and bald eagles. If you've never seen a bald eagle drop like a rock out of the sky and splash down into the still pond water and fly away with a pike or a walleye in its talons, you're missing out.

After my father tried to drown my mother, I had to quit beaver trapping. I didn't have a problem killing animals as long as it was done out of necessity and with respect, but leg traps kill by dragging the beavers under the water and holding them there, and death by drowning made my stomach turn.

What bothered me more than drowning beavers was that I didn't understand why my father continued to trap them at all. Our utility shed was piled high with furs. Mink, beaver, otter, fox, coyote, wolf, muskrat, ermine. My father always taught that it was important to show respect for the animals we killed. That we should think before we pulled the trigger, and we shouldn't be wasteful. That we shouldn't shoot the first animal we see because it might be the only one of its kind we see all day, and that would mean the population was small and needed to be left alone for a while. Yet every year he added more furs to the piles. When I was very small I used to think that one day he would load the furs into his canoe and paddle up the river and trade them like the French and Indians used to do. I used to hope he'd take me with him. But after my father tried to drown my mother, I started to question the whole endeavor. I knew what he did to my mother was wrong. Maybe his excessive trapping was also wrong. If the end result of all that trapping was nothing but stacks of furs piled higher than my head, what was the point?

I thought about things like this as I sat on our back porch after supper as summer turned to fall, paging through the **Geographics** until it was too dark to see, hoping to find an article I hadn't read. I used to like watching the evening wind blow across the grasses as the shadows spread over the marsh and the stars gradually came out, but lately the movement only made me restless. Sometimes Rambo would lift his head and scent the air and whine as he lay on the porch boards beside me, like he felt it, too. A sense of wanting, but not having; a feeling that there was something outside the boundaries of the marsh that was bigger, better, more. I'd stare at the dark band of trees along the horizon and try to imagine what lay beyond. When airplanes flew over our cabin, I'd shade my eyes and keep looking at the sky long after the planes were gone. I wondered about the people inside. Did they wish they were down in the marsh with me as much as I wished I was up in the air with them?

My father was worried about me, I could tell. He didn't understand the changes that were coming over me any more than I did. Sometimes I'd catch him studying me when he thought I wasn't watching, stroking his thin beard in the way he had that told me he was thinking long and hard. Usually this was the prelude to a story. A Native American legend, or a hunting or fishing story, or a story about something strange or funny or dramatic or scary or wonderful that had happened to him. I'd sit cross-legged with my hands folded respectfully in my lap the way he taught me and pretend to listen while my thoughts roamed. It wasn't that I was no longer interested in my father's stories. My father is one of the best storytellers I've ever known. But now I wanted to make my own.

ONE DREARY, rainy morning that fall, my father decided it was time for me to learn how to make jelly. I couldn't see why I needed to know. I wanted to take my father's canoe to check my trapline. There was a family of red fox living on the other side of the ridge where the deer liked to gather, and I was hoping to snare one so my mother could make me a foxtail hat with ear flaps like the one my father wore. I didn't care that it was raining. I wasn't going to melt, and whatever got wet would dry out again eventually. When my mother announced at breakfast that because it was raining she was going to make jelly and said she wanted me to help, I put on my coat anyway, because my mother couldn't tell me what to do. But my father could. So when he decreed that today was the day I was going to learn how to make jelly, I was stuck.

I would rather have helped my father. He was sitting at the kitchen table using a whetstone and a polishing cloth to sharpen and polish his knife collection, though the knives were already shiny and sharp. Our oil lamp was in the middle of the table. Normally we didn't light the lamp during the day because we were running out of bear grease, but it was extra dark in the cabin that morning because of the rain.

My mother was stirring a pot of hot apple mash on the counter with a wooden spoon to cool it while another pot boiled and foamed on the stove. The empty jars she'd washed and dried waited on folded kitchen towels on the table. A tin can of melted paraffin sat on the back of the stove. My mother poured a layer of hot paraffin on top of the jelly after it set to seal the jars so the jelly wouldn't get moldy, though mold grew anyway. She said the mold wouldn't hurt us, but I'd noticed she scraped it off before she ate her jelly and threw the moldy parts away. The washtub on the floor was heaped with apple peelings. As soon as it stopped raining, my mother would carry the tub outside and dump the peelings on her compost pile.

My hands were red from squeezing the hot apple mash through a piece of folded cheesecloth to separate the juice from the pulp. The kitchen was stuffy and hot. I felt like a miner chipping away at a coal seam deep underground. I peeled my T-shirt over my head and used it to wipe my face.

"Put your shirt on," my mother said.

"I don't want to. It's too hot."

My mother shot my father a look. My father shrugged. I wadded up my shirt and threw it into a corner and stomped up the stairs to my room and flopped onto my bed with my arms behind my head and stared at the ceiling and thought bad thoughts about my father and mother.

"Helena! Get down here!" my mother called up the stairs.

I didn't move. I could hear my parents argue.

"Jacob, do something."

"What do you want me to do?"

"Make her come down. Make her help. I can't do everything myself."

I rolled off the bed and dug through the piles of clothes on the floor for a dry T-shirt, buttoned a flannel shirt over it, and stomped back down the stairs.

"You're not going out," my mother said when I crossed the kitchen and grabbed my coat from the hook by the door. "We're not finished."

"You're not finished. I'm done."

"Jacob."

"Listen to your mother, Helena," my father said without looking up from the knife he was sharpening. I could see his reflection in the blade. My father was smiling.

I threw my coat on the floor and ran into the living room and threw myself on my bearskin rug and buried my face in its fur. I didn't want to learn how to make jelly. I didn't understand why my father wouldn't take my side against my mother, what was happening to me and to my family. Why I felt like crying though I didn't want to.

I sat up and wrapped my arms around my knees and sank my teeth into my arm until I tasted blood. If I couldn't stop myself from crying, I'd give myself a reason to.

My father followed me into the living room and stood over me with his arms crossed. The knife he'd been sharpening was in his hand.

"Get up."

I got up. Tried not to look at the knife as I stood as straight and tall as I was able. I crossed my arms over my chest and stuck out my chin and stared back. I wasn't challenging him. Not yet. I was only letting him know that whatever he was planning to do to me in punishment for my defiance was going to come at a cost. If I could go back in time and ask the eleven-year-old me what I was planning to do to my father in retaliation, I couldn't have said. All I knew was that there was nothing my father could say or do that would make me agree to help my mother make jelly.

My father looked back just as steadily. He hefted the knife and smiled. A sly, crooked smile that said I would have been a whole lot smarter if I'd done as he said, because now he was going to have a little fun. He took my wrist and held it tightly so I couldn't pull away. Studied the bite mark I'd left on my forearm, then touched the tip of the knife to my skin. I flinched. I didn't want to. I knew that whatever my father was planning to do would be worse if he knew I was afraid. And I wasn't afraid—not really, not of pain, anyway. I'd had plenty of experience enduring pain because of my tattoos. In hindsight, I think the reason I flinched was that I didn't know what he was going to do. There's a psychological component to controlling a person that can be just as powerful as the physical pain you inflict on them, and I think this incident is a good example.

My father drew the knife along my forearm. The cuts he made weren't deep. Just enough to make the blood well up. Slowly he connected the teeth marks until they formed a crude **O.**

He paused, studied his handiwork, then drew three short contiguous lines on one side of the **O** and four more on the other.

When he finished, he held up my arm so I could see. Blood ran down the inside of my arm and dripped off my elbow.

"Go help your mother." He tapped the tip of the knife against the word he'd cut into my arm and smiled again, like he'd be happy to keep this up for as long as he had to if I didn't do as he said, and so I did.

The scars have grown faint over time, but if you know where to look, you can still read the word **NOW** on the inside of my right forearm.

The scars my father left on my mother, of course, went much deeper.

# 15

I stare at the agate my father left on the stump. I don't want to touch it. This is exactly the sort of trick he used to pull when he was teaching me to track. Just when I thought I was at the top of my game, merrily anticipating the moment when I could shoot a bullet between his feet, he'd do something to throw me off: brush out his tracks with a leafy branch, or use a long stick to bend the grass where he wanted me to think that he had walked, or walk backward, or walk on the sides of his feet so he wouldn't leave heel or toe marks at all. Every time I thought I had mastered everything there was to know about tracking a person through the wilderness, my father would come up with something new.

Now it's an agate. That my father was watching for who knows how long, that he could sneak up while I was occupied and leave the agate for me to find proves my father is a better woodsman after thirteen years in a five-by-nine jail cell than I will ever be. Not only can he escape from a maximum security prison, he can make the people who are looking for him think he's in an area where he's not, then lure me here knowing that our shared history will lead me to this spot. I knew when I went looking for my father this morning that I would find him.

What I didn't anticipate was that he would first find me.

Rambo is barking like he thinks the rock is going to sprout legs and take off. I'll give it to him to sniff eventually, but first, I want to know how my father knew that the person who'd gone into the underbrush to relieve herself was me. I don't look at all like I used to. The black hair I wore in pigtails or braids is shoulder-length now, and shot through with so many highlights, it's almost blonde. After two kids my figure has filled out and rounded. I'll never be fat because I don't have the body type or the metabolism, but I'm not as skinny as I was the last time he saw me. I've also grown an inch, possibly two. Rambo could have been a clue, since he's the same breed as the dog that showed up on our ridge, but a brindled bear hound running around the Upper Peninsula woods during bear season isn't exactly a rarity. Unless I spoke his name out loud, I don't see how my father could have made the connection. And where and how did he get the agate? The whole thing stinks worse than the meat scraps we used to throw in our garbage pit. If my father thinks he's going to draw me into an adult version of our old tracking game, he should remember that the last three times we played this game, I won.

Only maybe my father didn't put the rock on the stump to gloat about how much better he is than I am at hunting and tracking. Maybe it isn't a taunt. Maybe it's an invitation. **I haven't forgotten you. I care about you. I want to see you one last time before I disappear.**

I pull out my shirttail and pick up the agate and hold it out for Rambo to smell. Rambo sniffs his way over the sticks and the brush to a spot on the road twenty feet in front of my truck. A set of treaded footprints points west. Prints like the kind that could have been made by the shoes of a dead prison guard. I go back to the truck, half expecting my father to jump out of the bushes and grab me like he used to when I'd walk back to the cabin after one of his scary sweat lodge stories.

I toss the rock on the front seat, then tie

Rambo in the back and signal him to lie down and stay quiet. I haven't forgotten how my father feels about dogs. I slide the ignition key from the ring and put it in my pocket, then make sure my phone is on mute and stick it in the other. Normally I leave my keys in my truck when I'm hunting—the U.P. isn't exactly crawling with car thieves, and you don't want your keys making noise in your pocket—but I'm not about to follow the trail my father laid down for me only to come to the end of it and discover he's stolen my truck. I lock the cab for extra insurance and check my knife and gun. The police say my father is armed and dangerous. So am I.

A quarter mile up the road, the prints turn in at the driveway of one of the cabins I wanted to check. I bypass the drive and cut a wide circle so I can approach at an angle from the back. There's less cover than I'd like. These woods are mostly tamarack and jack pine, thin and scraggly and dry as tinder, impossible to navigate without making noise. On the other hand, if my father is waiting for me inside the cabin, he already knows I'm here.

The cabin is old and small and set so far back into the clearing, it almost disappears into the forest. Moss and pine needles blanket the roof. Tall yellow flowers and rangy vines cover the sides. It looks like a fairy-tale cottage from one of my girls' picture books. Not the kind of cottage that belongs to an innocent childless couple or a poor woodsman; more the kind of cottage that's meant to entice unwary children inside. I keep a particular eye on the utility shed at the end of the drive where an old pickup is parked. I check under the truck carriage and up in the rafters. The shed is empty.

I skirt the edges of the clearing and go around the cabin to the back. The only window opens into a bedroom barely bigger than the bed, dresser, and chair someone managed to squeeze inside. The bed sags in the middle and doesn't look slept in.

I go to the side to check the next window. The bathroom fixtures are rust-stained, the towels old. A single toothbrush hangs above the sink in a holder on the wall. The water in the toilet is brown. A dark ring above the water level indicates it's been a while since the toilet was flushed.

The next window opens to a living room that could have been a twin to the living room at my grandparents': faded flowered sofa, matching armchairs, wooden coffee table with a bowl full of pinecones and driftwood and agates in the middle, glass-fronted corner cabinet crammed with knickknacks and salt and pepper shakers and Depression glass. Yellowed crocheted doilies on the arms and backs of the chairs. An old recliner badly in need of reupholstering. A coffee cup and a folded newspaper on the table beside it. The room looks undisturbed. If my father is waiting inside the cabin, he's not waiting here.

I go around to the front and step silently onto the porch. Stand still, listen, smell the air. When you're hunting humans, slow is the way to go.

After long minutes of nothing, I try the door. The knob turns freely, and I go inside.

I WAS FIFTEEN the first time I broke into a cabin. By then I'd dropped out of school, and the tutors the state sent over didn't know what to do with me any more than my grandparents did, so I had a lot of free time.

I wish I could say I broke into the cabin out of necessity—because I got caught in a rain shower or a snowstorm, something—but it was just a lark, an idea I got for something to do one day when I was bored. The cabin belonged to the parents of one of the boys I went to school with who liked to make trouble for me, and I thought it would be fun to turn things around and make trouble for him. I wasn't planning to do any damage; I just wanted to leave enough evidence behind that I'd broken in so he'd know I could. The cabin had one of those "This property is protected by" stickers on the door, but my grandparents' house had the same sticker, so I knew the warning wasn't real. My grandfather said that fake stickers worked just as well as real ones and were a lot cheaper than installing a security system.

My plan was simple:

1. Put on the pair of yellow rubber gloves I took from under my grandmother's sink.
2. Use my knife to pry the hinge pins off the front door.
3. Open a can of something from the kitchen and build a fire in the woodstove to cook it because I liked hot canned food better than cold.
4. Leave the can in the middle of the living room with the dead mouse I brought from my grandparents' woodpile inside it.
5. Put the door back on its hinges and leave.

The mouse was fresh, so I was counting on it stinking up the place enough that the next time anybody came in, the smell would be the first thing that would hit them. They'd find the can with the dead mouse inside and know that someone had broken in, but they wouldn't know who because of the gloves. After I came up with the mouse-in-a-can idea, I figured I'd break into all of the cabins belonging to all of the families of all of the kids who were giving me trouble, and it would be my calling card. The police would think the break-ins were random, but eventually my tormentors would figure out the connection and realize it was me. They wouldn't be able to say anything without pointing the finger at themselves, however, which I thought was the best part of my plan.

But it turned out not everyone is as cheap as my grandfather was: the security stickers were real. I was sitting in a chair by the woodstove, looking through a stack of **National Geographics** to see if they had the one with the article about the Vikings while I waited for my beans to boil, when a sheriff's car pulled up out front with its lights flashing. I could have ducked out the back—there wasn't a sheriff on Earth who could catch me after I disappeared into the woods if I didn't want to be caught—but the deputy who got out of the car was the same one who'd brought me back the last two times I'd run away, and we'd kind of developed a relationship.

"Don't shoot!" I called as I came out the front door with my hands up, and we both laughed.

The deputy made me put everything back the way I found it, then opened the car door like I was a movie star and he was my chauffeur. We traded hunting and fishing stories on the way home, and it was a lot of fun. I told him my father's story about falling into the bear den like it had happened to me, and he was impressed. When I asked if he would be my boyfriend because we seemed to be getting along so well, he told me he was married and had two kids. I couldn't see where that mattered, but he promised that it did.

The deputy took me to the police station. Apparently, breaking and entering was a more serious crime than running away. I was hoping he'd put me in the jail cell where my father was held so I could see what it was like, but he made me sit on a wooden bench in the hall while he called my grandparents. When my grandparents came, the deputy launched into a long lecture about how I was lucky the people who owned the cabin weren't going to press charges, but they could have, and then I would have been in real trouble, and I needed to obey the law and respect people's possessions so nothing like this ever happened again. I didn't mind. He was only doing his job. But when he started going on about how I should think about what would happen to me if I didn't stop behaving so recklessly, and asked if I wanted to end up in prison like my father, I was glad he wasn't my boyfriend. I decided the first chance I got, I'd break into another cabin to spite him. Maybe his.

After that, my grandfather made me work in his store full-time. Till then, I'd been working three days a week. My grandparents ran a combination bait and bicycle shop in an old wooden building on Main Street sandwiched between a real estate office and the drugstore. The bicycles were lined up in the front of the store so you could see them if you were walking by, and the bait tanks and refrigerators full of worms and night crawlers were in the back. I used to think the reason my grandfather chose to sell bait and bicycles was that they both started with the letter **B.** Now I know a lot of businesses in the U.P. sell a combination of things you wouldn't normally think would go together because it's so hard to make a living selling only one. I do all right with jelly and jam, but that's because a lot of my sales are made online.

My grandfather also said that because I was working full-time, I had to pay room and board. After that, if I wanted, I could save up the money that was left and buy a bicycle from him at cost. My grandfather had sold all the bikes and other things people sent me long before this, so I was glad to have the chance to get another one. He drew three columns on a piece of paper labeled **Wholesale, Retail,** and **Net Profit** and put numbers in them as examples to show how the retail business worked, which came in handy later when I started my own.

The bike I picked out was a Schwinn Frontier mountain bike in mirror blue. I liked that I could ride the bicycle both on the road and off. I know now there were better and more expensive bicycles my grandfather could have stocked, but nobody was going to make a living selling high-end bikes in the Upper Peninsula, even if they sold bait on the side.

Every time a customer came into the shop looking to buy a bike, I steered them away from mine. I didn't know my grandfather could order another one like it if that one sold. I realize that after three years, most people would think I should have understood more about how the commercial system worked, but I'd like to see them try starting from zero and see how well they do. Even now I occasionally run up against things I don't know. So when one of the boys from school bought the bike I'd been saving for, I figured it was over. I wheeled the bike out to his parents' pickup, dropped the bike on the sidewalk without helping them load it like I was supposed to, and kept right on walking. I didn't have any particular destination in mind;

I only knew my grandfather had cheated me out of the bike I was saving to buy and I wasn't going back.

My grandfather caught up to me after a few hours. By then it was well after dark. If my grandmother hadn't been in the passenger seat, I probably wouldn't have gotten in. Naturally I felt pretty stupid after we got everything sorted out and my grandfather promised to order another bike like the one that sold. Back then I felt stupid a lot.

I'm not telling these stories to make people feel sorry for me. God knows I've had enough of that. I just want people to understand why, after a few years, I felt like I needed to start over. Sometimes a person thinks she wants something, but then after she gets it, she finds out it wasn't what she wanted at all. That's what happened to me when I left the marsh. I thought I could make a new life for myself, be happy. I was smart, young, ready to embrace the outside world, eager to learn. The problem was that people weren't so eager to embrace me. There's a stigma to being the offspring of a kidnapper, rapist, and murderer that's hard to shake. If people think I'm exaggerating, they should think about this: Would they have welcomed me into their home knowing who my father was and what he did to my mother? Let me be friends with their sons and daughters? Trusted me to babysit their children? Even if someone says yes to any of these, I'll bet they hesitated before they did.

Luckily my father's parents died within a few months of each other not long after I turned eighteen and left to me the house where my father grew up. Because I was of age, their lawyer was willing to transfer the property without telling my mother or grandparents. As soon as the paperwork was ready, I packed a suitcase, told them I was moving but not where to find me, changed my last name to Eriksson because I had always loved the Vikings and figured this was my chance to be one, and cut my hair short and dyed it blonde. And just like that, The Marsh King's daughter was gone.

THE CABIN DOOR OPENS directly into the living room. The room is small, maybe ten by twelve, and the ceiling is so low, I could touch it if I stood on my tiptoes. I leave the front door open behind me. I have a problem with closed-in places that smell of damp and mold.

The television is on with the sound off. On the screen an announcer is mouthing the latest about the search for my father. Video footage plays in a box above the man's left shoulder: a helicopter stirring the surface of a pocket lake while patrol boats circle. At the bottom of the screen, a ticker tape scrolls: **Search continues** and **FBI brings in more manpower** and **Prisoner's body found?**

I stand as still as possible, trying to sense the sway of a curtain, a small intake of breath, a molecular displacement that would indicate I'm not alone. Beneath the mold and mildew I can smell bacon, eggs, coffee, the smoky residue of a gun that's been recently fired, and the sharp, metallic tang of fresh blood.

I wait. No sound. No movement. Whatever happened was over long before I arrived. I wait some more, then cross the living room and stop in the doorway to the kitchen.

A naked man is lying on his side between the table and the stove. Blood and brains spatter the floor.

**Stephen.**

# 16

## The Cabin

**The skald spoke of the golden treasure the Viking's wife had brought to her wealthy husband, and of his delight at the beautiful child which he had seen only under its charming daylight guise. He rather admired her passionate nature, and said she would grow into a doughty shield maiden or Valkyrie, able to hold her own in battle. She would be of the kind who would not blink if a practiced hand cut off her eyebrows in jest with a sharp sword.**

**Every month this temper showed itself in sharper outlines; and in the course of years, the child grew to be almost a woman, and before anyone seemed aware**

**of it, she was a wonderfully beautiful maiden of sixteen. The casket was splendid, but the contents were worthless.**

—HANS CHRISTIAN ANDERSEN,
**The Marsh King's Daughter**

Get your coat," my father said early one morning the winter I was eleven. This would be my last winter in the marsh, though I didn't yet know it. "I want to show you something."

My mother looked up from the hide she was working. As soon as she realized my father wasn't talking to her, she quickly put her head back down. The tension between my parents was as thick as fog. It had been like this since my father tried to drown my mother. "He's going to kill me," my mother whispered not long after, when she was sure my father wasn't around. I thought this might be true. My mother didn't ask for my help or expect me to side with her against my father, and I appreciated that. If my father truly wanted to kill my mother, there wasn't anything I could do.

My mother was working the deer hide my father tanned into buckskin. Aside from cooking and cleaning, this was her main winter job. Last winter she made a beautiful fringed buckskin overshirt for my father. This winter, as soon as she had enough buckskin, she was going to make one for me. My father promised to decorate my shirt with porcupine quills according to the design I drew for him with charcoal on a piece of birch bark because we were out of pencils and paper. My father was a talented artist. The shirt was going to look a lot better than my picture.

I put on my winter gear and followed my father outside. My spotted fawnskin mittens were too small for me now, but I was trying to get as much use out of them as I could before I had to add them to the discard pile. I wished my mother had made them bigger, but she said my fawn was so tiny that this was the best she could do. When my father shot his deer that spring, I was hoping for a doe that was pregnant with twins.

The day was sunny and cold. The sun reflecting off the snow was so bright, I had to squint. My father called this kind of weather a January thaw, but nothing was melting today. We sat on the edge of the porch and strapped on our snowshoes. We'd had a lot of snow that winter, and nobody was going anywhere without them. My father made my snowshoes from alder branches and rawhide the winter I was nine. He used a pair of Iversons that belonged to his father. When he got too old to go snowshoeing, my father promised he would give them to me.

We set off at a brisk pace. Now that I was almost as tall as my father, it was no problem keeping up. I didn't ask where we were going. My father used to surprise me with mystery outings like this, mostly in connection with teaching me how to track, but it had been a while. As I followed him toward the low end of our ridge, I tried to guess our destination. It wasn't hard. In the rucksack my father carried was a small lidded coffeepot in which to melt snow for tea, six biscuits that were hard as rocks but would soften after we soaked them, four strips of the dried venison and blueberry mixture my father called pemmican, and a jar of blueberry jam, so I knew we wouldn't be back in time for lunch. My father's rifle was locked in the storage room and Rambo was tied in the woodshed, so we weren't going hunting. We were carrying snowshoe poles, which meant we'd be walking a considerable distance. There was nothing between our ridge and the river except a few small ridges I'd already explored, and there was nothing on them that was worth hiking out to see anyway, so these couldn't be our destination. Taken all together, it was obvious we were heading for the river. I still didn't know why. I'd seen the river many times and in every season. All I could think was that my father had found some interesting ice formations he wanted to show me. If this was correct, the effort hardly seemed worth it.

When we came to the river at last, I expected my father to turn upstream or down and walk alongside it until we came to whatever it was I was supposed to see. Instead, he walked straight out onto the ice without breaking stride. This **was** a surprise. The Tahquamenon was swift and at least a hundred feet wide, and while most of the river was frozen, great sections of it were not. Yet my father walked purposefully toward the other side without so much as a backward glance, as if he was walking on solid ground. All I could do was stand on the shore and watch. Normally I'd follow my father wherever he led, but how could he possibly think the river was safe to cross? Ever since I was old enough to roam the marsh by myself, my father had warned me over and over that I must never venture onto the river during winter no matter how solid the ice looked. River ice was nothing like lake ice because of the currents. It could be thick in some places and thin in others—and, unless you were using an ice pole to test the thickness, which my father was not, there was no way to tell. If I fell through the ice into a lake or a pond, I'd be cold and wet but I wouldn't be in serious danger because marsh lakes and ponds were generally shallow. Even if I had to swim to get to a section where the ice was strong enough to stand on, I would manage. But if I fell into the river, the current would sweep me under the ice faster than I could draw a breath to yell for help, and no one would ever see or hear from me again.

This was what my father had taught me. Yet now he was doing the opposite. I'd always thought of my father as so powerful that he was nearly indestructible. Something like a god. I knew he was human, mortal, but if only half the stories he told were true, my father had gotten himself into and out of many dangerous situations. But not even my father could survive a fall into the river. And death by drowning was not the way I'd choose.

Only maybe . . . maybe this was the point. My father never did anything without a purpose. Maybe **this** was what he brought me to the river to see. He knew I was afraid of drowning. He also knew I was desperate to explore the other side of the river; I'd asked him to take me across in his canoe many times. I hadn't figured he knew how claustrophobic the marsh had become for me, or how much I longed to see or do something new, but maybe he did. Either way, he put the two together, the thing I wanted most and the thing I was most afraid of, and brought me to the river so I could face my fear instead of keeping it inside and letting it fester.

Quickly I climbed over the ice blocks along the shore and stepped onto the river before I could change my mind. My heart thudded. Inside my mittens, my hands were damp with sweat. I placed my feet carefully, trying to remember the path my father took so I could follow his footsteps exactly. The ice moved up and down as I walked, like the river was breathing, like it was a living thing and it was offended by this arrogant human girl-child who dared to walk across its frozen surface. I imagined the River Spirit reaching an icy hand up out of the water from one of the many gaps in the ice, grabbing my ankle, and pulling me in. I saw myself looking back from beneath the ice, my hair streaming and my lungs straining as the River Spirit pulled me down and down and down, my face as wide-eyed and terrified as my mother's.

I kept walking. The brown water rushing past in the open places made me dizzy. My mouth was sour with fear. I looked back to see how far I'd come, then looked at my father to see how far I had to go, and realized it was now just as far to run to safety in one direction as it was in the other. I wanted to stop, wave cheerily at my father to show him how brave and fearless I was. Instead I ran, flying over the ice as fast as a person wearing homemade snowshoes could run. My father stretched out his hand and helped me climb up the riverbank and into the trees. I bent over with my hands on my knees until my breathing slowed. The significance of what I had accomplished was almost overwhelming. I was afraid, but fear didn't stop me from doing what I wanted to do. **This** was the lesson my father wanted me to learn. The knowledge filled me with power. I spread my arms wide and looked up into the sky and thanked the Great Spirit for the wisdom he gave my father.

We turned east and walked downstream along the river. I was Erik the Red or his son, Leif Eriksson, setting foot on the shores of Greenland or North America for the very first time. Every tree, every bush, every rock, was a rock or a bush or a tree that I had never seen. Even the air felt different. On our side of the river, the marsh was mostly flat grasslands covered in standing water with only the occasional ridge. This side was all solid ground, with towering white pines so big that two people couldn't have wrapped their arms around them. There was enough wood in this forest to build a thousand cabins like ours, enough firewood to keep the families who lived in them warm for dozens of years. I wondered why the people who built our cabin didn't build it here.

As I snowshoed behind my father, I felt like I could walk for miles. Then I realized **I could.** There was nothing stopping me from walking wherever I wanted because I was no longer bounded by water. No wonder the marsh felt small.

Of course I also realized that however far we walked, at some point we were going to have to turn around and walk the same distance back. We were also going to have to cross the river again, and if we didn't time our return trip right, it could be dark by the time we did. I had no idea how we'd manage if that happened, but I wouldn't think about that now. My father had gotten me across the river once; he could do it again. All that mattered was that at last—**at last**—I was seeing and experiencing something entirely new.

The river got wider. In the distance I heard a low rumbling. At first the sound was so faint, I wasn't sure if it was real. But gradually the noise got louder. It sounded like the noise the river made when the ice broke up in the spring, only it wasn't spring, and the river was frozen solid. I wanted to ask what the rumbling meant, why it was getting louder, why the current was running stronger, but my father was walking so quickly, I could barely keep up.

We came to a place where a thick cable made

of strands of wire twisted together was strung across the river. On our side the cable wrapped around a tree. The bark had grown over the cable, so I knew the cable had been there a long time. I imagined the cable was similarly anchored on the other side. Hanging from the cable in the middle of the river was a sign. Except for the word **DANGER** at the top in big red letters, the writing was too small to read. I didn't understand why someone would go to all of the trouble of hanging a sign in a place where the only people who could read it would have to be in a boat. And what was the danger?

We kept walking. The snow got slippery and wet. The trees were coated with what looked like frost, but when I tugged on a branch, the coating didn't fall off like frost should.

And then the river disappeared. That's the only way I can think to describe it. Beside us, the river flowed swift and wide. A hundred yards ahead was nothing but sky. The river simply stopped, like it had been cut off with a knife. The disappearing river, the frost that wasn't frost, the roaring that sounded like thunder but never stopped—I felt like I'd stepped out of the real world and into one of my father's stories.

My father led me through a break in the trees toward the edge of an icy cliff. For one terrifying moment I thought he expected me to link hands and jump off like in the legends about Indian warriors and maidens forbidden to marry. Instead he put his hands on my shoulders and gently turned me around.

I gasped. Not fifty feet from where we were standing, the river exploded over the side of the cliff in a great wall of brown and gold water, crashing down endlessly onto the rocks below. Chunks of ice as big as our cabin clogged the river at the bottom. Thick ice coated the trees and the rocks. The sides of the waterfall were frozen into massive ice columns like the pillars of a medieval cathedral. Directly across from us a wooden platform extended over the top of the waterfall. Stairs led from the platform up a steep hill and into the trees. I'd seen pictures of Niagara Falls in the **Geographics,** but this was beyond anything I could have imagined. I had no idea that such a thing existed in our marsh—never mind that our falls were less than a day's walk away.

We stood and watched for a long time. Mist coated my hair, my face, my eyelashes. At last my father tapped my arm. I didn't want to leave, but I followed him into the trees and sat down beside him on a fallen log. Like everything else in this magical forest, the log was huge—at least three times the size of the biggest fallen log that I had ever seen.

My father smiled and waved his hand expansively. "What do you think?"

"It's wonderful," was all I could say. I hoped it was enough. The noise, the spray, the endlessly pounding water—I had no words to describe the magnitude of what I was thinking and feeling.

"This is ours, **Bangii-Agawaateyaa.** The river, the land, this waterfall, all belong to us. Long before the white man came, our people fished these waters and hunted these shores."

"And the wooden platform? Did we build that, too?"

My father's face darkened. Instantly I wished I hadn't asked the question, but it was too late to take it back.

"On the other side of the falls is a place the white men call a park. The white men built the stairs and the platform so people would give them money to look at our waterfall."

"I thought perhaps the platform was for fishing."

My father clapped his hands together and laughed loud and long. Normally I would have been pleased with his reaction, but I wasn't trying to be funny. As soon as the words left my mouth, I realized there were no fish in these waters. My father had told me our river emptied into a big lake called **Gitche Gumee** at a place the Ojibwa call **Ne-adikamegwaning** and the white people call Whitefish Bay. I also knew from the **Geographics** that salmon swim upstream through rapids to spawn in the rivers of the Pacific Northwest, but no fish could swim through this.

My father's laughter echoed back from the other side, high-pitched, like a woman's or a child's. My father fell silent, but the echo of his laughter continued. My heart pounded. **Nanabozho,** the trickster, it had to be, hiding on the other side of the river, magnifying my father's laughter at my foolishness and throwing it across the water to mock me. I jumped to my feet. I wanted to see what form that old shapeshifter had taken today. My father grabbed my hand and pulled me down. I raised my head anyway. If **Nanabozho** was visiting this forest, I had to see.

A new sound, like clanging metal, and two people ran down the stairs. This was not what I was expecting. Normally, **Nanabozho** appeared as a rabbit or a fox. But **Nanabozho** was the son of a spirit father and a human mother, so I supposed it was possible that he could take on human form. However, unless he could also split himself in two, the humans on the platform had to be real.

**People.** The first people other than my mother and my father that I had ever seen. They were wearing hats and scarves and coats, so I couldn't be sure, but if I'd had to guess, I would have said I was looking at a boy and a girl.

A boy and a girl.

**Children.**

More voices, deeper-pitched, and two more people came down the stairs. Grown-ups. A man and a woman. The children's mother and father.

**A family.**

I held my breath. I was afraid if I let it out, the sound would carry across the water and frighten them off. My father squeezed my arm, warning me to stay quiet, but he didn't have to. I didn't want to draw their attention. I only wanted to look. I wished we'd brought the rifle so I could watch them through the scope.

The family talked, laughed, played. I couldn't make out what they were saying, but I could tell they were having fun. When the father picked up the smaller child at last and sat it on his shoulders and carried it up the stairs, my legs were stiff with cold and my stomach was growling. The mother followed more slowly with the other child. I could hear them laughing long after the family disappeared.

My father and I crouched behind the log for a long time. At last he got up, stretched, opened the rucksack, and set out our lunch on the log.

Normally my father would have built a fire to make tea, but he didn't, so I ate snow to wash down my mother's biscuits.

When we finished eating, my father put everything back in the rucksack and turned to leave without speaking. As we hiked back to our cabin, all I could think about was that family. We were so close, it felt like I could have thrown a rock at them and hit them. Certainly I could have gotten their attention if I had put a bullet above their heads into the trees. I wondered what would have happened if I had.

I'VE BEEN TO TAHQUAMENON FALLS many times since. The falls are always impressive: two hundred feet across, with a vertical drop of almost fifty feet. Fifty thousand gallons of water pour over the lip every second during the spring runoff, making Tahquamenon the third most voluminous waterfall east of the Mississippi. Over five hundred thousand people from all over the world visit the falls every year. For some reason, the falls are especially popular with tourists from Japan. The park has a visitors' center, a restaurant/microbrewery, public bathrooms with flush toilets, and a gift shop where I sell my jams and jellies. The path to the falls is paved for easy walking, and the park service built cedar fences along the edges of the cliff so people won't fall off. People have died at the falls, like the man who jumped into the whirlpool at the bottom to retrieve his girlfriend's tennis shoe, but that's not the park service's fault.

Stephen and I brought the girls last March. This was the first time I'd been back during the winter. In hindsight, I should have anticipated what was going to happen. But at the time, I was thinking only about how much the girls were going to enjoy their first look at the falls. Stephen had been pushing for the outing for a while, but I wanted to wait until Mari was old enough to appreciate what she was seeing. Plus, it's ninety-four steps down to the viewing platform and ninety-four back up, so you don't want to bring along a child you have to carry.

I was standing at the railing on the viewing platform, watching Stephen and the girls laughing and throwing snowballs and just generally enjoying the day, when I turned to look across to the place where my father and I stood all those years ago. Instantly I was eleven years old again, crouching behind the log with my father, looking back across the falls to the platform where I now stood with Stephen and my girls. It was then I realized.

We were that family.

I was overwhelmed with sorrow for the eleven-year-old me. Most of the time when I look back at the way I was raised, I'm able to view things fairly objectively. Yes, I was the daughter of a kidnapped girl and her captor. For twelve years, I lived without seeing or speaking to another human being other than my parents. Put like that, it sounds pretty grim. But that was the hand I was dealt, and I needed to call a spade a spade if I was ever going to move forward, as my court-appointed therapist used to say. As if the analogy would mean anything to a twelve-year-old who had never seen a deck of cards.

But as I stood at the railing looking across the falls at the ghost of my past, my heart broke for the poor little wild child I used to be. So clueless about the outside world despite her precious **National Geographics.** A child who didn't know a ball bounced, or that when people greeted each other with their hands outstretched it was called shaking hands because their hands actually moved. Who didn't realize people's voices sounded different because she had never heard anyone speak other than her mother and father. Who knew nothing of modern culture or popular music or technology. Who hid from her first opportunity for contact with the outside world because her father told her to.

I also felt sorry for my father. He knew I was

restless. I'm sure he hoped that by showing me what he considered the marsh's greatest treasure, he could convince me to stay. But after I saw that family, all I wanted was to leave.

I turned away from the railing with no explanation for my tears except to say I wasn't feeling well and we needed to go home right away. Naturally the girls were disappointed. Stephen swung Mari onto his shoulders and started up the stairs without question. But as I followed more slowly with Iris, I could tell she didn't believe me.

# 17

The naked dead man lying on the cabin's kitchen floor is not my husband. The idea that this might be Stephen was only a momentary thought, onc of those illogical emotional reactions that pop into your head during the first few seconds after you've had a surprise or a shock that are just as quickly dismissed.

That the man is naked is disturbing. Easy to assume that when my father walked in on him, the man wasn't cooking his breakfast without any clothes on. Just as easy to figure the dead man isn't wearing clothes because my father made him take them off before he shot him. This means that not only did the man know he was about to die, but my father humiliated him during his final moments. But of course my father always had a sadistic side. I doubt that thirteen years in a maximum security prison have improved his disposition.

What bothers me more than the way my father killed the man is that my father didn't have to kill him at all. He could have tied him to a chair, gagged him if he didn't want to listen to the man's objections, fixed himself something to eat, changed clothes, taken a nap, played cards, listened to music, and otherwise hung around the cabin while the searchers beat the bushes for him down in the marsh, then gone on his way again after it got dark. Someone would have found the man eventually, most likely within the next couple of days once the searchers realized they'd been tricked and turned their attention north. If the man was even moderately resourceful, there are any number of ways he could have gotten free on his own. Instead, my father made him take off his clothes and get down on his knees and beg for his life, then shot him in the back of the head.

I pull out my cell. No service. I punch in 9-1-1 anyway. Sometimes a call or a text will go through. But this one doesn't. Instead another text alert appears on the screen. Four messages from Stephen:

**Where r u?**
**r u ok?**
**Call me**

**Come home. Pls. We need to talk**

I read the first text again, then look down at the man's body. Where am I? Stephen definitely wouldn't want to know.

I cross the kitchen to try the landline. No dial tone. Whether the man didn't pay his bill or my father cut the line doesn't matter. I go outside and walk up the driveway with my phone in hand to see if I can catch a signal. I don't care about looking for footprints or other signs that my father was here. Whatever game he's playing, I'm done. I'll drive until I get a signal—go all the way to state police headquarters and report the murder in person if I have to—then it's straight home to my husband. The police won't be happy I went looking for my father, and neither will Stephen, but that's the least of my problems. Stephen might think that going forward will be as simple as both of us saying "I'm sorry, I love you," but I know better. Always in the back of his mind will be the knowledge that the father of the woman he married is a very bad man. Stephen can pretend that nothing has changed. He might even fool himself into believing this is true. But in reality he'll never be able to forget that half of my genetic makeup comes from my father. He's probably at the computer right now, reading everything he can find about The Marsh King and his daughter.

And this time when the media vultures swoop down to rip me apart, it's going to be worse because of my girls. Stephen and I can try to shield them from the attention, but we may as well try to hold back a waterfall. Mari will probably be able to handle the notoriety. Iris not so much. Regardless, one day, Iris and Mari will know everything about me, about their grandparents, and about the despicable thing their grandfather did to their grandmother. Everything is online, including the **People** magazine article with that ridiculous cover. All they have to do is Google.

I hope when that time comes my girls realize I've tried to be a better mother to them than my mother was to me. I understand it was hard for her after we left the marsh. She came back to a world that had moved on without her. The kids she'd gone to school with had grown up, gotten married, had kids of their own, moved away. Without the notoriety her kidnapping brought her, it's hard to say how my mother's life would have turned out. I picture her marrying as soon as she graduated high school, having a couple of kids in quick succession, living in a trailer on the back of her parents' property or someone's empty cabin, washing dishes and cleaning house and cooking dinner and doing laundry while her husband delivered pizzas or cut pulp. Not that much different from her life in the marsh, when you think about it. If that sounds harsh, you need to remember that my mother was only twenty-eight when she left the marsh. She could have finished her education, made something of herself. I understand my father kidnapped her when she was at a vulnerable age; I know there's a terrible toll on children who grow up in a state of captivity. Confinement stunts them at the very point in their lives when they're supposed to be maturing emotionally and intellectually. I've often wondered if the doll my mother made for me on my fifth birthday was, really, for her.

But I was struggling, too. I had no friends. I'd dropped out of school. My grandparents hated me, or at least they acted like they did, and I definitely hated them for how they treated me. I hated the way my mother stayed in her bedroom all day, and I hated my father for whatever he did to her that made her afraid to come out. I thought about my father every day. Missed him. Loved him. Wanted more than anything for things to go back to the way they were before we left the marsh. Not the chaotic days immediately preceding our escape, but back to when I was little, to the only time in my life when I was truly happy.

I knew my mother was never going to be the kind of mother I desperately needed the day I found a man in her bed. I don't know how long she'd been seeing him. This could have been the first night he spent with her or the hundredth. Maybe he loved her. Maybe she loved him back. Maybe she was ready to put her past behind her at last. If so, I guess I put an end to that.

I'd gotten dressed and gone upstairs to use the bathroom. There were two twin beds in my mother's room, but after weeks of sharing her childhood bedroom, I'd had all the togetherness I could stand and moved to the couch in the basement.

The bathroom door was closed. I figured my mother was using it, so I went to her bedroom to get something to read while I waited for her to come out. My mother used to spend a lot of time in the outhouse when I was growing up, so I expected her to be a while. I used to think it was because she was so often sick, but in hindsight I think it was because the outhouse was the only place on our ridge where she was guaranteed to be left alone.

I stopped in the doorway when I saw a man lying on his side in my mother's bed. The covers were thrown back to expose his nakedness and his head was propped on his elbow. I knew what they'd been doing. Most fourteen-year-olds would. When you live with your mother and father in a tiny cabin and regularly hang out with them in a sweat lodge without any clothes on and have scores of **National Geographic** pictures of naked primitive people to peruse, you'd have to be pretty stupid not to figure out eventually what those squeaking bedspring noises meant.

The man stopped grinning when he saw it was me and not my mother. He sat up quickly and pulled the covers over his lap. I put a finger to my lips and pulled my knife and sat down on the bed opposite him with my knife pointing at his privates. The man bolted upright and threw his hands over his head so fast, I almost laughed. I waved my knife at the pile of clothes on the floor. He sorted through them, put on his shirt and undershorts and socks and pants, picked up his boots, and tiptoed out without either of us saying a word. The whole thing took less than a minute. My mother started crying when she saw that he was gone. As far as I know, he never came back.

After that, I started making plans to run away.

I'd been staying in the woods overnight whenever I felt like it since I'd left the marsh, but this time was different. More calculated. Permanent. I filled a gunnysack with everything I'd need to spend the summer at the cabin and maybe longer and snuck down to the Tahquamenon and stole a canoe. I figured I'd do a little fishing and hunting, maybe look for my father, and just generally enjoy being by myself for a change. The sheriff's deputy caught up to me the next day in a patrol boat. I should have realized that a missing canoe and a missing wilderness girl would lead straight to our cabin.

That was the first of many times I ran away. And in a way, you could say I've never stopped since.

A FLASH OF LIGHTNING, a crack of thunder, and the drizzle turns to rain. I drop my phone in my pocket and run up the driveway for the truck. Rambo is uncharacteristically silent. Normally he'd be barking to let me know he wants to get inside—never mind that I told him to lie down in the back and stay quiet. Rambo is as well-trained as it's possible for a Plott hound to be, but every breed has its limits.

I step off the driveway and take cover behind the biggest jack pine I can find, which isn't saying much. The tree is maybe ten inches in diameter, tops. I stand absolutely still. A hunter wearing camouflage with her back to a tree to break up her outline is all but invisible as long as she stays quiet. I'm not wearing camo, but when it comes to blending in and becoming one with the forest, I've had more practice than most. I also have excellent hearing—far better than anyone I've hunted with, with the possible exception of my father—which used to surprise me until I realized that this, too, was a consequence of the way I grew up. Without radio and television and traffic and the thousand other noises people are subjected to every day, I learned to discern the slightest of sounds. A mouse foraging through pine needles. A single leaf falling in the forest. The nearly inaudible wing beats of a snowy owl.

I wait. There's no whining coming from the back of the truck, no scrabble of claws against metal. I whistle one long note followed by three short ones. The first low-pitched, the next three slightly higher. The whistle I've trained my dog to answer won't fool a chickadee, but if my father is within hearing distance, the fact that it's been thirteen years since he's heard a chickadee whistle should work in my favor.

Still nothing. I take the Magnum from the back of my jeans and belly-crawl through the underbrush. The truck seems to be sitting low. I move in closer. Both tires on the driver's side have been slashed.

I stand up and steel myself and go over and look in the back. The truck bed is empty. Rambo is gone.

I let out my breath. Rambo's leash has been cut—no doubt with the same knife my father took from the cabin to slash my tires. I curse my lack of foresight. I should have known my father wouldn't lead me to this cabin simply because he wanted to see me again. This is a test. He wants to play our old tracking game one last time to prove once and for all that he is better at hunting and tracking than I am. **I taught you everything you know. Now let's see how well you learned.**

He took Rambo so I'd have no choice but to follow. Again, he's done this before. Back when I was around nine or ten and had gotten very good at tracking, my father came up with a way to make the game more challenging by raising the stakes. If I found him before the allotted time was up, usually before the sun went down but not always, I got to shoot him. If I didn't, my father would take away something that was important to me: my collection of cattail spikes, my spare shirt, the third set of bow and arrows I made from willow saplings that actually worked.

The last three times we played—not coincidentally, the last three times I won—we played for my fawnskin mittens, my knife, and my dog.

I go around to check the other side of the truck. Both tires on the passenger side are also flat. Two sets of prints angle away from the truck across the road and into the trees, man and dog. The prints are so easy to see, they may as well have been painted in neon colors and given direction arrows. If a person were to look down from above and draw a line through the prints from where I'm standing to extrapolate where the man and the dog are traveling, the line would end at my house.

Which means we're not playing for my dog. We're playing for my family.

# 18

## The Cabin

**It was sometimes as if Helga acted from sheer wickedness; for often when her mother stood on the threshold of the door, or stepped into the yard, she would seat herself on the brink of the well, wave her arms and legs in the air, and suddenly fall right in.**

**Here she was able, from her frog nature, to dip and dive about in the water of the deep well, until at last she would climb forth like a cat, and come back into the hall dripping with water, so that the green leaves that were strewed on the floor were whirled**

**round, and carried away by the streams that flowed from her.**

—HANS CHRISTIAN ANDERSEN,
**The Marsh King's Daughter**

For weeks after my father took me to see the falls, I couldn't stop thinking about that family. The way the children ran up and down the stairs. How their parents stood with their arms around each other and smiled as the boy and the girl threw snowballs and wrestled and laughed. I didn't know for sure if they were a boy and a girl because they were wearing scarves and hats and coats, so in my mind I made them one of each. I named the boy Cousteau because he wore a red hat like Jacques-Yves Cousteau did in the **National Geographic** pictures, and I named his sister Calypso after Cousteau's ship. Before I discovered the article about Cousteau, Erik the Red and his son Leif Eriksson were my favorite explorers. But they only sailed on top of the water, while Cousteau explored what was beneath. Whenever I tried to tell my father about Cousteau's discoveries, my father said the gods were going to punish Cousteau one day because he dared to go to a part of the Earth that man was never meant to see. I couldn't see why the gods would care. I would have liked to have known what was at the bottom of our marsh.

Cousteau, Calypso, and I did everything together. I made them older than the children on the platform so they would be better company for me and so they could help me with my chores. Sometimes I made up stories: "Cousteau and Calypso and Helena Swim in the Beaver Pond." "Cousteau and Calypso Go Ice Fishing with Helena." "Cousteau and Calypso Help Helena Catch a Snapping Turtle." I couldn't write the stories down because we didn't have pencils or paper, so I repeated the best ones over and over in my head so I wouldn't forget. I knew the real Cousteau and Calypso lived with their mother and father in a house with a kitchen like the ones in the **Geographics.** I could have made up stories that happened there: "Cousteau and Calypso and Helena Eat Jiffy Pop Popcorn While They Watch Television on Their Brand-New RCA Color Television Set," but it was easier to bring them into my world than it was to picture myself in theirs.

My mother called Cousteau and Calypso my imaginary friends. She wondered why I didn't play with the doll she made for me the way I played with them. But it was too late for that even if I'd wanted to, which I did not. The doll still hung from the handcuffs in the woodshed, but there wasn't much left. Mice had made off with most of the stuffing and the sleeper was shot full of arrow holes.

My father never said one word about that family—not on the way home from the falls, and not in the weeks that followed. At first his silence bothered me. I had many questions. Where did the family come from? How did they get to the falls? Did they drive a car, or did they walk? If they walked, they must have lived close by because the children were too small to hike very far and they weren't wearing snowshoes. What were the children's names—not the ones I gave them, but their real names? How old were they? What did they like to eat? Did they go to school? Did they have a television set? And did they see my father and me watching from the other side of the falls? Were they now wondering the same things about me?

I would have liked to have known at least some of the answers. I thought about packing the rucksack with enough supplies for two or three days and heading for the tree line while the marsh was frozen to see if I could find their house. Or if I couldn't find that family, perhaps I would find another that was just as interesting. I had always known the world was full of people. Now I knew that some of them were not so very far away.

One thing was certain: I couldn't stay in the marsh forever. It wasn't only that we were running out of things. My father was much older than my mother. One day, he would die. My mother and I could manage by ourselves as long as we had bullets for the rifle, but one day, my mother would die, too, and then what would I do? I didn't want to live in the marsh by myself. I wanted to take a mate. There was a boy in the article about the Yanomami who looked good to me. He wore a dead monkey around his shoulders like a cape and nothing else. I knew he lived in another part of the world and we would likely never meet. But there had to be other boys like him who lived closer who I could pair up with. I thought if I could find one, I could bring him back to the marsh with me and make my own family. A boy and a girl would be nice.

Until I saw that family, I wasn't sure how this could all work out. But now I had ideas.

MY FATHER WENT OUT three times during those weeks to shoot our spring deer, and each time, he came back empty-handed. My father said the reason he wasn't able to shoot a deer was that the land was cursed. He said the gods were punishing us. He didn't say for what.

The fourth time he brought me with him. My

father thought that if I took the shot, this would lift the curse. I didn't know if this was true, but if this meant I got to shoot another deer at last, I was happy to go along with it. Every year since I'd shot my first deer I asked my father if I could go deer hunting again, and every year my father said no. I didn't understand why he went to all of the trouble of teaching me how to shoot if he wasn't going to let me share the job of putting venison on our table.

Cousteau and Calypso stayed at home. My father didn't like it when I said their names or played with them. Sometimes I did this on purpose to annoy him, but not today. My father was so angry all of the time because of the curse, I was thinking of sending them away. ("Cousteau and Calypso Visit the Yanomami in the Rain Forest Without Helena.") Rambo was tied in the woodshed. Rambo was fine for flushing a bear from its den or treeing a coon, my father said, but not when it came to deer hunting because deer were too easily spooked. I couldn't see why this would be a problem. Even if Rambo scared the deer, he could chase them down easily, since he could run on top of the snow crust while the deer's thin legs would break through. Then all we would have to do was walk up and shoot one. Sometimes I wondered if the only reason my father made so many rules and restrictions was because he could.

I was in the lead because I was carrying the rifle. I liked that this meant my father had to follow where I wanted to go. I thought about the pet name he gave me, **Bangii-Agawaateyaa,** and smiled. I was no longer his Little Shadow.

I was heading for the ridge where I shot my first deer because that ridge brought me luck. And I was still hoping to shoot a doe that was pregnant with twins.

When we came to the abandoned beaver lodge where my father used to set his traps, I signaled my father to get down, then pulled off my mittens and crouched beside him. I wet my finger to test the wind and counted to one hundred to give any deer who heard us time to settle down. Slowly I raised my head.

On the other side of the beaver lodge, halfway between us and the cedar swamp where the deer were supposed to be, standing out in the open as bold and as fearless as you please, was a wolf. It was a male, twice as big as a coyote and three times as big as my dog, with a massive head and a wide forehead and a heavy chest and a thick dark ruff. I'd never seen a wolf except for the skin in our utility shed, but there was no mistaking this was what it was. Now I understood why my father hadn't been able to shoot a deer. The land wasn't cursed—it was just home to a new hunter.

My father tugged on my sleeve and pointed

to the rifle. **Take the shot,** he mouthed. He tapped his chest to show where I should shoot so I didn't ruin the skin. I brought up the rifle as carefully as I knew how and sighted through the scope. The wolf looked back calmly, intelligently, like he knew we were there and didn't care. I slipped my finger through the trigger. The wolf didn't move. I thought about my father's stories. How **Gitche Manitou** sent the wolf to keep Original Man company while he walked the Earth naming the plants and the animals. How when they finished, **Gitche Manitou** decreed that **Mai'iigan** and Man should travel separate paths, but by then they'd spent so much time together they were as close as brothers. How to the **Anishinaabe,** killing a wolf was the same as killing a person.

My father squeezed my arm. I could feel his excitement, his anger, his impatience. **Take the shot,** he would have hissed if he could. My stomach got tight. I thought about the piles of furs in the utility shed. How because of my father's trapping, the beaver that used to live in the lodge we were crouching behind were all gone. How the wolf was so trusting, shooting **Mai'iigan** would be no different from shooting my dog.

I lowered the rifle. Stood up and clapped my hands and shouted. The wolf looked back a moment longer. Then, with two great, beautiful bounds, it ran off.

I knew when I decided not to shoot the wolf that I would end up in the well. I didn't know that my father would grab the rifle away from me and slam me across the face with the butt end so hard, I landed on my backside in the snow. I also didn't expect him to march me home to the cabin with the gun at my back like I was his prisoner. I wish I could say I didn't care. Still, I couldn't see where I could have done anything differently. I didn't like going against my father. I knew how much he wanted that wolf's skin. But so did the wolf.

I thought about these things as I squatted on my heels in the darkness. I couldn't sit because my father had filled the bottom of the well with deer antlers and rib bones and broken glass and shattered dishes—anything that would hurt or cut me if I tried to sit down. When I was little, I used to be able to curl up on my side and lie down in the leaf litter on the bottom. Sometimes I'd fall asleep. I think this was why my father started filling the well with debris. Contemplation time wasn't supposed to be comfortable.

The shaft was deep and narrow. The only

way I could fully stretch out my arms was if I put them over my head. I did this whenever my hands started to tingle. I would have had to grow another six feet to reach the cover.

I didn't know what time of day it was or how long I'd been in the well because the lid didn't let in any light. My father said the people who built the cabin made the lid this way so that children wouldn't fall in. All I knew was that my father would keep me in the well as long as he wanted to and let me out when he was ready. Sometimes I thought about what would happen if he didn't. If the Soviet Union dropped a bomb on the United States like the **Geographics** said Nikita Khrushchev wanted to do and the bomb killed my father and mother, what would happen to me? I tried not to think about things like that too often. When I did, it got hard to breathe.

I was very tired. My hands and feet were numb and my teeth chattered, but I'd stopped shivering, so that was good. My father let me keep my clothes on this time, and that helped. My front teeth were loose and the side of my face ached, but what I was really worried about was my leg. I cut it on something sharp when my father threw me in. I wiped up the blood with my shirttail and tied my scarf around my leg up high like a tourniquet, but I couldn't tell if it was working. I tried not to think about the time I shared the well with a rat.

"Are you okay?"

I opened my eyes. Calypso was sitting on the front seat of my father's canoe. The canoe rocked gently in the current. The day was sunny and warm. Cattail heads bent and nodded in the breeze. Overhead a hawk swooped and dived. In the distance, a red-winged blackbird called. The canoe was nosed into the reeds. Cousteau sat in the back.

"Come with us," Calypso said. "We're going exploring." She smiled and held out her hand.

When I stood my legs felt shaky, like they wouldn't hold me up. I took her hand and stepped carefully into the canoe. My father's canoe was a two-seater, so I sat down in the middle between them on the bottom. The canoe was made of metal. The bottom was cold.

Cousteau shoved his paddle into the riverbank and pushed off. The current was very strong. All Cousteau and Calypso needed to do was steer. As we floated downstream, I thought about the day we met. I was glad Cousteau and Calypso and I were friends.

"Do you have anything to eat?" I was very hungry.

"Of course." Calypso turned around and smiled. Her teeth were white and straight. Her eyes were blue like my mother's. Her hair was thick and dark and braided like mine. She reached into the rucksack between her feet and handed me an apple. It was as big as both my fists put together, a Wolf River, my father called it, one of three kinds of apples that grew near our cabin. I took a bite and juice ran down my chin.

I ate the apple, seeds and all. Calypso smiled and gave me another. This time I ate the apple down to the core. I tossed the core into the river for the fish to nibble and trailed my fingers in the water to wash the stickiness away. The water was very cold. So were the drips that splashed my head when Cousteau switched his paddle. We passed marsh marigolds and blue flag iris, Indian paintbrush and wood lily, St.-John's-wort and yellow flag iris and pondweed and jewelweed. I'd never seen so much color. Flowers that didn't normally bloom together were all blooming at the same time, like the marsh was putting on a show for me.

The current got stronger. When we came to the wooden sign that hung from the cable that spanned the river, I could read the whole thing: DANGER. RAPIDS AHEAD. NO ROWBOATS PAST THIS POINT. I ducked my head as we passed beneath.

The roar got louder. I knew we were going over the falls. I saw the canoe tipping forward when we reached the edge, plunging through the foam and the mist to disappear into the whirlpool at the bottom. I knew I was going to drown. I was not afraid.

"Your father doesn't love you," Cousteau said suddenly from behind me. I could hear him clearly, though the last time I was this close to the falls, my father and I had to shout. "He only loves himself."

"It's true," Calypso said. "Our father loves us. He would never put us in the well."

I thought about the day we met. How their father played with them. The way he smiled when he picked up little Calypso and carried her on his shoulders, laughing all the way up the stairs. I knew she spoke the truth.

I wiped my jacket sleeve across my eyes. I didn't know why my eyes were wet. I never cried.

"It's okay." Calypso leaned forward and took my hands. "Don't be afraid. We love you."

"I'm so tired."

"We know," Cousteau said. "It's all right. Lie down. Close your eyes. We'll take care of you."

I knew that this was also true. And so I did.

MY MOTHER TOLD ME I was in the well for three days. I wouldn't have thought a person could last that long without food and water, but apparently you can. She said when my father finally pulled the lid aside and lowered the ladder I was too weak to climb it, so he had to sling me over his shoulder like a dead deer and carry me out. She said she wanted to slide the lid to the side and lower food and water to me many times, but my father made her sit on a chair in the kitchen with the rifle pointed at her the whole time I was in the well, so she couldn't.

My mother said that after my father carried me into the cabin, he dropped me on the floor beside the woodstove like I was a sack of flour and walked away. She thought I was dead. She pulled the mattress off their bed and dragged it into the kitchen and rolled me onto it and covered me with blankets and took off all her clothes and crawled under the covers and held me until I got warm again. If she did all of this, I don't remember. All I remember is waking up shivering on the mattress though my face and hands and feet felt like they were on fire. I rolled off the mattress and put on my clothes and staggered to the outhouse. When I tried to pee, hardly anything came out.

The next day my father asked if I had learned my lesson. I told him I had. I don't think the lesson I learned was the one he wanted to teach me.

# 19

The prints in the road spell out a message that's impossible to miss: **I'm going to your house. Catch me—stop me—save them—if you can.**

I unlock the truck. Fill my pockets with as many rounds of ammunition as they will hold and take the Ruger from the rack over the window. Check the Magnum, adjust the knife at my belt. My father has two handguns and the knife he took from the old man's cabin. I have my handgun, my rifle, and the Bowie I've carried since I was a child. I'm calling us even.

I can't be sure if my father knows I have a family, just as I can't prove he knows I'm living on the property where he grew up. But I have to assume that he does. I can think of any number of ways he could have found out. Prisoners can't access the Internet, but my father has a lawyer. Lawyers have access to tax records, property records, marriage and birth and death certificates. My father could have pumped his lawyer for information about the people living on his parents' property without the lawyer even realizing my father was manipulating him. Maybe the lawyer staked out my house on some innocuous pretext at my father's request. If the lawyer saw me and happened to mention my tattoos when he reported back, my father would have known right away that this was me. I wonder—not for the first time—if I should have had the tattoos removed entirely, no matter how long and expensive the process. I can see now that I also should have changed my first name as well as my last. But how could I have known that nine years in the future these things would put my family in danger? I wasn't running from the law, or from organized crime, or hiding out like in a witness protection program. I was just an eighteen-year-old looking to make a fresh start.

There's another possibility as to how my father knows where I'm living, much more sinister and devious than the first. It's possible I'm living on his parents' property because my father put me there. Maybe his parents originally named **him** in their will, but he let the inheritance go to me so he could track me. I suppose it's possible I'm giving my father too much credit. But if my father plotted his escape in such a way that I would be forced to come looking for him on his terms, then I'm willing to admit I underestimated him. I won't do it again.

I check my phone. Still no signal. I send Stephen a text warning him to clear out, praying the text will go through, and turn west. Away from the trail my father expects me to follow. There's no question I could track my father if I wanted to. A person moving through the woods always leaves evidence behind, no matter how expertly they hide their trail. Twigs get broken. Dirt gets displaced. Grass bruises when it's stepped on. Moss crushes underfoot. Gravel gets pressed into the ground. Boots pick up material from the ground, which then gets transferred to other surfaces: grains of sand on a fallen log, bits of moss on an otherwise bare rock. What's more, my father is traveling with my dog. Unless he's carrying Rambo in his arms or on his shoulders, my three-legged canine is going to leave a trail that's impossible to miss.

But even if the rain weren't rapidly washing away all evidence of my father's trail, I'm not going to track him. If all I do is follow where he leads, I've already lost. I have to get out ahead of him. My father doesn't know my girls aren't home, but I know my husband is. We're less than five miles from my house. I've hunted this area often and know it well. Between this road and my house are two small creeks, a beaver pond, and a steep gully with a fair-sized stream at the bottom that my father will have to cross. The high ground is mostly second-growth aspen and scrub pine without a lot of cover, which means he'll have to stick to the low ground as much as possible. At the rate the rain is coming down, the creeks are quickly turning into torrents. If my father is going to make it across the stream at the bottom of the gully before it becomes a raging river, he's going to have to move fast.

My father knows all of this as well as I do from when he roamed these woods as a boy. What he doesn't know—what he can't possibly know unless he's somehow seen a recent satellite image of the area, which I have to doubt—is that between here and my house is a section of forest that was clear-cut three or four years ago. He also doesn't know about the rough road the loggers left behind that leads almost all the way to the wetland behind my house.

This is his first mistake.

I set off at a light jog. My father has at most a fifteen-minute head start. If I average five miles an hour to his three, I can get out ahead of him and cut him off. I picture him making his way through the underbrush, hiking up and down hills and wading through creeks while I'm barely breaking a sweat. Working so hard to hide his trail and I'm not even following it. He has no idea I'm about to get the better of him again. He can't imagine any outcome other than the one he's planned because in his universe, in which he's the sun and the rest of us orbit around him, things can only happen in the way that he decrees.

But I'm no longer the adoring child he used to manipulate and control. Thinking so is his second mistake.

I will find him, and I will stop him. I put him in prison once; I can do it again.

I PULL MY PHONE from my jacket pocket without breaking stride and check the time. Half an hour. It feels a lot longer. I estimate I'm halfway to my house. It could be more, but it's possibly less. It's hard to tell where I am exactly because the trees I normally would have used as landmarks are gone. The jack pines on the ridge to my right are nothing remarkable, certainly nothing I can use to gauge my progress, just the scrub the loggers couldn't be bothered to cut.

To my left, the land is so barren, the trees to my right look lush by comparison. There's nothing uglier than a forest that's been clear-cut. Acre after acre of scattered brush piles, deep skidder ruts, and stumps. Tourists imagine the U.P. is all beautiful and pristine wilderness, but what they don't know is that often just a few hundred feet from the main highways, great swaths of forest have been reduced to pulp.

The entire state used to be covered with magnificent stands of red and white pine until the late 1800s, when lumber barons claimed the climax forests as their own and rafted the logs down Lake Michigan to build Chicago. The trees the loggers cut today are all second-growth: birch, aspen, oak, jack pine. Once these are gone, the soil is so abused that nothing grows but moss and blueberries.

When my father and I cut firewood, we cut only the biggest trees, and then only what we needed. This actually helped the forest, because it gave the smaller trees room to grow. "Only when the last tree has died and the last river has been poisoned and the last fish has been caught will the white man realize he cannot eat money" was one of my father's favorite sayings. "We do not inherit the Earth from our ancestors; we borrow it from our children" was another. I used to think he made them up himself. Now I know they're famous Native American proverbs. Regardless, Native Americans understood the concept of sustainable forestry long before there was a word for it.

I keep running. There's no way to know for sure if taking the longer but potentially faster route will allow me to get out in front of my father. I do know it's going to be close. Running isn't as easy as I'd hoped. The logging road is a road in name only: rough, uneven, and canted so steeply in places that it feels like I'm running on the side of a cliff. Deep sand, rocks and tree roots sticking out, potholes as big as duck ponds. My breathing is ragged and my lungs burn. My hair and jacket are drenched from the rain and my boots and pant legs are soaked to the knees from splashing through puddles. The rifle slung over my shoulder bruises my back with every step. My calf muscles scream at me to stop. I desperately need to catch my breath, to rest, to pee. The only thing keeping me going is knowing what will happen to Stephen if I don't.

Which is when, off to my right, a dog barks. A sharp, distinctive yelp that any Plott hound owner would recognize instantly. I bend over with my hands on my knees until my breathing slows. I grin.

# 20

## The Cabin

**The Viking's wife looked at the wild, badly disposed girl with great sorrow; and when night came on, and her daughter's beautiful form and disposition were changed, the Viking's wife spoke in eloquent words to Helga of the sorrow and deep grief that was in her heart. The ugly frog, in its monstrous shape, stood before her, and raised its brown mournful eyes to her face, listening to her words, and seeming to understand them with the intelligence of a human being.**

**"A bitter time will come for thee," said the Viking's wife; "and it will be terrible for me too. It had been better for thee if thou hadst been left on the high-road,**

**with the cold night wind to lull thee to sleep." And the Viking's wife shed bitter tears, and went away in anger and sorrow.**

—HANS CHRISTIAN ANDERSEN,
**The Marsh King's Daughter**

The days and nights I spent in the well taught me three things: My father didn't love me. My father would do whatever he wanted with no regard for my safety or feelings. My mother was not as indifferent toward me as I thought. For me, these were big ideas. Big enough that each required a great deal of careful thought. After three days, Cousteau and Calypso and I were still trying to sort it all out.

Meanwhile, I learned that the good thing about almost dying from hypothermia, which is what the **Geographic** article about the failed 1912 Scott expedition to the South Pole called it, was this: as long as you didn't lose any fingers or toes to frostbite, as soon as you warmed up again you were fine. The warming-up part wasn't fun—far more painful than smashing your thumb with a hammer or the kickback from a rifle or getting a large tattoo—and I sincerely hoped I would never have to go through anything like that again. On the other hand, I now knew that I was a lot tougher than I thought I was, which had to count for something.

I didn't know if my father pulled me out of the well because he knew I had reached the limit of what I could endure or if he wanted to kill me and he got the timing wrong. This was what Cousteau and Calypso said. They might have been right.

All I knew was that from the moment I opened my eyes, everyone was angry. Cousteau and Calypso were angry with my father for what he did to me. My mother was angry with him for the same reason. She was also angry with me for making my father so angry that he wanted to kill me. My father was angry with me for refusing to shoot the wolf, and he was angry with my mother for helping me after he pulled me out of the well. I didn't remember my mother crawling under the covers to warm me, but there was a fresh bruise on her face that proved she did. And around and around it went. There was so much anger filling the cabin, it felt like there was no air left to breathe. My father stayed in the marsh by himself most of the time, and that helped. I had no idea if he was still trying to shoot our spring deer or if he was hunting the wolf. I didn't very much care. All I knew was that every evening he came back angrier than when he'd left. He said just looking at my mother and me made him sick, and this was why he stayed away. I didn't tell him that Cousteau and Calypso felt the same way about him.

Also, we were out of salt. When my mother discovered that all of the salt was gone, she threw the empty salt box against the wall and screamed that this was the last straw, and why didn't my father do something about it before now, and how was she supposed to cook without salt? I expected my father to slap her for yelling at him and talking back, but all he did was tell her that the Ojibwa never had salt until the white men came, and she'd just have to get used to doing without. I was going to miss it. Not all the wild foods we ate tasted good, even after they were boiled in several changes of water. Burdock root definitely took getting used to. And I never did like wild mustard greens. Salt helped.

The next morning, however, everything was quiet. My mother fixed the hot oat cereal we ate for breakfast without saying anything about salt. I didn't particularly like how it tasted, and I could tell by the way my father pushed his spoon around his bowl and left half his cereal behind when he got up from the table that he didn't, either. My mother ate hers like nothing was wrong. I assumed this was because she had a secret salt stash hidden somewhere in the cabin that she was keeping for herself. After my father strapped on his snowshoes and slung his rifle over his shoulder and went out into the marsh for the day, I spent the rest of the morning and most of the afternoon looking for it. I searched the storage room, the living room, and the kitchen. I didn't think my mother would hide her stash in the bedroom she shared with my father, and I knew she wouldn't hide it in my room. Though it would have been a good trick if she had, and it was something I would have done if I was her and she was me, my mother wasn't that smart.

The only place left to look was the closet under the stairs. I wished I had searched the closet before it started snowing and the cabin got dark. When I was little, I used to shut myself inside the closet and pretend it was a submarine or a bear's den or a Viking's tomb, but now I didn't like small, dark places.

Still, I wanted that salt. So the next time my mother went to the outhouse, I pushed the kitchen curtains open as far as they would go and propped one of our chairs against the closet door so it wouldn't swing shut. I would have liked to use the oil lamp to search the closet, but we weren't allowed to light the lamp when my father wasn't home.

The closet was very small. I don't know what

the people who built our cabin used to put in it, but for as long as I could remember, the closet had been empty. When I was little I fit inside with room to spare, but now I was so big, I had to sit with my back against the wall and my knees drawn up to my chin. I closed my eyes so the darkness would feel more natural and quickly patted down the walls and the backs of the stairs. Cobwebs stuck to my fingers. The dust made me sneeze. I was looking for a loose board or a knothole or a nail sticking out that could be used as a hook—any place a box or a bag of salt could hide.

In the space between a stair riser and the outside wall, my fingers touched paper. The people who built our cabin nailed newspapers to the outside walls as insulation to keep out the cold, but this didn't feel like newspaper, and anyway we'd used up all of the newspaper as fire starter long ago. I pried the paper loose and carried it to the table and sat down with it next to the window. The paper was rolled into a tube and tied shut with a piece of string. I untied the knot and the paper fell open in my hands.

It was a magazine. Not a **National Geographic.** The cover wasn't yellow and the paper was too thin. It was too dark to make out details, so I opened the door to the woodstove and stuck a sliver of cedar into the coals until it caught fire and lit the lamp, then pinched out the taper and put the taper in our dry sink so I didn't accidentally burn down the cabin. Then I pulled the oil lamp close.

Printed in big yellow letters at the top of the page against a pink background was the word 'TEEN. I assumed this was the magazine's name. There was a girl on the cover. She looked to be about the same age as me. She had long blonde hair, though hers was loose and curly instead of straight and braided like mine. She was wearing an orange, purple, blue, and yellow sweater with a zigzag pattern like my leg tattoos. A+ LOOKS MAKE THE GRADE it said on one side of her picture, and MAGNETIC MAKEOVERS: ATTRACTIVE HOW-TO'S on the other. Inside the magazine were more pictures of the same girl. A caption beneath one of the pictures said her name was Shannen Doherty and she was the star of a television show called **Beverly Hills, 90210.**

I turned to the table of contents: **Earth S.O.S.—How You Can Help; Fad Dieting: Safe or Scary?; Clip 'N' Keep Booklet: Bonus Fashion Planner; Hottest New TV Hunks; Mr. Right: Could He Be Wrong for You?; Teens with AIDS: Heartbreaking Stories.** I had no idea what the titles meant or what the articles were about. I flipped through the pages. **Hot looks for school** the caption said beneath a picture of a group of children standing beside a yellow bus. The children looked happy. No ads for kitchen appliances that I could see; instead the ads were for things called "lipstick" and "eyeliner" and "blush," which as far as I could tell were what the girls used to color their lips red and their cheeks pink and their eyelids blue. I wasn't sure why they'd want to.

I sat back, tapped my fingers on the table, chewed my thumb knuckle, tried to think. I had no idea where this magazine came from, how it got here, how long it had been hidden in the closet. Why anyone would make a magazine about only girls and boys.

I pulled the lamp closer and paged through a second time. Everything was described as "hot" and "hip" and "cool." The children danced, played music, had parties. The pictures were bright and colorful. The cars didn't look at all like the ones in the **Geographics.** They were sleek and low to the ground like weasels instead of big and round and fat like beavers. They also had names. I especially liked a yellow car the magazine called a Mustang because it had the same name as a horse. I assumed this was because the car could go very fast.

Outside on the porch my mother stomped the snow from her boots. I started to snatch the magazine off the table, then stopped. It didn't matter if my mother saw me looking at it. I wasn't doing anything wrong.

"What are you doing?" she cried as she shut the door behind her and shook the snow out of her hair. "You know better than to light the lamp before Jacob gets home." She hung her coat on the hook by the door and hurried across the room to turn off the lamp, then stopped when she saw the magazine. "Where did you get that? What are you doing with it? That's mine. Give it to me."

She reached for the magazine. I slapped her hand away and jumped to my feet and put my hand on my knife. That this magazine belonged to my mother was absurd. My mother had no possessions.

She took a step back and held up her hands. "Please, Helena. Give it to me. If you do, I'll let you look at it whenever you like."

As if she could stop me. I waved my knife toward her chair. "Sit."

My mother sat. I sat down across from her. I laid my knife on the table and put the magazine between us. "What is this? Where did it come from?"

"Can I touch it?"

I nodded. She pulled the magazine toward her and slowly turned the pages. She stopped at a picture of a dark-haired, dark-eyed boy. "Neil

Patrick Harris." She sighed. "I had **such** a crush on him when I was your age. You have no idea. I still think he's handsome. **Doogie Howser** was my favorite TV show. I also loved **Full House** and **Saved by the Bell.**"

I didn't like that my mother knew things I didn't. I had no idea what she was talking about, who these people were, why my mother acted like she knew them. Why she seemed to care about the boys and girls in this magazine as much as I cared about Cousteau and Calypso.

"Please don't tell Jacob," she said. "You know what he'll do if he finds this."

I knew exactly what my father would do with this magazine if he knew about it—especially if he thought the magazine was important to her. There was a reason I kept my favorite **Geographics** under my bed. I promised—not because I wanted to protect my mother from my father, but because I wasn't done looking at the magazine yet.

My mother flipped through the pages a second time, then turned the magazine around and pushed it toward me. "Look. See this pink sweater? I used to have a sweater just like this. I wore it so much, my mother used to say I would have slept in it if she'd let me. And this one." She turned back to the cover. "My mother was going to buy a sweater like this one for me when we went shopping for school clothes."

It was hard to imagine my mother as a girl like the ones in this magazine, wearing these clothes, going shopping, going to school. "Where did you get this?" I asked again, because my mother still hadn't answered my question.

"It's . . . a long story." She pressed her lips together like she did when my father asked her a question she didn't want to answer, like why she let the fire go out, or why his favorite shirt was still dirty even though she claimed she'd washed it, or why she hadn't fixed the holes in his socks or brought in more water or firewood, or when was she going to learn how to make a decent biscuit.

"Then you'd better get started." I locked eyes with her the way my father did, letting her know I wasn't going to take silence for an answer. This was going to be interesting. My mother never told stories.

She looked away and bit her lip. At last she sighed. "I was sixteen when your father told me I was going to have a baby," she began. "Your father wanted me to make the diapers and baby clothes you'd need out of the curtains and blankets we had at the cabin. But I didn't know how to sew." She smiled to herself like her not knowing how to sew was funny. Or like she was making this story up.

"I managed to cut a blanket into diapers using one of his knives, but there was no way I could make clothes for you without scissors or sewing needles or thread. And we still needed diaper pins to get the diapers to stay on you. Your father stormed off when I told him—you know how he gets. He was gone a long time. When he came back, he said we were going shopping. This was the first time I'd left the marsh since . . . since he'd brought me here, so I was very excited. We went to a big store called Kmart and got everything you'd need. While we were in the checkout line, I saw this magazine. I knew your father would never let me have it, so when he wasn't looking, I rolled it up and hid it under my shirt. When we got back to the cabin, I hid it in the closet while he was unloading the things we bought. It's been there ever since."

My mother shook her head like she couldn't believe she was ever that brave. If it wasn't for the magazine on the table between us, I wouldn't have believed it, either. I pictured her going to the closet whenever my father and I were away, taking the magazine from its hiding place, carry–ing it to the kitchen table or outside to the back porch if it was a sunny day, reading the stories and looking at the pictures when she was supposed to be cooking and cleaning. It was hard to believe she had been doing this since before I was born and my father had never caught her. That this magazine was the same age as me.

An idea began to form. I looked at the date on the magazine's cover. If my mother took this magazine when she was pregnant with me and I was almost twelve, then this magazine was also almost twelve. This meant that the girl on the cover wasn't a girl at all—she was a grown woman like my mother. So were the rest of the children.

I'll admit, I was disappointed. I liked it better when these boys and girls were the same as me. I understood the concept of dates and years, of course, and why important events had their year-number attached to them so people could know which came first and which came later. But I'd never really thought about the number of the year I was born, or what year it was now. My mother kept track of the weeks and the months on the calendar she drew with charcoal on our kitchen wall, but I'd always been more interested in what the weather would be like on a given day and the seasons.

Now I realized that the numbers of my years were important as well. I subtracted the dates on the **Geographics** from the date of the current year and felt like my father had punched me in the stomach. **The** Geographics **were fifty years old.** Far older than the **'Teen** magazine. Older than my mother. Older even than my father. My Yanomami brothers and sisters weren't children; they were old men and women. The boy with the double row of dots tattooed across his cheeks whose picture I showed to my father so he could do the same to me was not a boy at all; he was an old man like my father. Cousteau—the real Jacques-Yves Cousteau—was a grown man in the **Geographic** pictures, which meant he must be very old. He might even be dead.

I looked at my mother sitting across the table, smiling like she was happy I found her magazine because now we could read it together, and all I could think was, **Liar.** I'd trusted the **Geographics.** I'd trusted my mother. She knew the **Geographics** were fifty years old, yet she let me believe that everything they said that was happening in the present was current and true. Color television and Velcro and a vaccine to cure polio weren't recent inventions. The Soviets didn't just send the dog Laika into orbit on **Sputnik 2** as the first living creature to orbit the Earth. Cousteau's amazing discoveries were fifty years old. Why would she do this to me? Why had she lied to me? What else was she not telling me?

I grabbed the magazine off the table and rolled it up and stuck it in my back pocket. After this, she was never getting it back.

Outside there was a noise. It sounded like my father's chain saw, only it was almost dark and my father wouldn't cut firewood at night. I ran to the window. A small yellow light was coming toward us from the direction of the tree line. It looked like a yellow star except that it was moving and it was close to the ground.

My mother came over to the window and stood beside me. The noise got louder. She cupped her hands against the glass so she could see.

"It's a snowmobile," she said when she turned away at last, her voice full of wonder. "Someone is coming."

# 21

Rambo doesn't bark again, but once was enough. My gamble paid off. Not only have I caught up to my father, Rambo's bark proves he is not so very far away. Picture the quarter-mile section of road between the place where my father's trail began and the logging road where I'm running as the base of an isosceles triangle. My house is the apex, and the paths my father and I are traveling are the sides. The closer we get to my house, the quicker our paths will converge.

I could pinpoint his location more precisely if Rambo would bark a second time, but frankly I'm surprised he was able to bark at all. I guess the pants my father stole from the man he murdered didn't come with a belt. Back at the cabin, my father used to fasten his belt around my dog's nose as a muzzle when we were hunting and my father didn't want him to bark, or when Rambo was tied in the woodshed and my father got tired of listening to him wanting to be let out. Sometimes my father put the muzzle on Rambo for no reason at all that I could see and left it on a lot longer than I thought he should. I've read that one of the signs that a person might become a terrorist or a serial killer when they grow up is if they were cruel to animals when they were a child. I'm not sure what it means if they're still cruel as an adult.

I shield my eyes against the rain and scan the crest of the ridge, half expecting my father's head to poke over the top at any second. I move off the road into the trees. Wet pine needles muffle my footsteps. I shake the rain from my hair and slide the Ruger from my shoulder, holding the rifle with the barrel pointing down so I can swing it up at the first sign of trouble. The ridge is steep. I climb as quickly and quietly as I can. Normally I'd use the scrub trees as handholds, but jack pines are brittle and I can't risk the sound of a branch snapping off.

I near the top, drop to my belly, and crawl the rest of the way using my feet and elbows, the way my father taught me. I set up the Ruger's bipod and sight through the scope.

Nothing.

I pan slowly north and south, then check the other side of the ravine for movement. It's movement that gives a person away. If you're fleeing someone through a forest, the best thing you can do is go to ground as quickly as possible and stay absolutely still. I scan every conceivable hiding place a second time on the chance that my father made Rambo bark on purpose to draw me out, then pack up the Ruger and work my way down the ridge and start climbing the next.

I repeat the process twice more before I come to the top of the fourth ridge and feel like cheering. At the bottom of the slope, not more than fifty feet below me and fifty yards south, walking purposefully up the middle of a creek that normally would be little more than ankle-deep but that now reaches almost to his knees is my father.

**My father.**

I've found him. Outpaced him. Outsmarted him in every way.

I set up the Ruger one last time and watch my father through the scope. He of course looks older than I remember. He looks thinner. The dead man's clothes hang loosely on his frame. His hair and beard are gray, and his skin is wrinkled and sallow. In the photo the police are circulating, my father looks as scraggly and wild-eyed as Charles Manson. I assumed they chose the most intimidating picture they could find so there'd be no question my father is dangerous. In person, he looks even worse: cheeks as hollow as a cadaver's, eyes sunk so deep into their sockets that he looks like the **wendigo** from his old sweat lodge stories. Now that I'm seeing him for the first time as an adult, I realize precisely how unhinged he looks. I suppose, to my mother, he always did.

My father has my dog in a choke hold, the cut end of the leash wrapped several times around his left hand. He carries a Glock in his right. I imagine the other guard's weapon is beneath his jacket in the back of his jeans. Rambo trots along easily on the creek bank beside him. Not for the first time, I marvel at how effortlessly my dog moves with only three legs. The vet who put him back together after the bear incident told me a lot of hunters would have put down a dog that severely injured. I took this to mean that if I couldn't afford the surgery to fix him, she'd understand. Most of the people who live in the Upper Peninsula have a hard enough time taking care of their families, let alone paying for an expensive operation for an animal, no matter how much they want to. I could tell she was happy when I told her I'd rather give up bear hunting than give up my dog.

I track my father through the scope as he continues toward me, unaware. I used to fantasize about killing him when I was a child—not because I wanted to, but because he'd planted the idea when he changed the rules of our tracking game. I'd watch him for a long time after I found him, thinking about what it would be like if I shot him instead of the tree. How killing my father would make me feel. What my mother would say when she found out I was now the head of our family.

As I watch him walk ever closer, I think again about killing him—this time, for real. From this distance and angle I could take him down easily. Put a bullet through his heart or head, and the game would be over without his even realizing I'd won. I could shoot him in the gut. Make him bleed out slowly and painfully as payback for what he did to my mother. I could shoot him in the shoulder or in the knee. Hurt him badly enough that he wouldn't be going anywhere without a stretcher. Go home, call the police as soon as I can pick up a signal, and tell them where to collect him.

So many choices.

Back at the cabin, my father and I used to

play a guessing game where he'd hide some small object he knew I'd like in one hand—a piece of smooth white quartz or an unbroken robin's egg—and I had to choose which hand held the treasure. If I guessed correctly, I got to keep it. If not, my father threw the treasure in our garbage pit. I remember trying so hard to reason it out. If my father held the treasure in his right hand the last time we played, did that mean that this time the treasure would be in his left? Or would he hold it in his right hand again to trick me? Perhaps several times? I didn't realize then that reason and logic had nothing to do with the outcome. No matter which hand I chose, the odds of guessing correctly remained the same.

This is different. This time there **is** no wrong call. I take off the safety. Slip my finger through the trigger and hold my breath and count to ten.

And shoot.

I WAS TERRIFIED the first time I shot my father. I remain astounded that he let me do it. I try to imagine putting a gun in Iris's hands and telling her to point it at me and pull the trigger—and, oh, yes, make sure you miss—and I simply can't picture it. I doubt I would ever consider doing such a thing with Mari, either, no matter how good a shot she turns out to be. It's reckless to the point of being suicidal. And yet this is exactly what my father did.

This happened the summer I was ten. We didn't play our tracking game in the winter because after there was snow on the ground, following my father's trail would have been too easy, and we didn't play in the late fall or in the early spring after the leaves had fallen or before the trees had budded out for the same reason. Only when the foliage was lush and dense was tracking a person through the forest a true challenge, my father said. This is also the time of year when the bugs are at their worst. You have to admire the self-control it must have taken him to sit in the swamp for hours while he waited for me to find him, bugs swarming and biting but my father resisting the urge to swat or even to twitch.

My father explained the new game rules at breakfast. After I found him, I had two options. I could shoot into the tree he would be hiding behind, either beside him or above his head, or I could shoot into the dirt near his feet.

If I didn't find him—or worse, if I was too scared to take the shot when I did—I would have to give up something that was important to me. We would begin with the **National Geographic** issue with the pictures of the Vikings that I'd hidden under my bed. I don't know how my father even knew it was there.

My father took me in his canoe to a ridge where I had never been. I was blindfolded to make it harder to judge how far we'd traveled and how much time had passed, and also so I wouldn't be able to see which direction he went when we got there. I was very nervous. I didn't want to shoot my father. I did want to keep my **Geographic.** I thought a lot about my two options. Shooting into the dirt would be easier and safer than shooting into a tree because the bullet would bury itself in the sand and be less likely to ricochet and hurt either me or my father. Also, if I missed the dirt shot and accidentally hit my father, shooting him in the leg or in the foot would be a lot less traumatic than shooting him in the chest or head.

But shooting into the dirt was the coward's shot, and I was no coward.

"Stay here," my father said as the canoe nudged the shore. "Count to a thousand, and then you can take the blindfold off."

The canoe rocked as he got out. I heard splashing as he waded toward the shore, a rustling as he made his way through the vegetation—arrowroot and cattails, most likely—and then nothing. All I could hear was the wind moving through the pines that my nose had already told me grew on this ridge and the papery sound of aspen leaves knocking against each other in the breeze. The water was quiet, and the sun was hot on my head. The light felt slightly warmer on my right side than on my left, which meant that the canoe was facing north. I wasn't sure how this was going to help, but it was nice to know. The Remington sat heavy on my knees. Beneath the blindfold, I was beginning to sweat.

Suddenly I realized I had been so busy gathering clues about my surroundings, I had forgotten to count. I decided to begin with five hundred to make up for lost time. The question was, did my father expect me to count to the full one thousand as he had instructed, or did he expect me to take off the blindfold before I finished counting and start looking for him sooner? It was hard to know. Most of the time I did exactly what my father told me to do because there was always some kind of punishment at the end of it if I didn't. But this was different. The whole point of tracking my father was learning to outthink him. Deviousness and trickery were part of the game.

I took off the blindfold and tied it around my forehead to keep the sweat out of my eyes and climbed out of the canoe. My father's trail was easy to follow. I could see clearly where he had waded through a patch of sedges—not arrowroot and cattails as I had supposed—and climbed onto the bank. The disturbances in the pine needles in the clearing he crossed before disappearing into the bracken ferns on the other side were also readily visible. I assumed the fact that I could follow my father's trail so easily meant that I had gotten very good at tracking. Looking back, I'm sure he left an easy trail that day because he wanted the game to reach its conclusion, and for that, he needed to be sure that I found him.

I almost lost the trail at the top of the ridge when the footprints ended at a smooth, bare rock. Then I saw a tiny pile of sand where it shouldn't have been. I picked up the trail on the other side and followed it to the edge of a small cliff. Bent bracken ferns and loose rocks showed where my father had climbed down. I followed the trail through the Remington's scope and found my father squatting on his heels on the far side of a beech tree a hundred feet away. The tree was fat but not fat enough: I could see both his shoulders sticking out.

I grinned. The gods were truly smiling on me this day. Not only had I found my father, shooting conditions were close to perfect. I had the high ground. There was no wind. The sun was at my back, and while that meant my father would be able to see me silhouetted against the sun if he happened to step out from behind the tree and turn around and look up, it also meant I would be able to see him clearly when I took my shot and would be less likely to miss.

I took cover behind a big red pine and held the Remington close while I considered my next move. The Remington was almost as tall as me. I dropped to my belly and pushed it in front of me until I was in a better position to shoot from beneath a bush. I braced the Remington against my shoulder and looked through the scope. My father hadn't moved.

I slipped my finger through the trigger. My stomach got tight. I pictured the crack of the rifle, my father's head snapping up in surprise. I saw him stepping out from behind the tree and walking up the hill to pat my head and congratulate me for making the shot. Or perhaps he would look down in dismay as his shoulder turned red and charge up the hill like a wounded rhino. My hands shook. I didn't understand why I had to shoot him. Why my father had changed the rules of our game. Why he'd taken something that was fun and made it into something dangerous and scary. I wished that things could always stay the same.

And with that thought, I understood. Things had to change because **I** was changing. I was growing up. This was my initiation, my chance to prove that I would be a worthy member of our tribe. To a Yanomami man, courage was valued above everything. This was why they were always fighting other tribes and stealing each other's women and why they would fight to the death even though they were shot full of arrows rather than quit and be branded a coward. According to the **Geographic,** almost half the Yanomami men had killed a man.

I braced the Remington more securely against my shoulder. My hands were no longer shaking. It's impossible to describe the mix of terror and exhilaration I felt when I pulled the trigger. I imagine it's similar to what a person feels when they jump out of an airplane or dive off a cliff, or the way a heart surgeon feels when she makes her first cut. I was no longer a little girl who loved and admired her father and hoped one day to become like him. I was his equal.

After that, I couldn't wait till I got the chance to shoot him again.

THE CRACK OF THE RIFLE and the snap of the branch above my father's head are nearly simultaneous. The branch falls into the creek directly in front of him. Exactly where I intended it to fall. The same move that ended our last hunting and tracking game.

My father freezes. He looks up to where the shot originated with his mouth hanging open like he can't believe I beat him again, let alone in the same way. He shakes his head and holds his arms to the side in surrender. Rambo's leash is wrapped around his left hand. The Glock dangles from his right.

I keep my finger on the trigger. Just because a man looks like he's beaten doesn't mean he's ready to give up. Especially when that man is as devious and manipulative as my father.

"Jacob." The name feels foreign on my tongue.

**"Bangii-Agawaateyaa."**

I shudder, and not because of the rain. **Bangii-Agawaateyaa.** Little Shadow. The name he gave me when I was a child. The name I haven't heard spoken since. I can't begin to articulate how these words coming out of my father's mouth after all these years make me feel. All of the anger and hatred and resentment I've been holding on to for more than a decade evaporate, ice on a woodstove. I feel like a part of me I didn't even realize was broken is now whole. Memories wash over me: my father teaching me to track, to hunt, to snowshoe, to swim. How to sharpen my knife and skin a rabbit and button my shirt and tie my shoes. Naming the birds, the insects, the plants, the animals. Sharing the marsh's endless secrets: a cluster of frog eggs floating on the still pond water beneath an overhanging branch, a fox den burrowed deep into the sand on the side of a hill.

Everything I know about the marsh that's worth knowing, this man taught me.

I tighten my grip on the Ruger. "Toss your weapons."

My father looks back for a long time before he flings the Glock into the bushes. He pulls a Bowie from inside his right boot and tosses the knife after the gun.

"Slowly," I say as he reaches behind his back for the second handgun. If I were him and he was me, this is the moment I'd make my move. I'd whip out my weapon, shove it against Rambo's head, and use my adversary's weakness for her dog to disarm her.

My father brings the second Glock out from behind him slowly as I instructed. His arm goes back like he's going to throw it, but instead of letting go when his arm reaches its apex, he drops to one knee and shoots.

Not at Rambo.

At me.

The bullet slams into my shoulder. For the briefest of moments, all I feel is shock. **He shot me.** Deliberately, and with no thought to the consequences except to take me down.

I didn't beat him. I didn't save my family. I

didn't win, because my father changed the rules of our game once again.

Then my shoulder explodes. Someone stuck a stick of dynamite inside of me and set it off. I was hit by a baseball bat and run through with a hot poker. I got run over by a bus. I clap my hand over the wound, fall to the ground, and writhe as the pain washes over me in waves. Blood gushes between my fingers. **Grab the Ruger,** my brain tells my hands. **Shoot him like he shot you.** My hands don't answer.

My father climbs the ridge and stands beside me looking down. The Glock points at my chest.

How incredibly stupid I am. I thought I was being strategic when I shot the branch instead of him. How tragically the consequences of my decision are going to play out. The truth is I didn't **want** to kill my father. I love him, even though he doesn't love me. He used my love for him against me.

I hold my breath as I wait for my father to finish me off. He looks down for a long time, then sticks the Glock in the back of his jeans and kicks the Ruger down the other side of the ridge. He rolls me onto my back and pockets my Magnum. I don't know how he knew I was carrying, but he did. He pulls a pair of handcuffs from his back pocket—no doubt the same cuffs he was wearing when he escaped from prison—and yanks my arms in front of me despite my wounded shoulder and snaps the cuffs over my wrists. My whole body shakes with the effort not to scream.

He takes a step back, breathing heavily.

"And **that,**" he says, looking down with a triumphant grin, "is how you beat someone at hunting and tracking."

# 22

## The Cabin

**Early in the autumn, the Viking again returned home laden with spoil, and bringing prisoners with him. Among them was a young Christian priest, one of those who contemned the gods of the north. In the deep stony cellars of the castle, the young Christian priest was immured, and his hands and feet tied together with strips of bark.**

**The Viking's wife considered him as beautiful as Baldur, and his distress raised her pity; but Helga said he ought to have ropes fastened to his heels, and be tied to the tails of wild animals.**

**"I would let the dogs loose after him,"**

**she said, "over the moor and across the heath. Hurrah! that would be a spectacle for the gods, and better still to follow in its course."**

**But the Viking would not allow the young Christian priest to die such a death as that, especially as he was the disowned and despiser of the high gods. The Viking had decided to have him offered as a sacrifice on the blood-stone in the grove. For the first time, a man was to be sacrificed here.**

**Helga begged to be allowed to sprinkle the assembled people with the blood of the priest. She sharpened her glittering knife; and when one of the great, savage dogs, who were running about the Viking's castle in large numbers, sprang towards her, she thrust the knife into his side, merely, as she said, to prove its sharpness.**

—HANS CHRISTIAN ANDERSEN,
**The Marsh King's Daughter**

Someone is coming," my mother said again as we stood together at the kitchen window, as if she couldn't believe her own words unless she said them twice.

I was surprised as well. My father was always so careful about not drawing attention to our cabin: cutting firewood on the low end of our ridge so the sound of his chain saw didn't carry; shooting the rifle only when necessary to get the venison we needed; never leaving the marsh to restock our supplies even though we were running out of things it would have been nice to have; hiding from that family so we wouldn't accidentally lead them to our cabin; running practice drills so my mother and I would know what to do in case anyone showed up on our ridge. It was hard to believe that after all of that, someone had actually come.

I pressed my nose against the glass and watched the snowmobile's headlight bob and weave toward us. It was too dark to make out details, but I knew what a snowmobile looked like. Or rather, I knew what a snowmobile looked like fifty years ago. I was still struggling to comprehend the enormity of my mother's deception.

My mother shook her head slowly, like she was waking up from a long sleep. She yanked the curtains shut and grabbed my hand. "Quick. We have to hide."

**Hide where?** I wanted to say. I knew this was

what my father wanted. I also knew what he'd do to us if we didn't follow his instructions. But it was too late to run out into the marsh and roll around in the muck to disguise ourselves, even if the marsh wasn't frozen. Whoever was driving the snowmobile had already seen our cabin. They were coming straight toward us. There was a fire in our woodstove, smoke coming from our chimney, firewood in our woodshed, footprints in the snow. Inside, our coats were hanging by the door, our dishes were laid out on the table, the rabbit stew was bubbling away on our woodstove. And what about Rambo?

**Rambo.**

I grabbed my coat and ran out to the woodshed. Rambo was whining and pulling at his chain so hard, I was afraid he was going to choke. I unbuckled his collar and turned him loose, then crouched between a row of firewood and the shed wall to watch through the slats. The engine's pitch changed as the snowmobile began climbing our ridge. Moments later it whipped past my line of sight in a cloud of snow and exhaust. I ran to the other side of the woodshed and climbed on top of the woodpile and crouched with my knife at the ready, the way my father taught me. The snowmobile stopped directly below me. The noise was so loud, my ears rang long after the driver turned the engine off.

"Hey, boy." The driver whistled and patted his leg as Rambo barked and circled. I couldn't see his face because he had on a helmet like the kind deep-sea divers wore—or rather, the kind of helmet a deep-sea diver **used** to wear—but I could tell it was a man by his voice. "Come 'ere, boy. Come on. It's okay. I won't hurt you."

Rambo stopped barking and ran up wagging his tail and rested his chin on the man's knee. The man pulled off one glove and scratched Rambo behind his ear. I wondered how he knew this was where my dog liked to be scratched.

"Good boy. What a good dog you are. Yes, you are. Yes, you are." I'd never heard anyone talk so much to a dog.

The man nudged Rambo aside and climbed off the snowmobile. He wore thick black pants and a black jacket with a stripe down the sleeves in a shade of green I'd never seen. The snowmobile had the same colored stripe on the side with the words ARCTIC CAT written in white letters. He pulled off his helmet and left the helmet on the seat. The man had yellow hair like my mother and a big bushy beard like a Viking. He was taller than my father, and younger. His clothes made a rustling sound like dry leaves when he walked. I couldn't imagine they'd be any good for hunting, but they looked warm.

The man climbed our porch steps and rapped his knuckles on the door. "Hello! Anybody home?" He waited, then hit the door again. I wasn't sure what he was waiting for. "Hello!"

The cabin door opened and my mother came out. I couldn't see her expression because the light was behind her. I could see that her hands were shaking.

"I'm sorry to bother you," the man said, "but can I use your phone? I got separated from my group and lost the trail."

"Our phone," my mother said softly.

"If you don't mind. My cell's battery died."

"You have a cell phone." My mother giggled. I had no idea why.

"Um, yeah. Right. So if I could use yours to let my buddies know I'm all right, that'd be great. I'm John, by the way. John Laukkanen." The man smiled and put out his hand.

My mother made a choking sound, then grabbed his hand like a drowning person grabbing a lifeline. She held on to his hand long after their hands stopped going up and down.

"I know who you are." She glanced around the yard, then quickly pulled the man inside.

---

I STARED AT THE CABIN long after the door shut. More lies. More tricks. More deception. My mother knew this man. He came to see her while my father was gone. I didn't know what the man and my mother were doing inside our cabin, but I knew it was wrong. I sheathed my knife and climbed down from the woodpile. The snowmobile crouched in our yard like a big black bear. I wanted to slap it on its rump and run it off. Call my father to come with his rifle and shoot it. I tiptoed across our back porch and peeked through a gap in the curtains. My mother and the man were standing in the middle of the kitchen. My mother was talking and waving her hands. I couldn't hear what she was saying. She looked scared and excited. She kept glancing at the door, like she was afraid my father would walk through at any second. I wished he would.

The man just looked scared. My mother kept talking and gesturing until, at last, he nodded. Slowly, like he didn't want to do what my mother was asking him to do, but he had to, like I did when my father told me I had to help my mother make jelly. My mother laughed and stretched up on her toes and threw her arms around the man's neck and kissed his cheek. The man's cheeks turned red. My mother laid her head on his shoulder. Her shoulders shook. I couldn't tell if she was laughing or crying. After a moment the man put his arms around my mother and patted her on the back and held her close.

I sank down on my heels in the snow. My own cheeks burned. I knew what a kiss meant. A kiss meant you loved the person you were kissing. This was why my mother never kissed my father. I couldn't believe my mother kissed this man, this stranger, after she brought him into our cabin while my father was away. I did know what my father would do to them if he was here. I took out my knife. Crept silently across the porch and flung open the door.

"Helena!" my mother cried. The man and my mother pulled apart as cold air swept the cabin. Her face was flushed. "I thought you were . . . Never mind. Hurry. Shut the door."

I left the door open. "You have to leave," I told the man as harshly as I could. "Now." I waved my knife so he'd know I meant business. I'd use it if I had to.

The man backed away, put up his hands. "Whoa. Easy. Put the knife down. It's okay. I'm not going to hurt you." Talking to me like I was my dog.

I made my face as hard as my father's and

took a step closer. "You have to go. **Now.** Before my father comes back."

My mother's face turned white when I mentioned my father, as it should. I didn't know what she was thinking when she brought this man into our cabin, how she thought this might end.

She sank down into a chair. "Helena, please. You don't understand. This man is our friend."

"'Our friend'? **Our** friend? I saw you kiss him. **I saw you.**"

"You saw . . . Oh, Helena. No, no—I was only thanking John because he's going to take us away. Put your knife down. We have to hurry."

I looked at my mother—excited, hopeful, happy, like this was the best day of her life because this man showed up on our ridge. All I could think was that she was out of her mind. I knew she didn't like living in the marsh, but did she really think she could leave now, in the cold and the dark? Get on the snowmobile behind this stranger and let him take her away without my father's permission? I couldn't imagine why she would think for a second that I would agree to this plan.

"Please, Helena. I know you're scared—"

I most certainly was not.

"—and this is all very confusing."

I was not a bit confused.

"But you have to trust me."

Trust her? The magazine in my back pocket burned like an ember. After this, I would never trust my mother again.

"Helena, please. I'll explain everything, I promise. But we have to hur—"

She broke off as my father's footsteps clomped across the porch.

"What's going on?" he roared as he burst into the room. He sized up the situation in an instant and swung his rifle between the man and my mother like he couldn't decide which of them he should shoot first.

The man held up his hands. "Please. I don't want any trouble—"

"Shut up! Sit down."

The man fell into one of our kitchen chairs like he'd been pushed. "Look here, now. There's no need for the gun. I just wanted to use your phone. I got lost. Your—um, wife let me in, and—"

"I said **shut up.**" My father spun on his heel and smashed the rifle butt into the man's gut. The man gasped and toppled off the chair and rolled around on the floor, moaning and clutching his stomach.

"No!" my mother screamed, and covered her face.

My father handed me the rifle. "If he moves, shoot him." He stood over my mother and drew back his fist. The man scrambled to his knees, crawled toward my father, grabbed my father's ankle. I knew I should shoot. I didn't want to pull the trigger.

"Leave her alone!" the man cried. "I know who you are. **I know what you did.**"

My father froze, whirled around. There was an article in one of the **Geographics** that described a person's face as being "black with rage." My father looked like that now. Angry enough to kill us all.

He roared like a wounded black bear, advanced on the man, kicked him in his kidney. The man cried out and fell facedown on the floor. My father grabbed the man's left wrist and planted his foot on the man's elbow, then twisted the man's arm higher and higher behind his back until the bone snapped. The man's scream filled the cabin, mixed with my mother's, my own.

My father grabbed the man by his broken arm and yanked him to his feet. The man screamed again. **"Please! No! Oh, God—no! Stop! Please!"** he yelled as my father marched him across the yard to the woodshed. My mother sobbed. My hands shook. I looked down and realized I was still holding the rifle. The rifle was pointed at my mother. My mother was looking at me like she thought I was going to shoot her. I didn't tell her the safety was on.

My father came back into the cabin. His jacket was bloody and his knuckles were red. He took the rifle from my shaking hands and locked it in the storage room. I waited in the kitchen with my mother. I wasn't sure what he wanted me to do.

When he came back his expression was calm, like nothing had happened, like this was an ordinary day and he didn't just break the arm of the first person to show up on our ridge. This could have meant one of two things: his anger was spent or he was just getting started.

"Go to your room, Helena."

I ran up the stairs. Behind me I heard the sound of a fist hitting flesh. My mother screamed. I shut the door.

LONG AFTER the cabin was quiet, I lay on my bed with my arms behind my head and stared at the ceiling. Memories crowded out my dreams.

My father and I were swimming in the beaver pond. He was teaching me how to float on my back. The sun was warm and the water was cold. I lay on my back on top of the water with my arms straight out to the sides. My father stood beside me. The water came up to his waist. My father's hands were beneath my back holding me up, though I could hardly feel them. "Legs up," he said when my feet started to droop. "Stomach out. Arch your back." I pushed my stomach out and curled my shoulders back as far as they would go. My face dipped under the water. I sputtered, started to sink. My father caught me, lifted me up. I tried again. Later, after I learned to float, it was so easy, it was hard to remember a time when I didn't know how.

My father was helping me bait my fishhook. The hook was very sharp. The first time I picked up a fishhook from my father's tackle box, it got stuck in my thumb. It hurt, but not as much as when my father pulled it out. After that I was careful to hold the hook only by the loop at the top. Our bait can was full of worms. We dug the worms from the wet soil at the low end of our ridge. I fished through the dirt in the can and took one out. The worm was slippery and wet. My father showed me how to slide the hook into the middle of the worm and loop the worm around the hook and stick it again through its tail and head. "It doesn't hurt," he said when I asked how the worm felt about this. "Worms can't feel anything." If this was true, I asked, then why did the worm twist and wiggle? My father smiled. He said it was good that

I was learning to think for myself and patted my head.

My father and I were sitting in the sweat lodge. My father was once again telling the story about the time he fell into the bear's den. This time I noticed that whenever my father told the story, he changed the details to make the story more exciting. The hole was deeper, my father fell farther, it was harder for him to climb out, the bear started to wake up when my father landed on its back, the cub's neck was broken. I could see that while it was important to always tell the truth, when you were telling a story, it was okay to change the facts to make the story more interesting. I hoped when I grew up, I would be as good a storyteller as he was.

I got up and crossed the room to the window and looked out over the moonlit yard. Rambo was moving around in the utility shed. The snowmobile was beneath me. The man in the woodshed was quiet.

I had loved my father when I was little. I still did. Cousteau and Calypso said my father was a bad man. I know they cared about me, but I couldn't believe that this was true.

IN THE MORNING my father cooked breakfast while my mother stayed in bed. The oat cereal he fixed was bland and tasteless. It was hard to believe that yesterday the thing I was most concerned about was not having salt. All I could think about now was my mother's betrayal. Not only the lie she told about the **Geographics,** but the way she betrayed my father. I knew he beat her for bringing the man into our cabin and this was why she was still in bed. I didn't like when my father beat my mother, but there were times like now when she deserved it. My father said that because my mother was alone in our cabin with another man, this meant my mother had committed something called adultery, and when an Ojibwa woman commits adultery, her husband had the right to mutilate her or even kill her as he saw fit. My mother wasn't Native American, but because she was my father's wife she had to live by his rules. I knew she deserved to be punished, but even so, I was glad I didn't tell my father I saw her kiss the man.

I scrubbed out our cereal bowls and cooking pot with cold water and a handful of sand and carried a mug of hot chicory to the man in the woodshed as my father instructed. The morning was sunny and bright. The snowmobile looked bigger in the daylight, shiny and black and as sparkly as a fresh snowfall, with a windshield the color of wood smoke and that extraordinary green stripe. It was nothing like the pictures in the **Geographics.** I left the mug on the porch step and picked up the helmet. It was heavier than I'd expected, with a piece of dark curved glass in front shaped like a shield. Inside the padding was thick and soft. I put on the helmet and sat down on the seat with my legs on either side the way the man did and pretended I was driving. I used to wish we had a snowmobile. If we'd had a snowmobile, we could have checked our ice-fishing lines in half the time it took to snowshoe from hole to hole. I asked my father once if we could trade some of his furs to get one. That led to a long lecture about how Indian ways were better than white men's inventions, and faster wasn't always better. But I thought that if our people had had snowmobiles back in the day, they would have used them.

I climbed off the snowmobile and picked up the mug and crossed the yard to the woodshed. The chicory was no longer steaming. The man was handcuffed to the post in the corner. His hair was bloody and his face was swollen. His jacket and pants were gone. He was wearing white thermal underwear like my father and I wore in the winter and nothing else. His feet were pushed into the woodchips and sawdust to keep them warm, though I could see his toes sticking out. His arms were handcuffed above his head. His eyes were closed and his beard rested on his chest. He didn't look much like a Viking now.

I stopped in the doorway. I wasn't sure why. This was my woodshed, my cabin, my ridge. I had every right to be here. This man was the one who didn't belong. I think I was afraid to go in because I didn't want to be alone with this man and possibly commit adultery. My father was the one who told me to bring the man a cup of chicory, but adultery was a new concept. I wasn't sure how it worked.

"Are you thirsty?" An obvious question, but I didn't know what else to say.

The man cracked open one eye. The other was swollen shut. My father often told me that if I was ever in a situation where I had to take someone captive, no matter how badly I had to beat them, I should always make sure they had one good eye so they could see me coming and anticipate what I might do so I wouldn't lose my psychological edge. When the man saw me standing in the doorway, he scrambled as far away as the handcuffs would let him, so I could see that what my father said was true.

"I brought you something to drink." I knelt in the sawdust and held the cup to his lips, then took out the biscuit I'd hidden in my coat pocket and broke it into pieces and fed it to him. The feel of his whiskers on my fingers and his breath against my skin made me shiver. I'd never been this close to a man who was not my father. I thought again about adultery and brushed away the crumbs that fell on the man's chest.

The man looked better when he finished, though not by much. A cut over his eye was bleeding, and the left side of his face was swollen and purple from where my father had hit him. The broken arm stretched over his head was going to be a problem. I'd seen animals die from less.

"Is your mother all right?" he asked.

"She's okay." I didn't tell him that my mother's left arm was similarly broken. "A matched pair," my father said that morning when he told me how last night he'd twisted my mother's arm behind her back the same as he did to the man.

"Your father is crazy." The man jutted out his chin to indicate the woodshed, the handcuffs, his lack of clothing.

I didn't like when he said this. This man didn't know my father. He had no right to say bad things about him.

"You shouldn't have come," I said coldly. "You should have left us alone." Suddenly, I had to know. "How did you find us?" The question didn't come out the way I meant it. It sounded like I thought we were lost.

"I was riding trail with a couple of my buddies and took a wrong turn. We'd been drinking," he said, as if this was some kind of explanation. "Whiskey. Beer. Never mind. I drove a long time looking for a trail marker. Then I saw the smoke from your cabin. I didn't know that this cabin . . . that your mother . . ."

"What about my mother?" I didn't care how badly this man was hurt. If he said he came here because he was in love with my mother, I was going to hit him on his broken arm.

"I didn't know that your mother has been here all along. That after all these years, someone had finally found her, and that your father . . ." He stopped and looked strangely at me. "My God. You don't know."

"Know what?"

"That your mother . . . your father—"

"What about me?" my father demanded.

The man shrank back as my father's shadow filled the doorway. He closed his good eye and started to whimper.

"Go inside, Helena," my father said. "Your mother needs you."

I grabbed the empty mug and jumped to my feet and ran past my father to the cabin. I rinsed the cup and put it in our dry sink, then stood at the kitchen window for a long time, watching through the slats in the woodshed as my father punched and kicked the man while the man screamed and yelled. I wondered what the man was going to tell me.

# 23

My shoulder throbs. I have no idea how badly I'm wounded. It's possible the bullet only grazed my shoulder and a couple of stitches will put me to rights. It's just as possible the wound is much worse. If the bullet hit an artery, I'm going to bleed out. If it hit one of the major nerves, I could lose the use of my arm. For now, all I know is that it hurts. A lot.

If this was your typical accidental shooting, I'd be riding in the back of an ambulance on the way to the hospital while medics worked to stabilize me instead of sitting on the ground with my back against a tree. Doors would fly open when we arrived, orderlies would rush out and roll me inside. Doctors would treat the wound, give me something to stop the pain.

But this shooting was no accident.

After my father shot and handcuffed me, he dragged me by my shoulders to a large red pine and pulled me up and propped me against it. I don't even want to try to describe how that felt.

Rambo is gone. I think I yelled "Home!" when my father charged up the hill to disarm me, but it's hard to know if I actually shouted the command or only thought it. Those first few seconds after my father shot me are a blur.

I blink. Force my thoughts away from the pain. Try to stay focused. What a fool I was to think that my father would surrender. I should have killed him when I had the chance. Next time, I will.

My father is sitting on the ground with his back against a log. My Magnum is in his hand. My knife hangs from my belt at his waist. My cell phone is dead, and I'm not talking about the battery. After my father found the iPhone Stephen gave me for our last anniversary, he tossed it into the air and shot it.

My father is relaxed, completely at ease—and why shouldn't he be? He has every advantage, and I have none.

"I didn't want to hurt you," he says. "You made me do it."

Typical narcissist. No matter what happens, it's always the other person's fault.

"You shouldn't have left," he goes on when I don't answer. "You ruined everything."

I'd like to point out that I wasn't to blame for the way our lives fell apart. If my father was capable of the smallest logic, I'd tell him that the life he imagined was always unattainable, that his delusion that he could create a life in the marsh according to his wants and preferences ended the moment I was conceived. I was the chink in his armor, his Achilles' heel. My father raised me and shaped me into a version of himself, but in so doing he sowed the seeds of his own demise. My father could control my mother. He could never control me.

"She's dead," I say. "Mother."

I don't know why I'm telling him this. I can't even say for sure how my mother died. All I know is what I read in the papers: that she died unexpectedly at her home. It seemed an appropriate place for her to pass away. When I lived at my grandparents', those four pink bedroom walls plastered with butterflies and rainbows and unicorns all but smothered me. Whenever the noise and the turmoil of the world beyond the marsh got too much for me, I had to go outside. As long as I could look up and see the trees moving, I was okay. My mother was the opposite. Looking back, I think the reason she spent so much time in her room after we left the marsh is that it was the last place she'd felt safe.

My father snorts. "Your mother was a disappointment. I often wished I'd taken the other one."

"The other one"? The other girl she was playing with that day? It guts me to hear him speak so dispassionately of my mother's abduction. I think about the day he kidnapped her, how she fell for his story about the dog, how terrified she must have been when she realized my father meant to harm her. There had to have been a point when she was helping him look for his nonexistent dog when she realized he wasn't telling the truth. **I should go home now,** she would have said. Probably more than once. **My parents will be looking for me.** Tentatively, like she was asking permission, because back then little girls weren't taught to be assertive like they are now. Maybe my father promised to get her an ice cream if she'd help him look a little longer. Maybe he tempted her with a ride in his canoe. My father can be convincing when it suits his purpose.

Whatever my mother was thinking or feeling, the moment she got into his canoe, she was done for. For the first few miles east of Newberry, the Tahquamenon River cuts through hardwoods and is relatively narrow. Maybe my mother thought about jumping over the side and swimming to shore once she realized she was in trouble. Maybe she held her breath each time they came around a bend, thinking they'd pass by a fisherman or a family and she could yell for help. But as soon as the river opened out into the marshland, she had to have known it was over. I think the marsh is beautiful, but to my mother the endless waving grasses must have looked as desolate as the moon. Did she realize then that there **was** no dog? That my father had tricked her? That she would never see her girlfriend, her house, her room, her clothes, her toys, books, and movies, or her parents ever again? Did she cry? Scream? Fight? Or did she slip into the fugue state that was her refuge for the next fourteen years? My mother never shared the details of that day, so I can only guess.

"You planned this from the beginning," I say as understanding dawns. "You attacked the guards in the Seney Stretch because you knew I'd come looking for you if you escaped close to my home. You've taken me hostage because you want me to drive you to Canada and leave you there." Of course there's the matter of the four flat tires on my truck, but I'm sure my father has planned a way to get around that.

He smiles. It's the same smile he used to get

when he was teaching me to track. Not when I'd gotten it right. When I'd gotten it wrong.

"Almost. You're not leaving me at the border, **Bangii-Agawaateyaa.** You're coming with me. We're going to be a family. You. Me. Your girls."

Time slows to a crawl as this settles in. My father has to know I will never willingly fetch my girls and go away with him, even if I were physically able to form words and sentences to tell him. I'll die first, and gladly. I can't believe I wanted to see him again. That I ever loved this man. A man who murders as easily as he draws a breath. Who thinks that because he wants a thing, he should have it. My mother. Our cabin. **My girls.**

"Yes, your girls," he says, as if he can see straight inside my head. "Surely you didn't think we'd leave without them?"

**We?** But there is no we. This is entirely about him. It always has been. I think about how my mother and I did everything according to my father's preferences without realizing this was what we were doing—eating what and when he said we could, wearing what he told us to, getting up and going to bed at the times that he decreed. I'll never subject Mari and Iris to that kind of control. And what about Stephen? Where does my father think my husband will be in all of this? Stephen would go to the ends of the Earth to track down his daughters. Any normal parent would. There's no way this can end except badly.

Then there is the fact that my father knows I have two daughters. He's been in prison for thirteen years, and we've had no contact during that time. I'm not one of those parents who chronicle their kids' lives online, and even if I did, prisoners can't access the Internet. I keep a low profile, don't do anything that will put me in the public eye for reasons that should be obvious by now to anyone who knows my history. I make my living selling homemade jam and jelly, for God's sake. And yet somehow, my father knows about my family.

Or does he?

"What makes you think I have children?"

My father reaches into the dead man's jacket and pulls out a dog-eared copy of **Traverse** magazine. I recognize the cover. My heart sinks. He tosses the magazine at my feet. The magazine falls open to the photograph of me and Stephen and the girls standing in front of the old lightning-scarred maple beside our driveway. The tree is distinctive—especially if it's standing beside the driveway of the homestead where you grew up. The article doesn't name my girls, doesn't have to. The picture told my father everything he needed to know.

Stephen was so proud when the piece ran. He set up the interview a couple of years ago after the economy went bust and gas prices went up and tourism fell off and jam sales were slow. Seeing my name and picture in a magazine was just about the last thing I wanted, but I couldn't think of a reason to tell Stephen no without telling him the truth. He said the publicity would boost my online sales, and he was right about that—after the article ran I started getting orders from transplanted Michiganders from as far away as Florida and California.

I honestly thought I'd covered my tracks well enough that the article wouldn't be a problem. Maybe that sounds naive, but it's easier to reinvent yourself in the U.P. than you might think. The towns may be only thirty to fifty miles apart, but each is like its own separate world. Folks keep to themselves—not only because the people who live in the U.P. are naturally independent and self-reliant, but because they have to. When you have to drive fifty miles to go to a Kmart or see a movie, you learn to be content with what's around you.

Everyone knew all about The Marsh King and his daughter. But by the time I moved from Newberry to Grand Marais, I didn't look anything like the twelve-year-old wild child in the newspaper pictures. I'd grown up, cut my hair, dyed it blonde, changed my last name. I even wore makeup when I was in public to hide my tattoos. As far as anybody knew, I was just the woman who bought the old Holbrook place, and that was fine by me.

If I'd had any idea that a copy of the magazine would one day find its way into the prison library and my father's cell, I never would have agreed to do the piece. In the photo my girls' faces are smudged. How many times did my father run his fingers over their pictures as he plotted and dreamed? The idea of his playing doting grandfather to my daughters . . . playing with them, tickling them, telling them stories . . . I simply can't conceive of it.

"Tell me, do your girls help you make jelly and jam?" He leans in close and presses the Magnum against my chest. I can smell the bacon the old man was cooking for his breakfast on my father's breath. "You thought you could hide from me? Change your name? Deny I'm your father? You're living on my **land,** Helena. Did you really think I wouldn't find you?"

"Don't hurt them. I'll do anything you want as long as it doesn't involve my family."

"You're not in a position to make demands, Little Shadow."

There's no warmth when he says my pet name, no twinkle in his eyes. Maybe the charm I remember from my childhood has been snuffed out by the years in prison. Maybe it was never there. Memories can be tricky, especially those from childhood. Iris will tell a story with absolute conviction about something she thinks happened, even though I know it isn't true. Maybe the man I remember never existed. Maybe the things I think happened never did.

"You won't get away with this," I can't stop myself from saying.

He laughs. It's not a pleasant sound. "You can get away with anything. You of all people should know that."

I flash back to my last day in the marsh. I'm afraid that this is true.

He waves the Magnum in the direction of my house and stands up. "Time to go."

I push myself to my feet using the tree as balance. I start walking. Father and daughter, together again.

# 24

## The Cabin

But there was one time of the day which placed a check upon Helga. It was the evening twilight; when this hour arrived she became quiet and thoughtful, and allowed herself to be advised and led; then also a secret feeling seemed to draw her towards her mother.

The Viking's wife took her on her lap, and forgot the ugly form, as she looked into the mournful eyes. "I could wish that thou wouldst always remain my dumb frog child, for thou art too terrible when thou art clothed in a form of beauty. Never once to my lord and husband has a word passed my lips of what I have to

**suffer through you; my heart is full of grief about you."**

**Then the miserable form trembled; it was as if these words had touched an invisible bond between body and soul, for great tears stood in the eyes.**

—HANS CHRISTIAN ANDERSEN,
**The Marsh King's Daughter**

I thought about the man in the woodshed all the rest of that day. I wondered what he was going to tell me about my father and mother that I didn't know. It must have been important, because my father beat the man for almost telling. I wanted to sneak out to the woodshed many times to ask him, but my father stayed close to the cabin, hauling water and splitting firewood and sharpening his chain saw, so I couldn't.

I spent the entire day inside. It was without a doubt the longest, dullest, least exciting, and most boring day of my life. Worse than the day my father made me help my mother make jelly. I didn't want to take care of my mother, though I was sorry about her broken arm. I wanted to run the snare line, check our ice-fishing holes, tag along with my father when he went to shoot our spring deer even though I was mad at him for breaking my mother's arm—anything but stay inside. It felt like I was being punished, and I hadn't done anything wrong.

Even so, I did everything my father and mother told me, and I did it cheerfully and without complaining in the hope that this would make everyone happy again and things would go back to normal. I washed the dishes, swept the floors, chopped a frozen chunk of venison into pieces with the hatchet and put it on the stove to boil as my mother instructed. I brought her a cup of yarrow tea every time she asked, and I brought her a bowl of leftover rabbit soup for lunch. I helped her sit up to drink and eat, and I fetched a pot from the kitchen for her to pee in and emptied the pot in the outhouse when she was done. My father said that yarrow tea would help stop the bleeding, though it didn't seem to be working. The sling he made for her broken arm from one of our kitchen towels was stained and crusty. So were the sheets. I would have washed them if I could.

I honestly didn't realize how much work she did until I had to do everything myself. I was standing on a step stool leaning over the woodstove, trying to decide if the venison I was cooking for dinner was ready to eat ("Stick a fork in the meat and pretend the fork is an extension of your teeth," my mother said when I asked how I was supposed to know when the meat was done), when my father opened the back door and stuck his head inside.

"Come," he said.

I moved the pot to the back of the stove and put on my winter gear gladly. It was almost dark. The day had been sunny and bright, but now the clouds were rolling in and the temperature was dropping and the wind was kicking up like it was going to snow. I breathed deeply in the frosty air. I felt like a prisoner who'd been let out of jail, or a zoo animal that had been released into the wild after a lifetime in captivity. As I followed my father across the yard, it was all I could do to keep from jumping.

My father carried his favorite knife in his hand, a seven-inch KA-BAR with a carbon steel blade and a leather-wrapped handle, like U.S. Marines used during World War II, though he got his when he was in the Army. The KA-BAR is an excellent combat knife, useful for opening cans and digging trenches and cutting wood or wire or cable as well as fighting hand to hand, though I preferred my Bowie.

Then I saw that we were going to the woodshed. The scars on my forearm tingled. I didn't know what my father was planning to do to the man, but I could guess.

The man scrambled back as far as the handcuffs would let him when we went inside. My father squatted on his heels in front of the man and tossed his knife from hand to hand, letting the man get a good long look while he smiled as if he knew what he was going to do but he couldn't make up his mind where to start. He stared at the man's face for a long time, then let his gaze trail slowly down the man's chest to his groin. The man looked like he was going to throw up. Even I felt queasy.

Suddenly my father grabbed the man's shirt and stuck his knife through the fabric. He sliced the shirt open all the way from the neck to the man's waist, then touched the tip of the knife to the man's chest. The man squeaked with fear. My father pressed harder. The knife pierced the skin. The man yelped. When my father began cutting letters into the man's chest, the man screamed.

My father worked on the man's tattoos for a long time. This is what my father called them, though the words he cut into the man's chest didn't look much like tattoos to me.

My father stopped when the man passed out. He stood up and went outside and cleaned his hands and knife in the snow. As we walked back to the cabin, my head was dizzy and my knees were weak.

When I told my mother about the man's tattoos, she pulled up her shirt and showed me the words my father had written on her: **Slut. Whore.** I didn't know what the words meant, but she said that they were bad.

THE NEXT MORNING my father went into the marsh to shoot our spring deer without first torturing the man in the woodshed. He said we needed the meat more than ever now that we had one more mouth to feed. But my father wasn't giving him anything to eat. Plus, we had enough vegetables in the root cellar to last until the ducks and geese came back, in addition to the cans and other food supplies in the storage room.

I thought my father was only pretending to go hunting, that he was really hiding somewhere close by to keep an eye on me to see if I would do as I was told when he was away. I was in charge of the man while he was gone. I was supposed to give him one cup of hot chicory in the morning and another at night, and nothing else. I didn't see how he could survive drinking only chicory. My father said that was the point.

My father called the man The Hunter, though I knew his name was John. My mother told me The Hunter's last name was spelled like it was pronounced, **Lauk-ka-nen,** with all of the syllables accented the same. I had to say it twice before I got it right. She said that Finnish last names might look like they were hard to pronounce because of all the double consonants and vowels, but they're really not. Unlike English where some letters are silent, like the **b** in **dumb** or the **w** in **sword,** Finnish is written almost exactly like it's spoken.

My mother said that she and The Hunter grew up in the same town, in a place called Newberry, and that she went to school with his youngest brother before my father brought her to the marsh. She said she used to have a crush on The Hunter's youngest brother, though she never told him. I thought about the boy in the **'Teen** magazine with three names, Neil Patrick Harris, who my mother also wanted to crush. It seemed a strange thing to do to a person.

My mother told me her last name was Harju, which was also Finnish, which I did not know. She said her grandparents moved from Finland to Michigan not long after they were married to work in the copper mines. I knew from the maps in the **Geographics** that Finland was sometimes included as part of Scandinavia along with Denmark, Sweden, and Norway, and that the Scandinavians were descended from the Vikings. This meant my mother was a Viking, and so was I, which made me very happy.

I couldn't remember the last time my mother talked this much. I now knew her last name, though I realized suddenly that I did not know mine. Perhaps I didn't have one, in which case I decided I would like to be called "Helena the Brave." I knew the name of the town where my mother grew up. I knew my mother was a Viking, and that I was a Viking, too. I would have liked to learn more, but my mother said she was tired of talking and closed her eyes.

I put on my jacket and went out to the woodshed. I was hoping The Hunter would tell me more about the town where he and my mother grew up. I wondered if other Vikings lived there. I also wondered what it was about my mother and father that I didn't know.

The woodshed smelled very bad. The cuts on The Hunter's chest were swollen and red. His chest was smeared with brown, like my father filled The Hunter's tattoos with excrement instead of soot.

"Help me," The Hunter whispered. At first I thought he was whispering because he was afraid my father would hear. Then I saw the dark bruise on his throat. I understood now why last night, The Hunter had suddenly stopped screaming. "Please. I have to get out of here. Get the handcuff key. Help me."

I shook my head. I didn't like what my father was doing to The Hunter, but I also knew what he would do to me if I helped The Hunter get away. "I can't. My father has the key. He carries it on his key ring all the time."

"Then chop the ring out of the beam. Cut the beam with your father's chain saw. There has to be something you can do. **Please.** You have to help me. I have a family."

I shook my head again. The Hunter had no idea what he was asking. I couldn't chop the ring loose even if I wanted to. The iron ring and the post it was fastened to were very strong. My father said the people who built the cabin made the ring and post this way so they could chain their bull inside the woodshed, and that back then, the woodshed had been filled with straw instead of wood. When I asked if this meant our woodshed used to be a bullshed or a strawshed, he laughed. And while I had watched my father use his chain saw many times, I'd never used it myself.

"Helena, your father is a bad man. He belongs in prison for what he did."

"What did he do?"

The Hunter glanced toward the doorway

and shivered like he was afraid my father would hear, which was ridiculous because there were big gaps in the slats, and if my father was hiding outside listening in, we would have seen him. He looked at me for a long time.

"When your mother was a girl," he began at last, "somewhere around the same age as you, your father took her. He stole her from her family and brought her here, even though she didn't want to come. He kidnapped her. Do you understand what kidnapping means?"

I nodded. The Yanomami often kidnapped girls and women from other tribes to be their wives.

"People looked everywhere for her. They're still looking. Your mother wants to go back to her family. And your father belongs in prison because of what he did. Please. You've got to help me get away. If you do, I promise I'll take you and your mother on the snowmobile with me when I go."

I didn't know what to say. I didn't like that The Hunter said my father belonged in a prison, like Alcatraz or the Bastille or Devil's Island or the Tower of London. I also didn't understand why he seemed to think that kidnapping was wrong. How else was a man supposed to get a wife?

"Ask your mother if you don't believe me," he

called as I got to my feet and started back to the cabin. "She'll tell you I'm telling the truth."

I FIXED MY MOTHER a cup of yarrow tea and carried it to her room. While she drank it I told her everything The Hunter had said. When I finished, she was quiet for so long, I thought she had gone to sleep. At last she nodded.

"It's true. Your father kidnapped me when I was a girl. I was playing with my girlfriend in the stationmaster's empty house by the railroad tracks when your father found us. He said he'd lost his dog and asked if we had seen a little brown cockapoo running around. When we told him we hadn't, he asked if we would help him look for it. Only it was a trick. Your father led me to the river. He put me in his canoe and brought me to the cabin and chained me in the woodshed. When I cried, he beat me. When I begged him to let me go, he stopped giving me anything to eat. The more I fought, the worse it got, so after a while, I did whatever he told me. I didn't know what else to do."

She pulled up a corner of her blanket and wiped her eyes. "Your father is a bad man, Helena. He tried to drown me. He put you in the well. He broke John's arm and mine. He **kidnapped** me."

"But the Yanomami take women from other tribes as wives. I don't understand why kidnapping is wrong."

"How would you like it if someone came to our cabin and took you away without asking if you wanted to go with them? What if this meant that you could never hunt and fish or wander the marsh again? If someone did that to you, what would you do?"

"I would kill them," I said without hesitation. And I understood.

WHEN MY FATHER CAME BACK from the marsh that afternoon, I made sure I was busy in the kitchen so I wouldn't have to watch him beat and torture The Hunter. But I could still hear him scream and yell.

"He's going to kill me," The Hunter said much later when I brought his evening chicory. His face was so bruised and swollen, he could barely talk. "Take the snowmobile. Tomorrow, as soon as your father is gone. Take your mother. Send someone back for me."

"I can't. My father has the snowmobile key."

"There's an extra key in a compartment in the back. In a metal box, stuck to the top. The snowmobile isn't hard to drive. I'll teach you. Please. Get help. Before it's too late."

"Okay," I said, not because The Hunter wanted me to do this, or because I believed my father was a bad man who belonged in prison like my mother and The Hunter said, but because The Hunter was going to die if I didn't.

I sat down cross-legged in the sawdust and listened carefully as he told me everything I needed to know. It took a long time. The Hunter was in a lot of pain. I think my father broke his jaw.

THE NEXT TWO DAYS followed a pattern. I cooked breakfast for myself and my father. Spent the rest of the day hauling water and keeping the fire going and cooking and cleaning while my father went out into the marsh. Pretended everything was as it should be. That my mother and The Hunter weren't dying, that my father was not a bad man. I tried to concentrate on the good things I remembered from when I was growing up, like the way my father gave me the boards and nails I needed to build my duck pen, even though he must have known that wild ducks can't be kept in captivity the same as chickens; how he called me Helga the Fearless as I'd asked him to after I'd read the article about the Vikings; the way he carried me on his shoulders when I was little as we roamed the marsh.

On the third morning, Cousteau and Calypso called a powwow. My mother was in her bedroom. The Hunter was in the woodshed. Rambo was in the utility shed. My father was in the marsh. The three of us were sitting Indian-style in the living room on my bearskin rug.

"You have to leave," Cousteau said.

"Now," Calypso added. "Before your father comes back."

I wasn't so sure. If I left without my father's permission, I could never return.

"What about my mother?" Thinking about her broken arm and how I had to help her sit up to eat and drink. "She can't ride the snowmobile. She won't be able to hold on."

"Your mother can sit in front of you," Calypso said. "You can reach around and hold her up while you steer."

"And The Hunter?"

Cousteau and Calypso shook their heads.

"He's too weak to sit behind you," Cousteau said.

"His arm is broken," Calypso added.

"I don't want to leave him. You know what my father will do if he comes back and The Hunter is here while my mother and I are gone."

"The Hunter wants you to leave," Calypso said. "He said so himself. If he didn't want you to go, he wouldn't have told you how to drive the snowmobile."

"And Rambo?"

"Rambo can run behind. But you have to go. Now. Today. Before your father comes back."

I bit my lip. I didn't understand why it was so hard to make up my mind. I knew my mother and The Hunter couldn't live much longer. I'd seen enough animals die to know the signs. If my mother and I didn't leave the marsh today, most likely, she never would.

Cousteau and Calypso said they knew a story that would help me decide. They said that when I was very little, my mother told this story to me. The story was called a fairy tale. This meant that even though the story wasn't real, it still had a lesson, like my father's Indian legends. They said my mother loved fairy tales when she was a girl. She had a book of stories written by a man called Hans Christian Andersen, and another by two men who called themselves the Brothers Grimm. They said my mother told these fairy tales to me when I was a baby. Her favorite was called "The Marsh King's Daughter" because it reminded her of herself.

The story was about a beautiful Egyptian princess and a terrible ogre called The Marsh King and their daughter, who was named Helga, who was me. When Helga was a baby, a stork found her sleeping on a lily pad and carried her away to the Viking's castle because the Viking's wife had no children and she had always wanted a baby. The Viking's wife loved little Helga, though during the day, she was a wild and difficult child. Helga loved her foster father and she loved the Viking life. She could shoot an arrow and ride a horse and was as skilled with her knife as any man.

"Like me."

"Like you."

During the day, Helga was beautiful like her mother, but she had a wicked, wild nature like her real father. But at night, she was sweet and gentle like her mother, though her body took on the form of a hideous frog.

"I don't think frogs are hideous," I said.

"That's not the point," Cousteau said. "Just listen."

They told me how The Marsh King's daughter struggled with her dual nature; how sometimes she wanted to do what was right, and other times she did not.

"But how does she know which is her true nature?" I asked. "How does she know if her heart is good or bad?"

"Her heart is good," Calypso said with conviction. "She proves this when she rescues the priest her father captured."

"How does she do this?"

"Just listen." Calypso closed her eyes.

This meant she was going to tell a long story. My father did the same thing. He said that closing his eyes helped him remember the words because then he could see the story in his mind.

"One day the Viking came home from a long journey with a prisoner, a Christian priest," Calypso began. "He put the priest in the dungeon so the priest could be sacrificed to the Viking gods the next day in the forest. That night, the shriveled frog sat in the corner alone. Deep silence reigned all around. At intervals, a half-stifled sigh was heard from its innermost soul: the soul of Helga. It seemed in pain, as if a new life were arising in her heart.

"She took a step forward and listened, then stepped forward again and seized with her clumsy hands the heavy bar which was laid across the door. Gently, and with much trouble, she removed the iron bolt from the closed cellar door and slipped in to the prisoner. He was slumbering. She touched him with her cold, moist hand, and as he awoke and caught sight of the hideous form, he shuddered as if he beheld a wicked apparition. She drew her knife, cut through the bonds which confined his hands and feet, and beckoned to him to follow her."

The story sounded familiar. They told me I used to know this story. If I did, I'd forgotten.

"You really don't remember?" Calypso asked.

I shook my head. I didn't understand why they remembered my mother's story and I did not.

"The shriveled frog led him through a long gallery concealed by hanging drapery to the stables and then pointed to a horse. He mounted upon it, and she sprang up also before him and held tightly by the animal's mane. They rode forth from the thick forest, crossed the heath, and again entered a pathless wood. The prisoner forgot her hideous form, knowing that the mercy of God worked through the spirits of darkness. He prayed and sang holy songs, which made her tremble. She raised herself up and wanted to stop and jump off the horse, but the Christian priest held her tightly with all his strength and then sang a pious song, as if this could loosen the wicked charm that had changed her into the semblance of a frog."

Calypso was right. I **had** heard this story before. Memories I didn't know I possessed swirled like pond ripples at the edges of my consciousness and came into focus. My mother singing to me when I was a baby, whispering to me, cradling me in her arms. Kissing me. Hugging me. Telling me stories.

"Let me tell the next part," Cousteau said. "The next part is my favorite."

Calypso nodded.

I liked how Cousteau and Calypso never disagreed.

"The horse galloped on more wildly than before," Cousteau began, waving his arms with great enthusiasm to indicate how the horse had run. His eyes sparkled and danced. His eyes were brown like mine, though his hair was yellow like my mother's, while Calypso's hair was brown and her eyes were blue.

"The sky painted itself red, the first sunbeam pierced through the clouds, and in the clear flood of sunlight the frog became changed. It was Helga again, young and beautiful, but with a wicked demoniac spirit. The priest held now a beautiful young woman in his arms, and he was horrified at the sight.

"He stopped the horse and sprang from its back. He imagined that some new sorcery was at work. But Helga also leaped from the horse and stood on the ground. The child's short garment reached only to her knee. She snatched the sharp knife from her girdle and rushed like lightning at the astonished priest.

"'Let me get at thee!' she cried. 'Let me get at

thee, that I may plunge this knife into thy body. Thou art pale as ashes, thou beardless slave.' She pressed in upon him. They struggled with each other in heavy combat, but it was as if an invisible power had been given to the Christian in the struggle.

"He held her fast, and the old oak under which they stood seemed to help him, for the loosened roots on the ground became entangled in the maiden's feet and held them fast. Then he spoke to her in gentle words of the deed of love she had performed for him during the night, when she had come to him in the form of an ugly frog to loosen his bonds and to lead him forth to life and light; and he told her that she was bound in closer fetters than he had been, and that she could recover also life and light by his means. She dropped her arms and glanced at him with pale cheeks and looks of amazement."

I was amazed as well. This story was nothing like the ones my father told.

"Helga and the priest rode forth from the thick forest, crossed the heath, and again entered a pathless wood," Cousteau continued. "Here, toward evening, they met with robbers. 'Where hast thou stolen that beauteous maiden?' cried the robbers, seizing the horse by the bridle and dragging the two riders from its back. The priest had nothing to defend himself with but the knife he had taken from Helga, and with this he struck out right and left. One of the robbers raised his ax against him, but the young priest sprang on one side and avoided the blow, which fell with great force on the horse's neck so that the blood gushed forth and the animal sunk to the ground.

"Then Helga seemed suddenly to awake from her long, deep reverie; she threw herself hastily upon the dying animal.

"The priest placed himself before her to defend and shelter her, but one of the robbers swung his iron ax against the Christian's head with such force that it was dashed to pieces. Blood and brains were scattered about, and he fell dead upon the ground.

"Then the robbers seized beautiful Helga by her white arms and slender waist, but at that moment the sun went down, and as its last ray disappeared, she was changed into the form of a frog. A greenish white mouth spread half over her face; her arms became thin and slimy while broad hands with webbed fingers spread themselves out like fans. The robbers in terror let her go, and she stood among them, a hideous monster."

"Frogs aren't—"

Calypso put a finger to her lips.

"The full moon had already risen," Cousteau

continued, "and was shining in all her radiant splendor over the Earth, when from the thicket, in the form of a frog, crept poor Helga. She stood still by the corpse of the Christian priest and the carcass of the dead horse. She looked at them with eyes that seemed to weep, and from the frog's head came forth a croaking sound, as when a child bursts into tears."

"So you see, her evil nature is strong," Calypso said, "but her good nature is stronger. This is what the story teaches. Will you let your good nature win? Will you take your mother away?"

I nodded. My legs were stiff from sitting. We stood up and stretched and went into the kitchen to collect my mother's coat from the hook by the door, along with her boots, hat, and mittens.

"Are we leaving?" my mother asked as we laid out her winter gear on her bed.

"We are," I told her. Calypso put her arm behind my mother's shoulders and helped her sit up. Cousteau swung her legs over the side of the bed. I knelt on the floor and put her boots on her feet, then worked her good arm into her coat sleeve and zipped the coat shut over the sling.

"Can you stand up?"

"I'll try." She put her right hand on the bed and pushed. Nothing happened. I wrapped her arm around my neck and put my other arm around her waist and pulled her to her feet. She wobbled, but stayed standing.

"We need to hurry," I said.

My father wouldn't be back for several hours if he didn't shoot a deer today. He would come back much sooner if he did.

I helped my mother to the kitchen. She was so weak, I didn't know how we were going to get her on the snowmobile, though I didn't tell her that.

"I'm sorry, Helena," she said between gasps. Her face was white. "I have to sit down. Just for a minute."

I wanted to tell her that she could rest after she got on the snowmobile, that my father could be on his way home even now, that every minute we delayed might make all the difference, but I didn't want to scare her. I pulled out a chair. "Stay here. I'll be right back." As if she was going anywhere without us.

Cousteau, Calypso, and I stood on the porch and looked out over the yard. There was no sign of my father.

"Do you understand?" Cousteau asked as we descended the porch steps and crossed the yard to the woodshed. "Do you know what you have to do? The priest sacrificed himself so that Helga could be saved."

"You have to save yourself and your mother," Calypso said. "This is what The Hunter would tell you if he could."

We stopped in the doorway. The woodshed smelled as bad as a **wendigo**'s breath. Urine and feces; death and decay. The Hunter's broken arm was swollen and black. His shirt was ripped and his chest was so caked with blood and pus, I could no longer read the words my father had written. His head hung to the side. His eyes were closed and his breathing was shallow and ragged.

I went inside. I wanted to thank The Hunter for what he did for my mother and me. For bringing us the snowmobile so we could leave the marsh, for giving me the opportunity to return my mother to her parents, for telling me the truth about my mother and father.

I said his name. Not the name my father called him, but his real name.

He didn't answer.

I looked back toward the doorway. Cousteau and Calypso nodded. Calypso was crying.

I thought again about all of the things my father would do to The Hunter when he came back and discovered that my mother and I were gone. I took my knife from its sheath.

I remembered to stand to the side.

# 25

The rain has stopped. I'm trying to figure out if I can use this to my advantage. I realize that sounds desperate. That's because I am. My father killed four men in twenty-four hours. Unless I figure out a way to stop him, my husband is going to be the fifth.

We're less than a mile from my house. Just ahead is the beaver pond. Beyond that, the wetland, the grassy meadow that borders our property, and the chain-link fence surrounding our backyard that was supposed to keep my family safe and predators out.

I am in the lead. My father covers me with my Magnum from behind. The handguns he took from the dead prison guards are tucked in the waistband of his jeans. I'm walking as slowly as I can. It's not nearly slow enough. I've run through my options a dozen times, which didn't take long, because there aren't many. I can't use misdirection and lead my father away from my house, because my father knows exactly where to go. I can't overpower him and grab one of the three handguns, because I've been cuffed and shot.

There's only one option that could conceivably work. The deer trail we're following hugs the edge of a high cliff. At the bottom is the creek that drains the beaver pond. As soon as we come to a place that's relatively clear of trees, I'm going to throw myself off. It has to be a place with a steep slope where I will tumble all the way down so that when my father sees me lying motionless in the creek at the bottom, he'll conclude I'm too injured to climb up or dead and go on without me.

Diving headfirst off a cliff and rolling down a hill with a wounded shoulder is going to hurt. A lot. But if I'm going to fool my father, the fall has to look real. Something big and dramatic. Something that involves genuine risk. Something where I might actually die. My father will never suspect a trick because he can't imagine that anyone would be willing to sacrifice herself for her family.

The idea of my father continuing to my

house while I play dead at the bottom of a cliff might sound counterintuitive, but it's the only way I can think of to separate myself from him. The deer trail we're following takes the long way around the wetland behind my house. The moment my father is out of sight, I'll cross the creek and climb the slope on the opposite side, cut through the marshland below the beaver pond, circle back to the trail ahead of my father, set up my ambush, and do what I have to do. I don't want to hurt my father, but he brought this on himself. He changed the rules of our game when he shot me. Now there are no rules.

If my father doesn't continue on to my house and decides instead to follow me down the cliff intending to pull me out of the river and drag me up the hill and force me to keep going as his prisoner, I'll be ready. I'll lock my arms around his neck and choke him with the handcuffs; pull him into the creek with me and drown alongside him if that's the only way to stop him.

But I'm betting it won't come to that. I know how my father thinks. His narcissism is going to work now in my favor. A narcissist can alter his plan to allow for changing circumstances, but he can't change his endgame. My father wants to possess my girls even more than he wants me. By leaving the marsh, I chose my mother over him.

By choosing her, I disappointed him. Kidnapping my daughters gives him another chance. He can mold and shape and coerce them into the new and improved versions of the daughter who betrayed him. All of which means that my father will go after my girls with or without me.

I hope.

I stumble once to set the stage. Fall to my knees and put out my arms to catch myself even though I'm wearing handcuffs because that's what a person who's not thinking clearly would do. The pain that blasts through my shoulder when my hands hit the ground makes me gasp. I cry out, curl into a ball, stay still. I could have choked it down if I had to—my father trained me well when it comes to enduring pain—but I want him to think I've reached my limit and am ready to break.

He kicks me in the ribs and rolls me onto my back. "Get up."

I don't move.

"Get up." He grabs me by the cuffs and hauls me to my feet. I cry out again. This time, the cry is real. I remember all of his past acts of cruelty: smashing my thumb to teach me to be more careful, torturing The Hunter for no reason other than that he could, handcuffing me in the woodshed when I was a toddler when he got tired of my following him around or asking questions. There's no way I will ever let this man get near my husband or my daughters.

"Now walk."

I walk, scanning the trail ahead for the best place to make my move. Every tree and rock calls up a memory. The boggy place where Iris picked a spring bouquet of trillium and mayflowers. The place where Mari turned over a rock and found a red-bellied salamander. The rocky outcropping where Stephen and I shared a bottle of wine on our first anniversary and watched the sun set over the beaver pond.

I stumble over a tree root. Twice is enough to establish a pattern. More than that and my father will become suspicious.

A break in the trees ahead looks promising. The slope is steeper than I'd like, a hundred feet to the bottom and close to sixty degrees, but it's covered in bracken ferns and not scrub pine. I doubt I'll find anything better.

I trip over nothing, then stumble toward the edge like I'm trying to stop myself from falling and throw myself over. Headfirst, because what person in her right mind would do such a thing?

My wounded shoulder slams into the ground. I bite my lip. Keep my arms and legs loose while I tumble down and down.

It takes longer than I expected to reach the bottom. At last I crash to a stop on a clump of branches the current pushed together, my face inches from the water, and stay still. I try not to think about how much I hurt as I listen for sounds of my father. Remind myself I'm doing this for my family.

All remains quiet. When my gut says I've waited long enough, I lift my head enough to scan the top of the cliff.

My plan worked. My father is gone.

I SIT UP. The pain that blasts through my shoulder makes me gasp. I fall back, close my eyes, try to breathe, sit up again more slowly. I unzip my jacket and slide it off my wounded shoulder. The good news is it looks like my father's bullet only grazed the skin. The bad news is I've lost a **lot** of blood.

"Are you okay?"

Calypso is sitting on the creek bank beside her brother. They look exactly as I remember. Cousteau still wears his red watch cap. Calypso's eyes are as blue as a summer day. They're wearing work boots and overalls and flannel shirts because, I now realize, at the time I created them that was the only kind of clothing I knew. I remember how I used to make up stories about our adventures.

Cousteau stands up and holds out his hand.

"Come on. You have to hurry. Your father is getting away."

"You can do it," Calypso says. "We'll help you."

I push myself to my feet and assess my surroundings. The creek isn't wide, no more than twenty feet, but judging by the angle of the slopes on either side, the middle is deep, possibly over my head. If I weren't wearing handcuffs, I could easily swim across, but as it is, I can't even put out my arms for balance. "Helena Drowns Because She Can't Swim While Wearing Handcuffs" is not a story I'd like to tell.

"This way." Cousteau leads me down the stream to a fallen cedar that spans the creek. It's a good idea. I step into the water on the upstream side of the log, bracing myself against the log to keep from being swept away. Broken branches and fallen leaves litter the bottom. The branches are slick. I take my time; place my feet carefully. The log shifts from my weight as I lean against it. I try not to think about what will happen if it breaks loose.

A flash of memory: My father and I were in his canoe. I was very small, perhaps two or three. As we came around a bend in the river, I leaned over the side to reach for a leaf or a branch or whatever it was that had caught my eye and tumbled out. I opened my mouth to yell and took in nothing but water. I remember looking up, seeing the sunlight refracted by the water above my head. Instinctively, I kicked, keeping my mouth closed, even though in no time it felt as though my lungs were going to burst.

Then my father grabbed my jacket. He lifted me out and pulled me into the canoe, then paddled quickly toward a sandbar. He beached the canoe, jumped out, and dragged the canoe onto the shore, then stripped me down and took off his shirt and rubbed me all over to warm me. When my teeth stopped chattering, he wrung the water out of my clothes and laid them out on the sand and held me on his lap and told me stories until my clothes dried.

This time, I'm on my own.

I keep going, one careful footstep after another, until at last I make it to the other side. When I climb up onto the creek bank and look up, the slope that looms over my head looks as daunting as Everest. I start climbing, working my way sideways up the loose limestone scree, hooking the handcuffs over a stump or a branch when I need to rest, pushing through the exhaustion and the pain, willing my body to function independently of my brain, looking for that trance state that long-distance runners use to keep going long after their bodies are screaming at them to stop.

All the while Cousteau and Calypso scamper

ahead like monkeys. "You can do it," they urge whenever I think I can't.

At last I reach the top. I throw a leg over and roll onto my back, gasping. Catch my breath, and stand up. I look around expecting Cousteau and Calypso to congratulate me on my herculean effort, but I am alone.

# 26

## The Cabin

Helga knelt by the corpse of the Christian priest, and the carcass of the dead horse. She thought of the Viking's wife in the wild moorland, of the gentle eyes of her foster-mother, and of the tears she had shed over the poor frog-child.

She looked at the glittering stars, and thought of the radiance that had shone forth on the forehead of the dead man, as she had fled with him over the woodland and moor.

It is said that rain-drops can make a hollow in the hardest stone, and the waves of the sea can smooth and round the rough edges of the rocks; so did the

**dew of mercy fall upon Helga, softening what was hard, and smoothing what was rough in her character.**

**These effects did not yet appear; she was not herself aware of them; neither does the seed in the lap of earth know, when the refreshing dew and the warm sunbeams fall upon it, that it contains within itself power by which it will flourish and bloom.**

—HANS CHRISTIAN ANDERSEN,
**The Marsh King's Daughter**

I stepped out of the woodshed and headed for the cabin. My hands shook. I didn't want to leave The Hunter hanging from the handcuffs. A corpse was supposed to be washed, groomed, dressed in fine clothing, and wrapped in birch bark before it was buried in the forest in a shallow grave. A priest or a medicine man was supposed to talk to the dead person to ease their passage from this world into the next, and offer tobacco to the spirits. I hoped my father would care for The Hunter according to Indian tradition and not throw his body in our garbage pit.

"Gas," Cousteau said. "You need to fill the snowmobile with gas so you don't run out."

"He's right," Calypso said. "You don't know how long The Hunter was driving before he came. The tank could be almost empty."

I felt like I should have thought of this myself, but things were happening so fast, it was hard to know what to do. I was glad Cousteau and Calypso were there to help me. I pushed the snowmobile over to our gravity-feed gas tank. My father kept track of how much gas we had by dipping a long stick through a hole in the top of the tank and drawing a line on the outside to show how much gas was left. He wasn't going to be happy that I took some without asking.

"Do you think this is the right kind?" I wished I'd thought to ask The Hunter while I had the chance.

"The snowmobile sounds like a chain saw," Cousteau said. "Use the chain saw mix."

My father cut the gas for his chain saw with a pint of oil for every two gallons, so I poured the oil in our big red metal can and topped it off with gas from the nozzle, then put as much of the mixture into the snowmobile as the tank would hold.

"Fill the can again," Calypso said. "Tie it on the back, just in case. You never know."

I ran to the utility shed for a piece of rope, ran back, tied the gas can in place, and pushed the snowmobile as close to the back steps as I could. Cousteau and Calypso waited on the porch while I went inside. My mother was still sitting at the table. Her head was resting on her arm and her eyes were closed. Her hair was straggly and wet. At first, I thought she was dead. Then she lifted her head. Her forehead was creased with pain and her face was white. She started to stand, swayed, sat back down. Getting her to the snowmobile was going to be harder than I thought.

I slung her good arm over my shoulder and hung on to her wrist, then slid my left arm around her waist and pulled her to her feet. Judging by the angle of the sun, it was almost noon. This time of year, it would be fully dark by the time we finished dinner. I hoped six hours would be enough.

I took a last look around our kitchen: at our table, the box stove, my father's underwear drying on the lines above it, the pie cupboard where we kept our dishes because my mother never made pies, the shelves lined with jelly and jam. I thought about packing a rucksack with food for our journey, but Cousteau and Calypso shook their heads.

We started down the steps. I was afraid my mother would fall and I'd never be able to get her back up, so Cousteau and Calypso stood on either side to catch her if she did. It took a long time to get her to the snowmobile. As soon as she was seated on it I hurried around to the other side and swung her leg around.

"Do you think I should I tie her on?" My mother was so wobbly, she could barely sit.

"It can't hurt," Calypso said.

"But hurry," Cousteau said.

As if I wasn't already working as fast as I could.

I ran to the utility shed for another piece of rope, ran back, looped it around my mother's waist, and tied the ends around the handles. I put on The Hunter's helmet. It was very heavy. The glass was so dark I could hardly see. I took it off and put it on my mother instead, then went around to the back of the snowmobile and opened the compartment and found the extra key. The Hunter said the snowmobile had something called an electric start, and all I had to do was turn the key. He said if the engine didn't start right away, which it might not because the snowmobile had been sitting for several days and the days and nights had been very cold, I should let go of the key quickly so I didn't burn out the starter, then keep doing this until the engine turned over. I hoped it wouldn't be as complicated as it sounded.

I squeezed between my mother and the gas can and reached around her to grab the handles. After two tries the engine roared to life. I leaned to the side so I could see past my mother and eased off the brake and opened the throttle. The machine leaped forward. I cut back on the throttle, and the machine slowed, just as The Hunter had said it would. I opened the throttle again, and the snowmobile jumped forward again. I drove slowly once around the yard to get a feel for the machine, then cut back the throttle and followed the trail The Hunter had left down the side of our ridge.

"Are you okay?" I shouted when I drove onto the marsh. My mother didn't answer. I didn't know if she couldn't hear me because of the helmet or because the engine was so loud. There was another possibility as to why my mother didn't answer, but I didn't want to think about that.

I opened the throttle as far as it would go. The wind stung my cheeks, whipped my hair. The extraordinary speed made me want to shout. I glanced over my shoulder. Rambo ran easily behind. The gauge The Hunter had said would tell me how fast I was going pointed to the number twelve. I had no idea Rambo could run so fast.

I thought about my grandparents as I drove. I wondered what they would be like. The Hunter said they had never stopped looking for my mother and they would be excited to see her again. I wondered if I would like them. I wondered what they would think of me. If they had a car, what it would be like to go for a ride in it. If I would one day take a trip with them on a train, or on a bus, or in an airplane. I had always wanted to visit the Yanomami in Brazil.

Then something whizzed past my head. At the same time, a sharp crack echoed across the marsh.

"Helena!" my father shouted. His voice was so angry and sharp, I could hear him clearly over the noise of the machine. "Get back here right now!"

I slowed. In hindsight, I should have gunned the engine and never looked back, but I was not in the habit of disobeying my father.

"Keep going," my mother said, suddenly alert. "Hurry! Don't stop!"

I stopped, looked back. My father was silhouetted on the top of our ridge with his feet spread like a colossus: rifle at the ready, long black hair whipping around his head like the snakes of Medusa. The rifle was pointed at me.

He shot a second time. Another warning shot, because if my father had wanted to shoot me, he would have. I realized then that stopping was a mistake. But I couldn't go back. If I did, my father would most certainly kill my mother and possibly me. But if I disobeyed and drove away, a bullet through my back would kill us both.

My father shot a third time. Rambo yelped. I jumped off the snowmobile and ran back to where Rambo flopped and ki-yied in the snow. I passed my hands over his head, his flanks, his chest. Saw that my father had shot my beautiful dog in the foot.

Another shot rang out. My mother screamed and fell across the handlebars, a bullet hole in her shoulder.

The Remington held four cartridges plus one in the chamber. My father had one shot left before he would have to reload.

I stood up. Tears streamed down my face. My father hated to see me cry, but I didn't care.

But instead of mocking me for my tears as I expected, my father smiled. To this day I can see his expression. Smug. Cold. Unfeeling. So sure that he had won. He pointed the rifle at me, then at Rambo, then at me, and back at Rambo again, toying with me the way he had with my mother and The Hunter, and I realized it didn't matter which of us he shot first. One way or another, my father was going to kill us all.

I dropped to my knees. Gathered Rambo into my arms and buried my face in his fur and waited for the bullet that would end my life.

Rambo trembled, growled, pulled away. He struggled to his three remaining feet and started limping toward my father. I whistled him back. Rambo kept going. My father laughed.

I jumped to my feet and spread my arms wide. "You bastard!" I shouted. I didn't know what the word meant, but my father cut the word into The Hunter's chest, so I knew it was bad. "You asshole! You son of a bitch!" Spewing all the words I could remember. "What are you waiting for? **Shoot me!**"

My father laughed again. He held the Remington on my struggling dog as Rambo limped ever closer. Rambo bared his teeth and snarled. He limped faster until he was headed for my father at an almost-run, baying like he was about to tear into a wolf or a bear.

I understood. Rambo was distracting my father so that I could get away. He would protect me, or die trying.

I sprinted for the snowmobile and jumped on and reached around my mother and opened the throttle wide. I didn't know if my mother was alive, if we would get away, if my father would shoot both her and me. But like Rambo, I had to try.

As we raced across the frozen marsh, the wind dried my tears. From behind came another gunshot.

Rambo yelped once and fell silent.

THE GUNSHOT REVERBERATED in my head long after the real echo was gone. I drove as fast as I dared, blind with tears, my throat so tight I could barely breathe. All I could see was my dog lying at my father's feet in the snow. Cousteau and Calypso and The Hunter and my mother were right. My father was a bad man. There was no reason for him to shoot my dog. I wished he had shot me. I wished I had waited longer after he went into the marsh before I started the snowmobile, driven faster, not stopped when he told me to. If I had done any of these things, my dog would be alive and my father would not have shot my mother.

My mother hadn't moved or spoken since my father shot her. I knew she was alive because my arms were wrapped around her and her body was warm, but I didn't know for how much longer. All I could do was drive—away from the marsh, away from my father.

Toward what, I didn't know.

I was following the trail The Hunter had left because that was what he'd told me to do. What I really wanted was to find Cousteau and Calypso. The real Cousteau and Calypso, not the ones I made up after I saw that family. I knew they lived close by. I was sure their mother and father would help.

I had long ago left the marsh and was now driving through trees—the same trees I used to want to explore when I stared longingly toward them on the horizon. It was very dark. I wished The Hunter had told me how to turn on the snowmobile's headlight. Or maybe he did and I'd forgotten. There was a lot to remember: **Keep the throttle high when you're pushing through deep powder. If the snowmobile pulls right, shift your weight left. When it pulls left, shift your weight right. When you drive up a hill, lean forward and shift your weight to the rear of the seat so the snowmobile doesn't flip. Or you can ride with one knee on the seat and the other foot on the side rail. Lean back when you go downhill. Shift your weight and lean into the curves.** And on and on.

The snowmobile was very heavy. Driving was harder than The Hunter had made it sound. The Hunter said that where he came from, even children drove snowmobiles, but if this was true, then Finnish children must have been very strong. Once I drove off the trail and got stuck. Twice we almost tipped over.

I was very afraid. Not of the woods or of the dark. Those things I was used to. It was fear of the unknown, of all the bad things that might happen. I was afraid the snowmobile would run out of gas and my mother and I would have to spend the night in the forest without food or shelter. I was afraid I would drive into a tree and wreck the engine. I was afraid we would end up as lost and desperate as The Hunter.

I was afraid my mother would die.

I drove for a very long time. At last the trail came to an end. I navigated down a steep hill and into the middle of a long, narrow clearing and stopped. I looked left and right. Nothing. No people, no town called Newberry, no grandparents searching for my mother as The Hunter had promised there would be.

Four tracks ran the length of the clearing, two on one side and two on the other. I couldn't tell which were The Hunter's. I worried about what would happen if I went the wrong way. I thought about the guessing game my father and I used to play that had two choices. Perhaps it didn't matter which way I went. Perhaps it did.

I looked up into the sky. **Please. Help me. I'm lost. I don't know what to do.**

I closed my eyes and prayed as I had never prayed before. When I opened my eyes, there was a small yellow light in the distance. The light was low to the ground and very bright. A snowmobile.

"Thank you," I whispered. There were times when I had wondered if the gods were real, like when my father put me in the well and they stayed silent, or when he beat my mother and The Hunter and the gods didn't intervene, but now I knew the truth. I promised I would never doubt again.

As the snowmobile came closer, the light became two. Suddenly there was a terrible honking, like a goose, only louder—like an entire flock of angry geese.

I shut my eyes and clapped my hands over my ears until at last, the honking stopped. There was a banging like a door had opened and closed, then voices.

"I didn't see them!" a man shouted. "I swear! They were sitting in the middle of the road with no headlights!"

"You could have killed them!" a woman yelled.

"I'm telling you, I didn't see them! What are

you doing?" he yelled at me. "Why did you stop?"

I opened my eyes and grinned. A man and woman. Cousteau and Calypso's father and mother. I found them.

WHEN THE POLICE FOLLOWED the trail I had left to rescue The Hunter, my father was gone. The Hunter still hung from the handcuffs in the woodshed. Everyone assumed that my father had killed him, because why wouldn't they? No one would think for a second that a twelve-year-old child could have done such a thing. Not when they had a kidnapper and rapist to pin the murder on.

Once the idea that my father had killed The Hunter was established, I was okay with letting it stand. I may not have been wise in the ways of the outside world, but I understood enough to know that confessing to The Hunter's murder wouldn't change anything except ruin my own life. My father was a bad man. He was going to jail for a very long time. Everybody said so. I had my whole life in front of me. My father had forfeited his.

That said, I guarantee I've paid for my crime. Killing a person changes you. It doesn't matter how many animals you've shot, snared, trapped, skinned, gutted, eaten. Killing a person is different. Once you've taken the life of another human being, you're never the same. The Hunter was alive, and then he wasn't, and mine are the hands that did it. I think about this every time I comb Iris's hair, or buckle Mari into her car seat, or stir a pot of jelly on the stove, or run my hands over my husband's chest; I look at my hands doing these normal, everyday things and think, **These are the hands that did it. These hands took another person's life.** I hate my father for putting me in the position where I had to make that choice.

I still can't understand how my father can kill so easily and without remorse. I think about The Hunter every day. He had a wife and three children. Whenever I look at my girls, I think about what it would be like for them if they had to grow up without their father. After we left the marsh I wanted to tell The Hunter's widow that I was sorry about what had happened to her husband. That I appreciated the sacrifice he made for my mother and me. I thought I could tell her when I saw her at the courthouse the day my father was sentenced, but by that time she'd filed a lawsuit against my grandparents for her share of the money they were making off our story from the tabloids, so my grandparents wouldn't let me. She won a big settlement in the end, and that made me feel better. Though, as my grandfather grumbled, all the money in the world wasn't going to bring back her husband.

Or my dog. Sometimes, I start to cry—which as you probably know by now is something I rarely do—and it's because I think of Rambo. I'll never forgive my father for shooting him. I've replayed the events that led up to that day more times than I can count, trying to see the places where I would have done something differently if I had known how things were going to turn out. The most obvious is when The Hunter asked for help the morning after my father handcuffed him in the woodshed. If I had done as he wanted me to before my father beat and tortured him until he was too weak to leave, most likely he would be alive today.

But The Hunter's death wasn't my fault. He was in the wrong place at the wrong time, the same as anyone who gets killed in a traffic accident, or a mass shooting, or a suicide bombing. The Hunter was the one who decided to go snowmobiling while he was drunk, not me. He was the one who got lost and then made a series of decisions that ultimately led to our ridge: turn left here instead of right, go around this clump of trees and not that one, drive into our yard to ask for help after he saw the smoke from our cabin. Certainly when he decided to hit the trail after he'd been drinking with his buddies he didn't have any idea that he would pay for that decision with his life. Yet it was his decision.

Likewise when my mother and her girlfriend decided to explore the abandoned house by the railroad tracks. As she and her girlfriend ran around the empty rooms, I'm sure she had no idea that, by the end of the day, it would be fourteen years before she saw her family again. Naturally they would have played somewhere else if they had known. But they didn't.

Likewise I doubt that when my father took me to see Tahquamenon Falls he had any idea he was setting in motion the events that would ultimately lead to the loss of his family. Just as when I decided to leave the marsh, I had no idea how badly things were going to turn out for my mother and me. I honestly thought that leaving would be as simple as driving away. I didn't anticipate my father would shoot my mother and my dog. That the last thing I would see before I drove into my uncertain future was Rambo lying motionless in the snow at my father's feet.

If I had known all of this before it happened, would I have done things differently? Of course. But you have to accept responsibility for your decisions, even when they don't work out the way you wanted.

Bad things happen. Planes crash, trains derail, people die in floods and earthquakes and tornadoes. Snowmobilers get lost. Dogs get shot. And young girls get kidnapped.

# 27

I take off running. Solid ground becomes wetland. Wetland becomes marsh. I shield my eyes against the rain and scan the opposite side of the pond. There's no sign of my father. Whether I managed to get out ahead of him or he's already at my house is impossible to tell.

I turn west into the marsh, heading for a thicket of tag alders near the end of the trail where the deer like to gather. I move quickly, jumping from grassy mound to grassy mound, keeping to areas of dry peat that are strong enough to hold my weight. A person who doesn't know the marsh as well as I do wouldn't be able to see the dangers that to me are as obvious as street signs: areas of fine silt that look solid enough to walk on but act like quicksand;

deep pools of water that can swallow a person in an instant. **Great black bubbles rose up out of the slime,** my mother's fairy tale says, **and with these, every trace of the princess vanished.**

When I come to the alder thicket, I drop to my belly and crawl the rest of the way using my feet and one elbow. The ground is wet, the mud crisscrossed with tracks. None of them recent. None of them human. It's possible my father left the trail when it got boggy and cut out cross-country. It's possible he's already at my house, sneaking in through the back door because the house is never locked, creeping down the hallway, forcing Stephen to hand over the keys to the Cherokee so he can go after our girls, shooting my husband when Stephen refuses to tell him where they are.

I shudder. I push the images away and lie down in the muddiest place I can find. Roll until every inch of me is covered, then wade through knee-deep water along the trail so I don't leave footprints while I look for the best place to set my ambush.

A moss-covered log lying across the trail looks big enough to hide behind. The way it sags in the middle tells me it's mostly rotten. My father will know better than to step on it. He'll have to step over. When he does, I'll be ready.

I break a sharp branch off a pine and stretch

out along the opposite side of the log, my ear to the ground, my makeshift spear beside me. I feel my father's footsteps before I hear them: faint vibrations in the waterlogged soil beneath the trail. The tremors are so slight, another person might think it was only their own heart beating, if they felt them at all. I hug the log closer and tighten my grip.

The footsteps stop. I wait. If my father suspects he's walking into a trap, either he'll turn around and leave me lying in the mud or he will lean over the log and shoot me. I hold my breath until the footsteps start up again. I can't tell if they're moving away from me or toward.

Then a boot crashes down onto my shoulder. I roll out from under it and jump to my feet. Dash forward and use all of my strength to jab my spear into my father's gut.

The spear breaks.

My father yanks what remains of my useless weapon out of my hands and throws it aside. He raises his arm, points my Magnum at me. I dive at his legs. He staggers and puts his arms out for balance. The Magnum falls. I grab for it. My father kicks it into the pool of water beside the trail and plants his boot on my handcuffed hands. No hesitation—I grab that boot and lift his foot off the ground. My father crashes down beside me. We roll, grapple. I work my arms over his head. The handcuff chain presses against his throat. I pull back as hard as I can. He gasps, takes my knife from the sheath at his waist and jabs and slices backwards at anything he can reach—my arms, my legs, my kidneys, my face.

I pull harder. The Glocks in the back of my father's jeans press against my stomach. If I could grab one, I could end this in an instant, but with my handcuffed arms around his neck, I can't. At the same time, with me pressed tight against him from behind choking him with the handcuffs, he can't grab a Glock and finish me. We're as stuck as a pair of bull moose who've locked horns. I picture my family walking this trail days or weeks from now and finding our decaying bodies frozen in one last embrace. I pull harder.

Then a dog barks. Rambo is running down the trail from the direction of my house, legs pumping, ears flapping.

"Attack!" I yell.

Rambo runs up and clamps his jaws around my father's leg, pulling and snarling. My father roars, stabs Rambo with the knife.

Rambo bites down harder. He rips, tears, shreds. My father screams and rolls. I roll with him. The moment my father is on his stomach I yank my arms back over his head and grab one of the Glocks and shove it in my father's back.

"Hold!" I order Rambo.

Rambo freezes. He keeps his grip on my father's leg, but there's a shift in his demeanor. He's no longer an animal tearing into his prey; he's a servant obeying his master. It takes a special breed and a lot of training for a dog to stand down like this in the heat of battle. I've seen lesser dogs so overcome with bloodlust as they tear into an elk or a bear, they completely ruin the hide.

My father doesn't move as I kneel on top of him. He knows better than to twitch.

"The knife," I say.

He flings my knife into the pool of water beside the trail.

I get to my feet. "Stand up," I order.

My father stands, puts his hands over his head, turns to face me.

"Sit." I wave him toward the log.

My father does as I say. The defeated look on his face is very nearly worth everything I've been through. I do not mask my disgust.

"Did you really think I'd go away with you? That I'd let you anywhere near my girls?"

My father doesn't answer.

"The handcuff key. Toss it over."

He reaches inside his jacket and tosses the key into the pool of water after my knife. A useless act of defiance. Cuffed or not, I can still shoot.

"We had a good life, **Bangii-Agawaateyaa,**" he says. "That day we went to see the falls. The night we saw the wolverine. You remember that, **Bangii-Agawaateyaa.**"

I want him to stop saying my name. I know he's only doing it to try to control the situation the way he always does, even though he has to know he's lost. Only . . . now that he's called up the memory, of course I can't help but see it. It was sometime after I shot my first deer, but before Rambo came to our ridge, which would have made me around seven or eight. I'd woken up out of a deep sleep with my heart racing. I'd heard a noise outside. It sounded like a baby crying—like I imagined a baby might cry—only louder. More like a scream. Like nothing I'd ever heard. I had no idea what it was. Animals can make terrible sounds, especially when they're mating, but if this was an animal, I couldn't put a name to it.

Then my father appeared in the doorway. He came over to my bed and wrapped my blanket around my shoulders and led me to the window. In the yard below, silhouetted in the moonlight, I saw a shadow.

"What is it?" I whispered.

**"Gwiingwa'aage."**

Wolverine.

I clutched the blanket tighter. Wolverines

are extremely ferocious, my father had often said, and would eat anything: squirrels, beavers, porcupines—sick or injured deer and moose. Perhaps even a small girl.

**Gwiingwa'aage** stalked into the yard. His hair was long and shaggy and black. I drew back. **Gwiingwa'aage** raised his head and looked up at my window and screamed.

I yelped and dashed for my bed. My father picked up my blanket and laid it over me, then stretched out beside me on top of the covers and held me in his arms while he told a funny story about Wolverine and his older brother Bear. After that, the wolverine's scream was no longer scary.

I know now that wolverine sightings in Michigan are extremely rare. Some say the animals never lived in the state at all, never mind that Michigan is nicknamed the Wolverine State. But memories aren't always about facts. Sometimes they're about feelings. My father had given a name to my fear, and I was no longer afraid.

I look down at my father. I understand he's done terrible things. He could spend a hundred lifetimes in prison and the scales of justice would never be balanced. But that night, he was just a dad, and he was mine.

"Okay," he says. "You won. It's over. I'll leave

now. I promise I won't go near you or your family."

He holds out his hands, palms up, and gets to his feet. I keep the Glock trained on his chest. I could let him go. God knows I don't want to hurt him. I love him, despite everything he's done. I thought when I went looking for him this morning that I wanted to return him to prison, and I do. But I also realize now that my connection to my father runs deeper than I ever imagined. Maybe the real reason I went after him was because I wanted to see him one last time before he disappeared. Now that I have, maybe that's enough. He's promising he'll walk away. He says it's over. Maybe it is.

Except that his promises mean nothing. I think about how a **wendigo** is never satisfied after killing and searches constantly for new victims. How every time he eats, he grows bigger, so he can never be full. How if the people hadn't killed him, the whole village would have been destroyed.

I ease back on the trigger.

My father laughs. "You won't shoot me, **Bangii-Agawaateyaa.**" He smiles, takes a step toward me.

**Bangii-Agawaateyaa.** Little Shadow. Reminding me of how I followed him everywhere he went. How, like his shadow, I belonged to him. How without him, I don't exist.

He turns and walks away. Reaches behind his back and takes the second Glock from his waistband and tucks it in the front of his jeans. His walk becomes a swagger. Like he truly believes I'll let him go.

I whistle two low notes. Rambo looks up, tenses. Ready to do whatever I command.

I flick my hand.

Rambo dashes baying after my father. My father whirls, grabs the Glock, shoots. The shot goes wild. Rambo leaps and locks his teeth around my father's wrist. The Glock falls.

My father slams his fist into Rambo's side. Rambo loosens his grip. My father hits him again and charges toward me. I stand my ground. At the last second, I raise my arms over my head as he slams into me. I slip the handcuffs over his head and down to his waist, trapping his arms by his sides, as we fall to the ground. I twist the Glock around and turn it toward me and shove it in his back, trying to angle the barrel in such a way that the bullet I fire will kill him and not me.

Suddenly his body goes slack, like he knows it's over, and there is only one way this can end.

**"Manajiwin,"** he whispers in my ear.

Respect. The second time in my life he's said this. A feeling of peace washes over me. I am no longer my father's shadow. I am his equal. I am free.

"You have to do it," Cousteau says.

"It's okay," Calypso says. "We understand."

I nod. Killing my father is the right thing to do. It's the only thing I can do. I have to kill him for my family, for my mother. Because I am The Marsh King's Daughter.

"I love you, too," I whisper, and pull the trigger.

# 28

The bullet that killed my father went through the same shoulder where my father had previously shot me—which, considering the alternatives, is actually a good thing. It would have been a whole lot worse these past months if both of my arms had been affected. Still, my recovery hasn't been fun. Surgery, therapy, more surgery, more therapy. Apparently the shoulder is a bad place to get shot. The doctors say there's no reason I won't eventually regain the full use of my left arm. Meanwhile, Stephen and the girls have gotten used to one-armed hugs.

Together, we are sitting in a circle around my mother's grave. It's a fine spring day. Sun shining, clouds scudding, birds singing. A tub of marsh marigolds and blue flag irises sits on top of the modest gravestone at my mother's head. The granddaughters I named for her two favorite flowers sit at her feet.

The flowers were my idea. Coming here was Stephen's. He says it's time the girls learned more about their grandmother, and that sitting beside her grave while I tell them stories about my mother will make more of an impression. I'm not so sure. But the marriage counselor we're seeing says both parties need to be willing to compromise in order to make a marriage work, so here we are.

Stephen reaches across my mother's grave and squeezes my hand. "Ready?"

I nod. It's hard to know where to begin. I think about what it was like for my mother when I was growing up. About all of the things she did for me that I didn't appreciate at the time. Trying to make my fifth birthday special. Warming me after my father put me in the well. How hard it must have been for her to nurture a child who was an echo of the man who kidnapped her. A child she genuinely and viscerally feared.

I could tell my daughters about the day I shot my first deer, or the time my father took me to see the falls, or the time I saw the wolf, but those stories are more about my father than my mother. And as I look at my daughters' innocent, expectant faces, I realize that every story from my childhood that I might possibly tell them also has a dark side.

Stephen nods encouragingly.

"When I was five," I begin, "my mother made me a cake. Somewhere in the stacks of cans and bags of rice and flour in the storage room she found a boxed cake mix. Chocolate with rainbow sprinkles."

"My favorite!" Iris exclaims.

"Fav-it," Mari echoes.

I tell them about the duck egg, and the bear grease, and the doll my mother made for me as a present, and end the story there. I don't tell them what I did with the doll. How my callous reaction to my mother's extraordinary gift must have pierced her heart.

"Tell them the rest of the story," Cousteau says. "About the knife, and about the rabbit." He and his sister are sitting quietly behind my daughters. Since my father died, they've been appearing more and more often.

I shake my head and smile as I remember the rest of that day, and how it ended with the first time my father acknowledged me with **"manajiwin."** Respect.

Iris grins back. She thinks I'm smiling at her.

"More!" she and Mari exclaim.

I shake my head and get to my feet. One day I'll tell my daughters everything about my childhood, but not today.

We gather up our blankets and start for the car. Mari and Iris dart ahead. Stephen runs after. Since my father's escape, he rarely lets the girls out of his sight.

I hang back. Cousteau and Calypso walk beside me. Calypso takes my hand.

"Helga understood all now," she whispers, her breath as soft as cattail fluff against my ear. "She was lifted up above the Earth through a sea of sound and thought, and around and within her was light and song such as words cannot express. The sun burst forth in all its glory, and, as in olden times, the form of the frog vanished in his beams and the beautiful maiden stood forth in all her loveliness. The frog body crumbled into dust, and a faded lotus flower lay on the spot on which Helga had stood."

The final words from my mother's fairy tale. I think about how the tale told me what I needed to do. How my mother's story ultimately saved us both. How my father may be the reason I exist, but my mother is the reason I'm alive.

I think about my father. When the medical examiner asked what I wanted done with my father's body, my first thought was to ask myself what he would have wanted. Then I thought about how his entire life was governed by his wishes and desires alone, and thought maybe I'd do the opposite. In the end, I picked the most practical and the least expensive. I'm not saying more than that. There's a fansite devoted to my father's exploits that sprang up not long after he died. I can imagine what the "Marshies" would do if they knew where my father was buried. I've tried several times to get the website taken down, but the FBI says as long as my father's fans don't break any laws, there's nothing they can do.

Stephen corrals the girls and waits for me to catch up.

"Thanks for doing this," he says, and takes my hand. "I know this is hard for you."

"I'm okay," I lie.

I think about how the marriage counselor also says a good marriage needs to be built on a foundation of honesty and trust. I'm working on it.

We crest the top of a small hill. At the bottom, a car is parked directly in front of our Cherokee. A news van is pulled up tight behind. A reporter and a cameraman wait beside them.

Stephen looks at me and sighs. I shrug. Since word got out that The Marsh King's daughter killed her father, the media has been relentless.

We haven't given a single interview and have trained the girls not to say a word to anyone with a notepad or a microphone, but that doesn't stop people from taking pictures.

I shake my head as we start down the hill and the reporter pulls a pen from her pocket and takes a step toward me. She doesn't know it, but I've already written everything I can remember from my childhood in a journal I keep hidden beneath Stephen's and my bed. I call my story "The Cabin," and dedicated the journal to my daughters on the first page, like a real book. One day I'll let them read it. They need to know their history. Where they come from. Who they are. One day I'll let Stephen read it, too.

I could sell the journal for a lot of money. **People** and the **National Enquirer** and the **New York Times** have offered to buy my story many times. Everyone says that since my parents are dead and I am the only one left who knows what happened, I owe it to my mother and father to tell their story.

But I will never sell. Because this isn't their story. It's ours.

## Acknowledgments

A novelist gets an idea. The idea grows into a story, and eventually, the story becomes a book—thanks to the help of the following creative, talented, incredibly insightful, and amazingly hardworking people:

Ivan Held and Sally Kim, my publisher and editorial director at Putnam. You made it happen. Thank you. Deeply, truly.

Mark Tavani, my editor. I loved working with you, and your keen eye and incredible insights exceeded my expectations.

The Putnam team: Alexis Welby, Ashley McClay, Helen Richard, the production staff, the art department, and everyone in sales and promotion. Thank you for making such a beautiful book!

Jeff Kleinman, my amazing agent. I can't begin to tell you what the past seventeen years have meant to me and my career. You made me the writer I am today.

Molly Jaffa, my talented and tireless foreign rights agent.

Kelly Mustian, Sandra Kring, and Todd Allen, my first readers. You applauded when the writing was working and held your noses when it wasn't. I couldn't have done it without you.

David Morrell. Your clear eye and generous heart made all the difference.

Christopher and Shar Graham, Katie and John Masters, Lynette Ecklund, Steve Lehto, Kelly and Robert Meister, Linda and Gary Ciochetto, Kathleen Bostick and Leith Gallaher (gone, but not forgotten), Dan Johnson, Rebecca Cantrell, Elizabeth Letts, Jon Clinch, Sachin Waikar, Tina Wald, Tim and Adele Woskobojnik and Christy, Darcy Chan, Keith Cronin, Jessica Keener, Renee Rosen, Julie Kramer, Carla Buckley, Mark Bastable, Tasha Alexander, Lauren Baratz-Logsted, Rachel Elizabeth Cole, Lynn Sinclair, Danielle Younge-Ullman, Dorothy McIntosh, Helen Dowdell, Melanie Benjamin, Sara Gruen, Harry Hunsicker, J. H. Bográn, Maggie Dana, Rebecca Drake, Mary Kennedy, Bryan Smith, Joe Moore, Susan Henderson, and so very many more wonderful friends who have my back and cheer me on. I'm honored to know you.

My family, for your love and support, and most especially, a huge heartfelt "Thank you" to my husband, Roger. Your unshakable faith in my ability to write this book means more than I can say.

noted - slight water damage on bottom edge - MAR 2021